FOOTPRINTS TO MURDER

FOOTPRINTS TO MURDER

Marcia Talley

This first world edition published 2016
in Great Britain and the USA by
SEVERN HOUSE PUBLISHERS LTD of
19 Cedar Road, Sutton, Surrey, England, SM2 5DA.
Trade paperback edition first published
in Great Britain and the USA 2017 by
SEVERN HOUSE PUBLISHERS LTD

British Library Cataloguing in Publication Data
A CIP catalogue record for this title is available from the British Library.

ISBN-13: 978-0-7278-8646-0 (cased)
ISBN-13: 978-1-84751-756-2 (trade paper)
ISBN-13: 978-1-78010-822-3 (e-book)

All Severn House titles are printed on acid-free paper.

Severn House Publishers support the Forest Stewardship Council™ [FSC™],
the leading international forest certification organisation.
All our titles that are printed on FSC certified paper carry the FSC logo.

MIX
Paper from
responsible sources
FSC
www.fsc.org   FSC® C013056

Typeset by Palimpsest Book Production Ltd.,
Falkirk, Stirlingshire, Scotland.
Printed and bound in Great Britain by
TJ International, Padstow, Cornwall.

This one is for Sherriel Mattingly

'But I don't want to go among mad people,' said Alice.
'Oh, you can't help that,' said the cat. 'We're all mad here.'

Lewis Carroll, *Alice's Adventures in Wonderland*

ACKNOWLEDGEMENTS

Thanks, always, to my husband, Barry, who is grateful that he didn't have to accompany me on any of the peculiar research trips for this one.

Thanks also to my daughters Laura Geyer and Sarah Glass, who know where all the bodies are buried and love me anyway.

Kudos to Leah Solat whose winning bid at a benefit auction for the Annapolis Opera Company bought her the right to play a character in this book. I hope that journalism is a refreshing change from presiding over non-profit organizations.

A special shout-out to my Oberlin College classmate, Cecelia Cloughly, who rose to the challenge and contributed generously to the Martin Luther King Internship Fund established by our class, hoping to be 'bumped off' in this novel. I apologize, in advance, for what I did to your French horn.

A tip of the hat to my friend and colleague, 'Cop Robin' Burcell, who graciously agreed to share her talent as a forensic artist with the attendees at my fictitious Sasquatch Sesquicentennial.

1,000,000 thanks to my colleagues in the Writers' Circle in Hope Town on Elbow Cay in the Bahamas, and to my partners in crime back in Annapolis, Maryland: Becky Hutchison, Mary Ellen Hughes, Debbi Mack, Shari Randall, Bonnie Settle and especially to Sherriel Mattingly, who will know why. They read it all first.

I'm grateful to Nan Fulton and Cindy Merrill, the 'Front Street Boutique Girls,' who put their stamp of approval on the title.

Hugs to Kate Charles and Deborah Crombie, dearest friends, confidantes and advisors. What would I do without FaceTime?

And, of course, to Vicky Bijur.

'How like a hateful ape,
Detected grinning 'midst his pilfered hoard,
A cunning man appears, whose secret frauds
Are opened to the day!'

Joanna Baillie, *Basil, A Tragedy*, Act 5, Scene III

ONE

November 8, 1721. 'The first night I lay in this habitation, there was a great alarm at nine at night. I inquired the cause of it and they told me there was in the neighborhood a beast of an unknown species, of a monstrous size, and the cry of which resembled no animal that we knew . . . It had already carried off some sheep and calves and killed some cows.'

Pierre-Francois Xavier de Charlevoix, Historical Journal, *Historical Collections of Louisiana. Pt. III.* NY, D. Appleton, 1851, pp. 157–159

The French thought a lot about the past. Guillaume Apollinaire hibernated in it, as I recall, while Marcel Proust had a good, 3000-page wallow while writing *A La Recherche du Temps Perdu.*

Me, I was driving west toward my past along Ohio Route 511, heading for Oberlin College and my fortieth class reunion. Past the Auto & Tire Works, past the IGA Foodliner, past the Lorain Laundramat where – what was his name, the waiter from Dascomb Hall? – took me on a date in the first semester of my freshman year. Perhaps he had found it romantic sharing a dryer – his tightie whities tangled up in my bra straps. I'll never know. We never progressed to date two.

After Tappan Square, I turned right on North Professor Street and slowed, looking for a dorm that hadn't existed during my time at Oberlin: Kahn Hall. I would have had to be blind to miss it – a huge crimson-and-gold banner was draped over the entrance: *Welcome Class of 1975.* How could it have been that long? I thought as I pulled into a driveway between Kahn and the next building. A student wearing an orange vest popped up from a folding chair, balanced her iPad mini on her forearm and directed me to a parking lot behind the dorm where I slotted my Volvo into a spot in the shade. After fluffing my recently lightened curls and refreshing my lipstick in the visor mirror, I collected my wheelie bag from the trunk and made my way back toward the dorm where I'd be staying. According to the reunion brochure, the modern building was totally dedicated to energy sustainability.

A classmate I didn't immediately recognize was in the lobby to greet me, printed nametags spread out in alphabetical order on the long table in front of her. 'Hannah Alexander!' she chirped. 'Gosh, I love your hair!'

I grinned, taking a split second to steal a glance at the nametag she wore, hoping she wouldn't notice. 'Candy,' I chirped as memories flooded back, 'so good to see you again.'

Candace Peters and I had been lab partners in Biology 101. Back then she'd been a fluffy, petite blonde who'd created a sensation by walking into Wilder Hall student union flaunting the first pair of hot pants most of us had ever seen. The woman handing over my nametag now had pink-blonde hair cut in a neatly-layered bob and – judging from the rolls of fat circling her abdomen – had long-ago lost the battle of the bulge. 'You haven't changed a bit,' she said.

I laughed out loud. Candy was such a liar! In 1975 I subdued my shoulder-length curls with a hot iron, parted my hair in the middle and flicked it out on the sides like one of *Charlie's Angels*. The thumbnail graduation photo printed on my nametag attested to that fact. I was much more wash-and-wear these days.

On the wall behind Candy's head, a glass dome-covered port-hole had been glowing green. As she handed me my nametag holder and a reunion information packet, the dome turned red. 'What's that?' I asked, gesturing toward the porthole with my free hand. 'Is the ship going down?'

'Oh, that!' she sniffed, glancing quickly back over her shoulder. 'It monitors the energy efficiency of the building. When it turns red . . .' She shrugged. 'Everyone's flushing toilets at the same time, I'd guess.'

'A lot of folks already here, then?' I asked as I slipped my nametag into the plastic holder and looped the cord over my head. 'Sorry to say, I haven't kept up with many of my classmates since graduation but I'm hoping to catch up with my roommate, Susan Lockley.' I ran my hand along the tabletop, scanning the nametags, but the space between 'Lindsay' and 'Loring' was empty.

Candy squinted at a checklist attached to a clipboard. 'Susan? Yeah. She checked in early this morning.'

'Can you tell me what room she's in?'

'Says here she's staying at the La Quinta in Elyria.' Candy looked up. 'I can give you the phone number there if you want.'

I smiled and waited as she wrote the number down for me on an Oberlin College Post-it note. The La Quinta, I knew, was a good twenty miles away, near the Cleveland Hopkins airport. Not everyone longs for the good old days of dorm living, I supposed.

After thanking Candy and promising to see her later, I dragged my suitcase up to the second floor, down the hall and through the door of the room that would be my home for the next three days – a student double, simply furnished with utilitarian blond-on-blond furniture. I opened my suitcase on the spare bed, retrieved my toiletry bag, then – thinking about the unisex bathroom I'd be sharing with others halfway down the hall – wished that I'd checked into the La Quinta, too.

From the semi-comfort of an ergonomically correct desk chair, I sent an 'arrived safely' text to my husband, a message he'd get whenever he and the Naval Academy training sloop he was chaperoning came within range of a cell-phone tower. Last I heard, the forty-four foot *Resolute* was offshore, somewhere between Cape May, New Jersey and Halifax, Nova Scotia, so it could be days before my message popped up in Paul's inbox.

Then I called Susan. She wasn't in her room, so I left my cell-phone number and asked her to call me back.

I was strolling across Tappan Square toward Gibson's Bakery where I'd hopefully still be able to connect with a tall cappuccino and a worship-worthy peanut-butter brownie when Susan texted me. 'Excited! See you at the president's reception tonight?'

'You bet,' I texted back. Then added as an afterthought: 'I'll be wearing a red rose in my lapel and carrying a rolled-up *New York Times*.'

'Goofball,' she texted. 'FB!'

I'd looked up Susan on Facebook, too, so I knew that she lived in Issaquah, just east of Seattle, and was owner/manager of

Scarborough Fairs, a conference management and event planning service. She had no private Facebook page, so whether there was still a Mister Lockley in the picture or a passel of successful Lockley children and darling grands would have to wait until we reconnected later that evening.

Marvin Krislov, like Oberlin college presidents before him since 1927, lived in a symmetrical, Flemish bond, two-and-a-half-story Georgian Revival home on Forest Street. As guests wandered in from points all over campus, college staff herded them down the driveway to a party tent in the backyard where wine, beer and hors d'oeuvres would keep the alumni happy until the speeches began later on. I went through the receiving line, perma-grin firmly in place, grabbed a glass of pinot grigio, some shrimp and something wrapped in bacon on a toothpick and merged with the crowd. I was nibbling on a cold shrimp, in deep discussion with John Congdon from the college development office about Oberlin's recent crowd-funding efforts, when someone boomed, 'Hannah Alexander!'

Still holding the toothpick, I turned.

The same abundant hair, now unnaturally blond. Same boyish face. Same straight, impossibly white teeth. I didn't have to check the guy's nametag to remember the jerk who was leering at me: Duane Edward Becker. We'd gone out a couple of times during our sophomore year. After a movie at the Apollo one evening I'd made the mistake of allowing him to kiss me goodnight. The next thing I knew, his hand had been snaking under my sweater, crawling up my back and skillfully unhooking my bra. One well-aimed knee had cut him off in mid-grope and we hadn't seen each other, except in passing, since.

'Duane,' I chirped. 'Have you met John Congdon?' I sent a wide-eyed, semi-desperate look to John, who picked up my SOS immediately.

'Duane,' he oozed, extending his hand and drawing the guy aside. 'Can't tell you how much the college appreciates your support.' He turned to me, a co-conspirator's grin lighting his face. 'Thanks to Duane, the Columbus Greater Medical Center is now matching charitable contributions.'

'So, what do you do at the Columbus Greater Medical Center?'

I asked, genuinely curious. With his thousand-dollar suit and boyish, Botoxed good looks, I figured he had to be somebody important.

'I'm Chief of Obstetrics and Gynecology,' Duane said.

That figured.

'There's somebody I'd like you to meet,' Congdon said then turned to me, his eyes twinkling behind his wire-rimmed glasses. 'Please excuse us, Hannah.' He seized Duane gently by the arm and steered him off into the crowd.

I snagged another shrimp from a passing server and made a mental note to up my annual donation to Oberlin College by at least a hundred dollars.

Over the course of my chat with John Congdon, my wine glass had grown mysteriously empty. I wandered over to the bar for a top up, then stationed myself near the receiving line, slowly sipping, waiting for Susan to show.

I didn't wait long. A white-haired woman dressed in navy slacks topped off by a festive, multicolored embroidered jacket was being efficiently passed from hand to hand along the receiving line. My college roommate still showed her love of all things Southwest in the turquoise and silver barrette that secured her shoulder-length hair to one side.

'Hey, you,' I said as she finished running the gauntlet.

'Hannah! You look wonderful!' Susan hugged me so hard that wine sloshed out of my glass and ran down my hand. 'Sorry,' she said as she released me.

'No damage done,' I told her, shaking my hand dry. 'That's why I drink white. Grab a glass for yourself and let's find a place to sit down.' While Susan waited in line for her wine I piled a plate high with cheese, crackers and cut-up vegetables then joined her at a table not far from the exit.

I brought her up to date on my family. Paul was still teaching math at the US Naval Academy and our daughter Emily's spa, Paradiso, was an unqualified success. There had been a Mister Lockley, I learned – Harold – but he passed away of a heart attack in 2010, leaving Susan and two grown sons, one in banking and the other in real estate. Between Susan and me there were eight grandchildren, and we'd both come prepared – *quelle surprise* – with iPhones loaded with pictures.

Susan was faster on the draw. I nibbled on cheese cubes while she paged through her photo album, then I did the same. As one impossibly cute grandchild after another scrolled past my thumb, I was vaguely aware that the tables around us were filling up, but it wasn't until someone thumped on the microphone that I realized the speeches were about to begin.

I glanced up. Duane Becker had escaped from John Congdon's clutches and was gliding my way, heading, I was certain, for the empty chair to my right. *Damn!* I leaned so close to Susan that our heads almost touched. 'Let's get out of here.'

Susan expertly pocketed her iPhone. 'Good idea. My engine only runs for so long on cheese cubes.' With a farewell glance at the podium where a line of speakers appeared to be gathering, she added: 'If we sneak out now, nobody but Duane will notice.'

We skedaddled.

Chatting amiably about our student days, we ambled up South Professor Street toward the Conservatory of Music. We skipped across the crosswalk painted like a piano keyboard, ducked around behind the Co-op Bookstore and made our way to Lorenzo's Pizzeria Restaurant, the best pizza joint in town – possibly in all of Ohio. 'The Beautiful Flame,' Lorenzo's wood-fired pizza oven, was parked in the lot nearby. Hauled on the back of a specially equipped flatbed truck, the oven made regular appearances at fairs and private events all around the state. The evening was balmy and it was tempting to sit outside under one of the umbrellas, but yellow jackets were buzzing around the patio tables so we opted instead for a table inside.

Although the joint was jumping, a server appeared promptly and handed us menus. 'A bottle of Chianti,' Susan told her without even consulting it. 'Sound good to you, Hannah?'

'Perfect. What could be better with pizza?'

After the server left to fetch the wine, I studied the menu. 'Lordy,' I said after a minute. 'There's something for everyone here. Veggie, vegan, gluten-free, dairy-free, soy-free, egg-free . . .'

'College town, Hannah. Duh.'

I chuckled. 'I can't imagine what a vegan, gluten-free pizza would taste like. No cheese? There ought to be a law.' I set the menu aside. 'If you have to spell it c-h-e-e-z-e, it's not. Do you ever wonder how we survived to adulthood, back before we learned that everything is bad for us?'

Susan looked up and grinned. 'Well, I'm famished. I'm throwing caution to the wind. Deluxe pizza for me, even if it proves to be fatal.'

When the server returned with our wine and a basket of bread-sticks, Susan ordered her pizza and a nine-incher with mushrooms, green pepper and olives for me.

'Tell me about Scarborough Fairs,' I said after the server disappeared into the kitchen.

'It's something I started out of my home about seven years ago. Now we manage a wide range of technical and non-technical conferences, tradeshows, workshops, seminars, symposia and the like.'

As a former librarian, I'd attended my share of conferences over the years, including ones like the American Library Association's Annual Conference. Just me in the big city with 17,000 of my closest friends. Managing a conference that huge had to be a major headache. 'So what does that entail?'

'Whatever the client wants, really, all the way from site selection to organizing the speakers. We're flexible.'

'We?'

'I used to handle everything myself but last year I had the good sense to hire an assistant. That's the only reason I was able to attend this reunion, as a matter of fact. I've got the Sasquatch Sesquicentennial in Flat Rock, Oregon coming up next weekend. Without Heather I'd be up to my eyeballs in last-minute registrations.'

I stared at Susan over the rim of my wine glass, wondering if I'd misheard. 'Sasquatch Sesquicentennial? You're kidding, right?'

Susan grinned again and waved a breadstick. 'Dead serious. And so are they. It's been about 150 years since some missionary named Zebulon Blackburn wrote an article for a local rag called *The Daily Mountaineer* describing a species of giant apes that came down from the mountains to steal salmon out of fishermen's nets. They've been looking for Sasquatch ever since.'

Sasquatch, Bigfoot, Swamp Ape, Yeti, Abominable Snowman

– tales of such elusive wild men perpetuated, especially on late-night cable television. As far as I knew, though, other than footprints, grainy photographs or shaky videos, no evidence had yet been found that conclusively proved their existence. As if reading my mind, Susan raised both hands and said, 'Hey, their money's good. Who am I to judge?'

'That's got to be one of the weirdest conferences I've ever heard of,' I said.

'Oh, I've seen my share of weird. Back when Harold was working for the World Bank in Washington, DC, I volunteered at the biennial meeting of the International Rhinologic Society.'

'Rhinologists, right? Nose doctors?'

She nodded and tapped her temple. 'Seared into my brain. They called it "The Nose: 2000 and Beyond." The logo was a profile of George Washington superimposed over the Capitol dome.' She leaned forward. 'Old George had quite a schnoz on him.'

I laughed out loud. 'You are making this up.'

'Well, you may scoff, Mrs Ives, but former first lady Barbara Bush was one of the speakers. And I still have the T-shirt.'

Our pizzas had arrived, served on elevated pizza tray stands. Susan sprinkled hers liberally with red pepper flakes. 'They had sessions like, I swear to God, "Your Nose is a Microbe Luxury Resort." You gotta love it.'

I took a bite of pizza and chewed appreciatively. 'Some of the Sasquatch sessions will be every bit as entertaining, I'll bet.'

'For sure,' she said. 'I've signed up a scientist from New Jersey. How could anyone pass up a program on scat analysis?'

From deep inside her handbag, Susan's iPhone began to chime. As she bent down to answer it, she added: 'They've even managed to snag Martin Radcliffe from *Don't You Believe It!*'

Radcliffe, I knew, was a professional debunker, host of a popular television show. Stir him into a mix of Bigfoot enthusiasts and the proverbial fur could fly.

Susan glanced at the display on her phone, frowned and punched the screen. 'Heather. What's up?'

I took another bite of pizza and waited.

'What? No, no, I can't!' Susan sprang to her feet and headed toward a side door marked exit, iPhone pressed to her ear. 'I understand completely, of course I do, but you just can't expect . . .'

When Susan returned five minutes later, her face flushed and frowning, my pizza was half gone. 'Bad news?' I asked.

Susan plopped into her chair, arms dangling at her sides. 'Heather's mom had a massive stroke. She has to bow out of the Sasquatch conference.' She pressed a hand to her forehead. 'I need more wine.'

I obliged, refilling her glass and scooting it across the tablecloth.

'I simply can't do it alone,' she said after chug-a-lugging half the Chianti in her glass. 'No way.'

'You don't have backup?'

'Heather *is* my backup.' She sighed. 'The business is at that awkward stage, Hannah. Too small for three employees but too big for two. I don't know what I'm going to do.' She set her wine glass down and studied me speculatively.

'What?' I asked after a bit, breaking the silence that hung between us like a blank cartoon balloon. I suspected that Susan was about to dragoon me into doing something, just like she had back in college. The last time I'd seen that look on her face she'd asked me to write a letter in fluent French to an exchange student from the Sorbonne she'd met at a party. *A toi, pour toujours.* Give me a break.

'You,' she said.

I held up both hands, palms out. 'No!'

'Didn't you say your husband was away on a sailing trip?'

'I did, but . . .'

Susan rested her elbows on the table and leaned closer. 'It's just a long weekend.'

'No.'

'Thursday night through to Sunday noon.'

'Absolutely not.'

'Have you ever been to Flat Rock, Oregon?' Susan asked.

'No, but I've never been to Outer Mongolia, either. One can live a long and happy life and never go to Outer Mongolia. I feel the same way about Flat Rock.'

'It will be fun, Hannah. Honestly. The people who attend these things are cheerful kooks. You wouldn't believe the crossover there is between Bigfoot believers, *Star Trek* fans and people who are convinced they've been abducted by space aliens.'

Paul *was* away, the grandkids were still in school, there was nothing of importance on my social calendar . . . I felt myself weakening. 'What would I have to do?'

A look of triumph brightened my former roommate's face. As if sensing victory, she relaxed into her chair. 'Supervise registration, keep an eye on catering, ride herd on the hotel technical staff to make sure all the equipment is where it needs to be and when, coordinate with the vendors . . . It'll be fun working together again, Hannah. Say yes.' She paused and added a heartfelt, '*Please*.'

'I'll have to think about it.'

Susan raised an eyebrow. 'Get this. One of the attendees is Randall Frazier.'

I frowned and shook my head. I'd never heard of Randall Frazier.

Seeing me hesitate, she said, 'Think superannuated Indiana Jones. Sweat-rimmed pith helmet and an ascot tucked into his smartly pressed safari suit. He's been chasing Bigfoot for more than thirty years. Now lives in the Hollywood Hills. They say Frazier once bribed a Tibetan monk with a bottle of Scotch to steal a yeti finger from a monastery and that what's her name, that actress with the bee-stung lips, married to the rock star?' She flapped a hand. 'Anyway, she smuggled the finger out of Nepal in her bra.'

I laughed. 'Is Frazier bringing the finger with him?'

Susan shrugged. 'You never know.'

'You drive a hard bargain, Susan Lockley.'

'Then you'll say yes?'

'I may live to regret it, but yes.'

TWO

*Spokane, Washington, 1840. 'They believe in a race of giants,
which inhabit . . . the snow peaks. They hunt and do all their work
at night. They are men stealers. They come to the people's lodges
at night when the people are asleep and take them . . . Their track is
a foot and a half long. They steal salmon from
Indian nets and eat them raw as the bears do. If the people are
awake, they always know when they are coming very near by
their strong smell that is most intolerable. It is not uncommon
for them to come in the night and give three whistles and then
the stones will begin to hit their houses.'*

Elkanah Walker, *Nine Years with the Spokane Indians:
The diary, 1838–1848, of Elkanah Walker.* Manuscript,
Walker Library at Washington State University, Pullman,
WA, 1840

My late mother was fond of saying, 'You can't get there from here.' As frustrated as I was trying to fly from Cleveland, Ohio to Flat Rock, Oregon – the closest airport being Roberts Field outside a little town I'd never heard of called Redmond – I had to smile, remembering her words.

Susan left on Tuesday morning, promising to arrange for someone to meet my flight once I had one. After noodling around on the Internet for an hour, Travelocity came up with a United flight via San Francisco, the final leg being a SkyWest regional puddle-jumper that would get me to Redmond just short of noon on Thursday. I paid for the flight using Susan's corporate credit card number, printed out the e-ticket and slipped it into the bag with my laptop. 'You trust me?' I had teased when Susan handed over her credit-card number and CVV code.

'Shouldn't I?'

'Muhwahaha!' I'd cackled. 'Rio de Janiero, here I come.'

'Skype me when you get there,' she'd said, laughing. 'I'll grab my bikini and meet you in Ipanema.'

And she went off singing, 'Tall and tan and young and lovely . . .' her hips lightly swaying.

Nothing could have been further from the big city lights and wanton gaiety of La Cidade Maravilhosa than the small but classy Roberts Field terminal outside of Redmond, Oregon. As we hustled along together following the signs toward baggage claim, a fellow passenger, a local, told me that a prominent California-based architectural firm had designed the upscale, multi-level terminal. The high desert sun poured through skylights overhead, spotlighting the original artwork that decorated the concourse. Granite walls and dark wooden beams provided accents throughout, drawing one's attention back to earth and emphasizing the region's close connection to nature. If the money lavished on the terminal was any indication, the hunters, fishermen, mountain climbers, rafters, kayakers, vacationers and, yes, even Bigfoot enthusiasts who flocked to the area contributed significantly to the robust health of the local economy.

At baggage claim, a burly guy looking for all the world like Paul Bunyan was waiting, holding a white board on which he'd scrawled 'Hives' in orange dry-erase marker.

Unless he was itching for a rash, I figured it was meant for me. 'I'm Hannah Ives,' I told him.

'I'm Scott.' The young lumberjack aimed a 1000-watt smile in my direction, melting the ice at the center of my cold, exhausted, jet-lagged heart. 'They sent me from the lodge.'

'Thank goodness,' I said.

'Which bag is yours?' he asked, eying the carousel.

'The pink hardcase.' I pointed. 'With the red bandana on the handle.'

'I'll get it,' he said. And did.

I followed my bag and the broad back of Scott's green plaid shirt into the parking garage, where he loaded my bag into the back of a non-descript white SUV. With a beep of his key fob, the side door slid open.

'I hope you don't mind,' he said, 'but I've got another pickup in . . .' he shot the cuff of his sleeve to check his watch, '. . . fifteen minutes. The American flight from Milwaukee,' he explained. 'There're sodas in the console cooler. Help yourself.'

Then he was gone without waiting to find out if I minded or not.

When you're desperately thirsty – I'd had nothing much to drink on the plane – nothing tastes better than an ice-cold Coca-Cola. I dug one out of his cooler, wrapped a napkin around the bottle to soak up the condensation then twisted off the cap. Leaning against the van's right rear fender, I drank deeply. I was halfway through the eight-ounce bottle when Scott reappeared, followed by . . .

My heart did a somersault. George Clooney?

No, not George Clooney exactly, I saw as the pair drew nearer, but someone eerily like the actor. Tall, tanned, early fifties, closely trimmed salt-and-pepper hair. He wore a black polo shirt tucked into a pair of slim-fitting blue jeans. Walking next to the man, obediently to heel, was a German shepherd.

A service dog? I wondered. What on earth could be wrong with the guy? He had muscles so gorgeous that they could have been Photoshopped. PTSD? Epilepsy? Depression? Dogs could even be trained to detect low blood sugar levels, I knew. But this animal wore no identifying vest to help answer my question.

While Scott loaded his new passenger's gear into the back of the SUV, the man introduced himself. 'Jake Cummings,' he said, 'and this is Harley.'

I told him my name then smiled at Harley. The dog sat politely near the door of the van as if awaiting instructions. 'May I?' I asked, indicating Harley. My fingers itched to give the dog a friendly scratch behind the ears. 'Service dogs can be touchy, I've heard.'

Jake grinned. 'He's not a service dog, Hannah. He's K-9. Retired. Be my guest.'

Harley accepted my petting with a lopsided, doggy grin.

I looked up at Jake in mid-scratch. 'K-9. Does that mean . . .?'

Before I could finish, he nodded and thumbed his chest. 'Milwaukee PD. Also retired.'

'You don't look old enough to be retired,' I said truthfully.

When I looked again, Harley was sniffing around the remains of what looked like a ham sandwich someone had tossed away.

'*Lass es!*' Jake said.

I majored in French but recognized the language at once. 'Your dog understands German?'

'Harley was trained in Frankfurt,' he said. '*Hier! Sitz.*'

No surprise, Harley obeyed.

'Appropriate,' I said with a grin. 'Harley being a German shepherd and all.'

Jake chuckled. 'Comes in handy, as it turns out. Not many petty criminals speak German so there's slim chance they'll countermand my orders.' He rested his hand on Harley's head. 'My previous dog was trained in Prague by the border patrol. She spoke Czech.'

'What's Czech for "sit"?' I wondered aloud.

'*Sedni.*'

'Well, if you insist,' I said with a grin as I climbed into the van and took my seat.

'Gave it twenty-five years,' Jake told me, referring to his early retirement as he waited for Harley to settle down on the floor of the van then climbed in after him. 'Injured my back tackling a suspect.' He shrugged it off. 'Just another day at the office.'

'Where are you heading?' I asked Jake as Scott circled the van round the airport, exited near the cell-phone waiting area and eased out onto Route 97 north.

'Flat Rock Mountain Lodge,' he said.

'The Sasquatch Sesquicentennial?' I asked.

Jake nodded. 'You?'

'The same,' I said. 'I'm one of the organizers, actually. Or rather my friend, Susan Lockley, is. I got drafted in at the last minute.'

'To do what?' he asked.

I shrugged. 'Name tags, registration, making sure there's enough veggie rollups and pita chips to go around.'

Jake laughed. 'I'll make life simple for you, then. I'm a meat man, through and through.'

Somehow, I'd guessed that.

'Downtown Redmond's over there,' Scott informed us from the driver's seat. He waved his hand in a northerly direction. 'Nice little town with an amazing antiques mall, or so they say. Not into antiques much myself.' He caught my eye in the rear-view mirror. 'I think you'll like Sisters better. We'll drive through there in about twenty minutes. Flat Rock's in the park, just on the other side of Sisters.'

Jake leaned forward and rested his forearms on the back of the front passenger seat. 'Sisters?'

'It's a town. Named after the three mountains just to the west of us. The early settlers called them Faith, Hope and Charity but nowadays they're just North, South and Middle Sister.' He chuckled. 'Some imagination, huh? Even Huey, Dewey and Louie would be better than North, South and Middle. Once the fog burns off you'll be able to see 'em. They're over ten thousand feet high.'

'Are you a Squatcher?' I asked Jake. I'd done my homework. Read the conference brochure that Susan had sent my way, familiarizing myself with the terminology.

He nodded again. 'I help monitor a database of Bigfoot sightings.'

'Have you ever seen a Bigfoot?' I asked.

'Only once,' Jake admitted. 'On a hunting trip to Canada with my dad and his brother. Been fascinated ever since.'

'Hah!' Scott snorted. 'It's bullshit if you ask me.' He glanced over his shoulder, said, ''Scuse my French, ma'am,' then turned his attention back to the road.

'Lived here long?' Jake asked our driver, not sounding the least bit offended.

'All my life,' Scott replied. 'Been over every square inch of the Deschutes National Forest and I've *never* seen a Bigfoot. Bears, sure. Wolves. Coyotes. The occasional buffalo. Ain't no such thing as Bigfoot.'

'There's going to be several hundred people at Flat Rock Lodge this weekend who are likely to disagree with you,' Jake said pleasantly.

The massive plaid shoulders shrugged. 'Reckon you're right.'

'Not everybody's a believer, though,' I said, remembering my conversation with Susan two nights earlier. 'Martin Radcliffe, for example. He'll be there.'

'Who's he?' Scott asked.

Jake answered for me. 'He's a professional debunker. Has a TV show on the History Channel – maybe you've seen it? Called *Don't You Believe It!*'

'Nah,' Scott muttered. His eyes drifted to the rear-view mirror. 'You ever watch *Forensic Files*, you being a cop and all?'

Jake rested a hand on Harley's head and stroked it gently. 'Uh, no. That would be a little like going to work early.'

I suppressed a grin. 'Do you know this guy Radcliffe, Jake?'

'Only by reputation,' he said.

As miles of pine forest spooled by outside my window, I asked, 'Why'd they pick Flat Rock for this conference anyway, Scott? It seems so remote.'

'There have been sightings here ever since the 1800s. The Indians talked about bear-like creatures that came down from the mountains at night to steal salmon.'

'Tsiatko,' said Jake. 'That's what the Native Americans called 'em. 'Stick Indians. They reportedly kidnapped children, too.'

'Sasquatch, Bigfoot, Yeti, Swamp Ape, Yowie . . . whatever,' Scott muttered. 'It's big business here, you know, so I don't like to make waves.'

'When you say it's big business, what do you mean?' I asked.

'I have two words for you, Mrs Ives: Prairie Flower.' He raised a hand from where it rested on the gear stick. 'I'll say no more.'

I stole a sideways glance at Jake, who shrugged, apparently as mystified by his comment as I was.

Harley's ears twitched. He glanced from Jake to me and back to Jake again before resting his muzzle on his paws and closing his eyes. If the dog knew anything about someone (or something) called Prairie Flower, he was staying mum.

Twenty miles further on, a carved wooden sign erected by the Kiwanis Club welcomed us to Sisters, a gentrified town of one- and two-story buildings featuring 1880s western-style facades. Boutiques, art galleries, restaurants, microbreweries and coffee shops lined both sides of the generously wide street, punctuated here and there by stately pine trees. By night, the streets would be illuminated by old-fashioned lanterns suspended from wooden cross beams; by day, floral hanging baskets brightened the scene. As we passed Dixie's Western Wear I made a mental note to stop by on my way back. I'd buy a pair of cowgirl boots – proper leather boots, too, the kind Santa Claus never brought me, despite years of pleading letters to the North Pole.

On the outskirts of Sisters the well-maintained highway ran remarkably straight through high desert sage; in the distance, pine forests formed a dark green skirt around the mountains, clearly visible now, still wearing their caps of winter snow. Traffic was light and Scott seemed in no particular hurry, avoiding the passing lanes and seemingly content to keep pace with the SUV and a long-distance trucker just ahead.

Just after the turnoff for Black Butte Ranch – 'fancy dancy' according to Scott, 'built by the lumber company back in the seventies' – he steered north onto an unpaved national forest road and we began a gradual, winding climb through a forest of ponderosa pine. We passed a yellow warning sign – Flood Hazard Area – pocked with bullet holes. Just when it seemed we'd run out of road and I began thinking how handy it was to have a cop and a K-9 on board in case Scott had driven us out to the middle of nowhere with murder on his mind, the curtain of trees parted.

I gasped.

Harley's head shot up.

'Damn,' said Jake. 'That's swanky.'

In the clearing before us stood a sprawling, three-story, red-roofed Swiss chalet built of white stucco accented with dark wooden shutters and carved gingerbread trim. Bright red geraniums filled the window boxes that decorated each balcony. Flat Rock Mountain Lodge was so relentlessly Bavarian that I expected Heidi and her grandfather to round the corner at any minute, followed by a herd of goats.

A paved trail lined with a low, split-rail fence snaked off and disappeared into the pine needles on our right. To the left, surrounded by the same rustic fencing, was a parking lot. 'Lots of cars here already,' I observed.

Scott brought the van to a stop under the portico. 'Most people arrive by car – either rent or drive their own,' he said as he opened his door and climbed out. I heard a beep and the door to my right slid open. Scott appeared almost at once, dragging a brass-colored bellman's luggage cart. 'I've got another pickup at the airport at two,' he said in way of explanation as he heaved Jake's and my bags unceremoniously onto the rolling cart. 'There's a minibus laid on at four for a big group from LA. A bit close, but it should get the lot of 'em here in time for the opening reception.'

'What a relief,' I said.

I must have sounded snarky because Jake frowned. 'You a skeptic, too, Hannah?'

I smiled. 'As the hired help, my opinion doesn't really matter. But, between you and me . . . and Harley here . . . let's just say that when it comes to Bigfoot, the jury is still out.'

Jake relieved a grateful Scott of the luggage cart. 'This conference will open your eyes,' Jake said as he pushed the cart with our bags on it into a lobby furnished with red plush-covered sofas, armchairs upholstered in a caramel-colored plaid and sturdy occasional tables painted off-white. A massive stone fireplace dominated the far end of the room, flanked by picture windows that soared from the weathered, oak-planked flooring straight into the rafters. In spite of warm, late-May temperatures, a small fire glowed in the grate and the four wing-back chairs facing the hearth were occupied. One of the occupants, a teenager, plugged into his iPod and nodding to some thankfully inaudible tune, had his bare feet deeply buried in the fur of – Dear Lord, help us! – an enormous bearskin rug. 'I wouldn't have wanted to meet *that* creature in the woods,' I said, indicating the rug that had me fixed in a glassy-eyed glare, teeth bared.

'At a conference like this, anything can happen,' Jake said.

Jake, Harley and I joined the line at the reception desk behind a well-dressed couple in their fifties who were loudly petitioning the desk clerk for a room change. She, with flyaway, improbably red hair, waved a printout under the young woman's nose. 'We don't want a double. We want a king. King. Sized. Bed,' she said, emphasizing each word. 'No smoking. Says so right here, doesn't it, Jim?'

Jim, balding and bespectacled, flushed, seeming to shrivel inside his three-piece suit as if willing himself to disappear. The clerk smiled, held her hand out for the printout, bowed her head and tapped a few keys. A minute later the pair trundled off behind a bellman pushing a cart loaded with two matching suitcases and an assortment of rectangular black boxes.

I checked in without incident.

'Don't forget to take a cookie,' the receptionist said, indicating a basket sitting on the counter nearby. The basket, woven in an intricate Native American design, was filled with waxed paper bags, each containing a homemade chocolate-chip cookie.

'Heat it up in the microwave,' she advised. 'To. Die. For.'

I didn't need to be told twice.

'See you at six-thirty?' Jake asked.

'I'll be around and about, I imagine.' I saluted him with my key packet, gave Harley a pat and headed for the elevators and my room on the third floor.

Once inside room 313, I dropped my bag on the bed then stepped out on the balcony to admire the view. Just beyond the parking lot below and to my right, acres of pine stretched off as far as the eye could see. On the left, however, just visible through a gap in the trees behind the tennis courts, I caught a glimpse of the enormous granite slab that must have given the lodge its name. Below that a ribbon of river danced and sparkled in the early afternoon sun.

Kudos to Susan for the view, I thought as I reluctantly slid the door closed. I ran a damp washcloth over my face, my fingers through my curls and freshened my lipstick. Then I headed back to the elevators, eager to track down my friend.

THREE

Nootka Sound, British Columbia, 1792. 'I do not know what to say about Matlox, inhabitant of the mountainous district, of who all have an unbelievable terror. [Native people] imagine his body as very monstrous, all covered with stiff black bristles; a head similar to a human one, but with much greater, sharper, and stronger fangs than those of the bear; extremely long arms; and toes and fingers armed with long curved claws. His shouts alone (they say) force those who hear them to the ground, and any unfortunate body he slaps is broken into a thousand pieces.'

Jose Mariano Mozino, *Noticias de Nutka: An Account of Nootka Sound in 1792.* Iris H. Wilson, trans. Toronto, McClelland and Steward, 1970, pp. 27–28

I found Susan by following a trail of yellow plastic Bigfoot prints that led from the lobby, past the coffee shop and down a long hallway to a registration desk set up just outside the Cascades

Ballroom. The minute Susan saw me, she leapt to her feet. 'Am I glad to see you!' Without giving me time even to click my heels, salute smartly and say, 'Reporting for duty, ma'am,' she turned and introduced me to the woman sitting next to her behind the table. 'Hannah, this is Carole Pulaski, one of the volunteers.'

Susan gestured to the chair she had just vacated. We did a quick do-si-do and switched places. 'It's going to be busy from now until registration closes at five-thirty,' Susan said. 'I have to check on the catering, so you'll have to excuse me, but Carole will show you what to do.'

After Susan left, I sat down on the folding chair, still warm, and tucked my knees under the long, skirt-covered table. While I wore slacks, I suspect Carole was grateful for the table skirt. Whoever had designed the black leather miniskirt she wore probably never envisioned anyone actually sitting down in it. She'd topped the skirt off with a Lycra animal-print scoop-neck T-shirt that was, in my opinion, at least two sizes too small, but when one was blessed with a full figure like Carole's it would be hard to resist the temptation to flaunt it. A drop-shaped polished agate suspended from a thin gold chain nested comfortably in the woman's cleavage.

Four trays of what I presumed were registration packets lay on the table in front of us. 'You have A to M,' Carole instructed. 'I'm handling N to Z.' Since A to M sat right in front of me, that was a no-brainer. Besides, I had to confess I was looking forward to seeing Jake Cummings again. 'Your badge will be in that batch, too.'

I thumbed through the envelopes, found my packet and opened it. My badge, like Carole's, had a Bigfoot silhouette printed in the upper right-hand corner. My name and hometown – Hannah Ives, Annapolis MD – was printed on it in Times New Roman, with my first name, 'Hannah,' several font sizes larger. A red stick-on ribbon invited conference attendees to 'Ask Me.' Good luck with that.

Carole reached under the table. 'Everyone gets one of these little bags of tchotchkes.'

'Swag?'

Carole laughed. 'Hardly. Van Cleef and Arpels was fresh out of diamond stick pins this year.'

I took the bag from her outstretched fingers. 'Been busy?' I asked, noticing that the tray in front of me still had at least fifty packets in it.

'They're having a break right now but I expect we'll be swamped in ten minutes or so, once the coffee runs out.'

'What's in the bag?' I asked, fingering the blue plastic drawstring that held it closed.

'Take a look.'

I undid the drawstring and upended the bag onto the tabletop. A fridge magnet shaped like a footprint dropped out. A koozie from Alpine Snowmobile Rentals to keep my canned drinks cold. Ponderosa Vacation Rentals was offering me a ten-day ski holiday rental for the price of seven. And there was an official-looking, gilt-edged gift certificate for twenty percent off the DVD of Brad Johnson's new video, *In the Steps of Bigfoot.*

I waved the certificate. 'Have you seen this video?'

Carole shook her head, setting the gold, double-hoop earrings she wore bouncing against her neck like miniature chandeliers. 'No one has. It's the one he's filming here at the conference.'

That was a surprise. Susan hadn't mentioned anyone filming the proceedings. Had I but known, I might have taken the time to have my eyebrows waxed. 'Who's Brad Johnson, anyway?'

Carole shrugged. 'I've never met him, but Ron – that's Ron Murphy, owns the Ford dealership? He's one of the conference organizers so he's read all the résumés. Ron told me the kid came out of NYU film school and did a bit of work in Hollywood. Guess this is his first big project. Hopes to sell it to the Discovery Channel or something.' She snorted. 'Fat chance!'

I tucked the loot back into the bag. 'Whoops, almost missed this one,' I said, taking genuine delight in a Bigfoot-shaped air freshener designed to hang on the rear-view mirror of my car. Pine scent. That would come in handy next time I took my daughter's labradoodle, Coco, to the doggie beach at Quiet Waters Park.

I was squinting at the small print on a keychain flashlight from a pool and spa company in Bend – 22 Years in Business! Our Spas are Made in Oregon! – when the last van from the airport arrived and the registration desk was deluged with conference attendees. As the clock ticked down to the time of the opening reception, each attendee seemed more anxious than the last.

By then I had my spiel down pat. *Tell me your name. Here's your packet – the badge holder is inside. Hospitality suite is down the hall, just past the restrooms. Simply follow the big yellow footprints. Ha ha ha. Please check your banquet ticket to make sure your entrée is correct. Blue for chicken, red for beef and if you asked for vegetarian, your ticket will be green.*

And, *Relax, you have plenty of time to check in. We've ordered tons of hors d'oeuvres.*

Then I'd shove a goody bag into their hands, smile and move on to the next customer.

I'd ducked under the table skirt, fishing for an errant goody bag when I heard a familiar voice. 'Hey, Hannah.'

I bumped my head on the way up. 'Ouch!' I said, gently rubbing the spot. Then, 'Hi, Jake.'

I found Jake's packet filed among the Cs and handed it over. When he opened it I was amused to see that Harley also had a nametag and a red banquet ticket. 'We're both meat and potato men,' Jake informed me with a wink as he clipped the tag to Harley's collar. 'See you at the reception?'

I shrugged and turned to Carole. 'What time do we finish up here, anyway?'

'Five-thirty or thereabouts.'

I smiled up at Jake. 'Then, yes, I'll be there, although if Susan has anything to say about it I'll be running around making sure the crab balls don't run out.'

'All work and no play?' Jake winked.

I felt suddenly warm and all a-fluttery. Tongue-tied, too. As I watched Jake stride away, long-limbed and lean, I gave myself a good talking-to. Don't flatter yourself, Hannah. He's sure to have noticed the wedding ring on your finger. The guy's simply a natural flirt.

'That's it, then,' Carole was saying when I came to. 'Only ten packets left. They'll have to wait until tomorrow.'

I helped her tuck the trays of registration packets and the box of goody bags under the table. 'Will they be safe here overnight?'

Carole rolled her eyes. 'We're in Flat Rock Freaking Oregon,' she said, as if that explained everything. Then she waved vaguely and hurried away.

Back in my room, I stripped off my limp, frankly embarrassing travel clothes and left them in a heap on the floor. After a quick shower I changed into the black slacks and colorful embroidered jacket I'd worn to the president's reception at Oberlin a few evenings before, then slipped into a pair of black Gucci nameplate flats I'd bought on sale at DSW for $149. Telling my reflection in the mirror, *That will have to do* – I picked up my iPhone and texted Susan: What next and where?

She replied: Catering office. Stat.

Oh, joy. An issue with the food already.

I found Susan standing guard over a platter of crudités arranged fan-shaped around a crystal bowl filled with what looked like ranch dip.

'Hannah, thank God. I have to run. Explain to this woman, please, the difference between vegetarian and vegan.'

With a wide-eyed, deer-in-the-headlights, what-did-I-do-wrong expression on her face, the young woman stammered, 'I'm just filling in; the catering manager is out tonight with a sick kid.'

I'd gone through a vegan phase, as Susan well knew, back when I was recovering from breast cancer. I'd loosened up a bit in recent years but was still careful to shop for groceries where I could be assured that any meat I decided to buy would be hormone and antibiotic free. 'What's in the dip?' I asked as Susan straight-armed her way out the door, leaving me alone with the nervous girl.

'Creamy ranch. It doesn't have meat in it, honest,' she said. 'I can show you the jar. You can read the ingredients for yourself.'

'Vegans eat no animal products whatsoever,' I explained, surprised that someone her age, which I judged to be around twenty, wouldn't already be familiar with twenty-first-century dietary trends. 'And that includes milk, eggs and honey.'

'Oh.' Clearly, this was a new thought.

'A vegan would eat a carrot stick plain,' I pointed out. 'Or dip it in salt, maybe with oil and vinegar on it.'

'I see.'

'You can leave the ranch dip on the tray but I suggest you label it so that there'll be no confusion.' I touched her arm. 'Look. Even a vegan who's never eaten a restaurant meal in her entire life isn't going to chance it by dipping into something white, but I know she would appreciate a head's up.'

Looking somewhat relieved, the young woman handed me a printout of the menu, presumably for my review and approval, although if I objected to something I didn't know what good it would have done now, just twenty minutes before cocktail hour was scheduled to begin. I made a production of skimming the menu, nodding, um-uming over each appetizer in what I hoped was an encouraging way, noting, in particular, the stuffed mushrooms, then handed it back. 'Cash bar?'

'Of course. One at each end of the dining room.'

'Good,' I said, thinking I was going to need a drink or three before the evening was over.

'Is there anything else?' she wondered.

'Not that I can think of. Point me in the direction of the reception?'

With an audible sigh of relief, the girl pointed.

I hustled along the carpeted hallway and pushed through a handful of attendees milling around one of the closed dining-room doors. I checked my watch, said cheerily, 'Just five minutes, folks!' opened the door and eased through.

When I caught up with Susan she was fluttering around the appetizer table, re-arranging the cocktail napkins and fussing with the nasturtiums that decorated the base of the centerpiece, an ice sculpture the size of a cat, carved in the shape of a Bigfoot taking an oh-so-casual stroll through the fruit platter. 'How can I help tonight?' I asked.

'Work the crowd. Meet and greet, especially the speakers.' She tapped her nametag. 'They have green ribbons.'

'That doesn't sound too onerous.' I snitched a mushroom. 'What about dinner?'

As I popped the mushroom into my mouth, Susan scowled, so I re-arranged the remaining mushrooms with a flick of my index finger, closing the gap and erasing all evidence of my premature sampling.

'It's a buffet with open seating. There's a table reserved for staff over near the lectern, but honestly? I'd rather you mingled with the attendees.'

'Who's speaking tonight?'

Susan's eyebrows shot up. 'Martin Radcliffe. I thought you knew.'

I ignored the not-so-subtle rebuke. 'Oh, right,' I said. 'He's talking about video fakery.'

'He concentrates on Bigfoot, of course, but he touches on bogus UFO videos and mentions Nessie hoaxes, too.'

'I thought the Loch Ness monster had been debunked ages ago,' I said.

'Hope springs eternal,' she said. 'You can even explore Loch Ness using Google Street View these days. Can I get you a glass of wine?' Susan asked unexpectedly. An apology, perhaps, for being a bit snarky.

'I wish,' I said, 'but I think I'd better have my wits about me. Perhaps later.' As she led me toward the bar nearest the podium, I added: 'I'm kind of surprised that the conference is starting with a focus on fakery. Most of these people are believers, surely.'

'True, but they are as eager as anyone – perhaps even more eager, to expose the fakers.'

I could see the logic behind that. 'So by showing how much of the so-called evidence out there *isn't* real, they can concentrate on what might actually be real.'

Susan grinned. 'Eliminate the pranksters in monkey suits, and then . . .' She winked. 'Anything can happen.'

Susan introduced me to each bartender in turn, saying, 'Anybody has an issue tonight, refer them to me or to Hannah here,' then sailed off again on another errand.

'A club soda with lime,' I told the bartender.

I had taken my first sip when the ballroom doors flew open and a man I recognized from a photograph in the conference brochure as Randall Frazier exploded into the room. All he needed was a safari hat and a pair of wire-rimmed spectacles and he'd be good to go for a charge up San Juan Hill. 'Where's the bar?' Frazier bellowed, loud enough to be heard by all his troops. A half-dozen neatly dressed men and women flowed into the room in his considerable wake.

'He's two minutes early,' I grumbled as I checked my watch.

The bartender shrugged, arranged the tip cup more prominently on the bar in front of him and said, 'It's show time.'

FOUR

Paris, France, 1784. 'There is lately arrived in France from America, a wild man, who was caught in the woods, 200 miles back from the Lake of the Woods, by a party of Indians . . . He is near seven feet high, covered with hair, but has little appearance of understanding and is remarkably sullen and subdued. When he was taken, half a bear was found lying by him, whom he had just killed.'

The London Times, January 4, 1784

As the room filled and the pre-dinner cocktail party progressed, I made it my goal in life to chat up Randall Frazier, the superannuated Indiana Jones who I kept my eye on as he migrated from one bar to the other, followed by his entourage. The man was down to one devoted fan, rapt, hanging on to his every golden word, when I crossed the room and pounced. 'Hannah Ives,' I said, extending my hand. 'One of the organizers. How's the conference going for you so far?'

His female companion, a petite, middle-aged woman dressed in a hot-pink tracksuit with matching athletic shoes – an outfit brought up to cocktail party standards by the addition of three-quarter-karat diamond ear studs – fixed me with eyes as green as the sea and shot shrapnel my way. Frazier, blustery but gentlemanly, introduced us. Monique Deschamps was from Montreal, I learned, and the author of the definitive Sasquatch work, *Bigfoot: Fact, Fiction and Fable*. 'Monique is here to promote her book,' Frazier explained, sounding like a proud father. 'It'll be on sale in the dealers' room.'

Monique's face softened and she flushed.

I promised to stop by her booth to check it out when the

exhibits opened in the morning. She must have decided that I, a lowly conference organizer, was no threat to her relationship with the great man because she took the opportunity to wander off and refill her plate, leaving us alone.

Based on what Susan had told me about Frazier, I wanted to quiz him about the enigmatic yeti finger but didn't know how to bring it up. I decided to ease into it. 'Did I read in the program that you're organizing an expedition to explore the lava tubes of Mount Saint Helens this coming August?' I asked.

'You heard correctly.' He brightened considerably. 'Interested in coming along to observe the filming?'

I laughed and sidestepped the question. 'Looking for Bigfoot, I presume?'

'Hope to find him, too, in spite of Radcliffe's naysaying. I'm pretty confident. A local Indian gal pinpointed the spot so we're not going in blind.'

'What kind of equipment do you need for a trip like that?' I asked.

'Leica night-vision binoculars, of course. I've also got a Nikon D1x top-end, single-lens reflex camera with shutter speeds up to 1/16,000th of a second that will freeze a cheetah running flat out, thermal imaging equipment and a ton of motion sensors. I even have access to a helicopter, although nowadays we're having pretty good luck using drones.' He leaned forward. 'Guy working for a real estate company in Sacramento was filming some property aerials and got footage of Bigfoot instead.'

'No kidding!' I said.

'Check it out on YouTube,' he said helpfully.

'Sounds expensive, an expedition like that,' I commented, taking a ladylike sip of club soda.

'Oh, it is, it is, but my sponsor has deep pockets. *Very* deep.'

I was thinking National Geographic or the Nature Channel when Frazier bumped my arm with his elbow and gestured with his long-neck bottle of Rainier 'mountain fresh' beer. 'Over there, hogging the shrimp platter.'

I turned slowly to see to whom he was referring. A portly gentleman dressed in a close-fitting dark blue business suit was dragging a shrimp by the tail through a shell-shaped bowl of cocktail sauce. As I watched, he tilted his head back, suspended the shrimp for a moment over his wide-open mouth then dropped it in. 'Smooth,' I commented.

Frazier laughed. 'Greg Gilchrist doesn't care what anyone thinks about him. He has more money than God.'

'Must be nice.'

'Mining,' he explained. 'He's chairman of Western Amalgamated Mining and Bank Amerika-Mexico, among others. Makes money faster than he can spend it. Gilchrist bankrolled my first expedition to Nepal. Perhaps you've heard of it?'

'It rings a bell,' I said, sensing an opening. 'Something about a monk and the finger from a yeti?'

Frazier waved his beer dismissively. 'That was a *huge* disappointment. Got the relic smuggled out of Nepal as far as London but the customs people picked it out of her carryon at Heathrow.'

'Her?'

'A famous actress.' He lowered his voice an octave. 'I'll say no more.'

'What happened to the finger after that?'

'Since it was an artifact they sent it to the British Museum for testing. Turns out to be old but definitely human.' He leaned closer. 'If you can't trust a monk, who can you trust? Paid good money for that finger, too.'

'And a bottle of Scotch?'

Frazier chuckled. 'You *have* done your homework, Hannah.'

'Your fame precedes you,' I said, glancing back to the buffet with stuffed mushrooms on my mind.

Clinging with laced fingers to Gilchrist's free arm and gazing at him adoringly in spite of his boorish behavior – or perhaps because of it – a leggy twenty-something dressed in a halter-top mini-dress tottered on a pair of strappy, high-heeled sandals. Her white-blonde hair, parted in the middle like a seventies rock star, fell straight as a stick to cover her bare shoulders. Her glossy red lips moved and parted. Gilchrist dredged another shrimp through the cocktail sauce and dropped it onto the woman's tongue, then bestowed a paternal kiss on her forehead.

'Who's she, then?' I asked Frazier.

'Nicole Baker,' he said.

'Nicole?' After a moment, I said, 'Her resemblance to Janice, the lead guitarist for Doctor Teeth and the Electric Mayhem is uncanny, don't you agree? Down to the inch-long false eyelashes.'

'Doctor Teeth?'

'The Muppets,' I explained.

'Meow.'

I shrugged and grinned. 'It's what I do.'

I decided not to comment on what was all too obvious. Nicole had to be a good forty years younger than her Sugar Daddy. As I watched, she returned the favor of the shrimp by sliding a carrot stick between his teeth. If they kept this up much longer I was going to need an insulin injection.

Fortunately Monique Deschamps sidled up to the mogul and his girlfriend just then, interrupting their tête-à-tête mid chicken skewer. Nicole had been demolishing it, one tidbit at a time, dragging the skewer seductively through her teeth.

Meanwhile, one of Frazier's fans tapped his shoulder, tackling him with a burning question about provisioning for the Mount St Helens expedition, so I excused myself, gladly leaving them to their discussion of down versus synthetic sleeping bags.

When dinnertime rolled around, I hung back from the buffet at first, hoping I might bump into Jake and Harley, but when they didn't show up I joined the queue at the buffet table. I passed up the fried chicken and the sliced beef swimming in gravy, but a Southwestern beans and rice concoction labeled 'Ranchero' looked appetizing so I spooned a portion onto my plate then moved on, closing in on the steam tray of broccoli and cauliflower smothered in cheese sauce.

'Oh, dear,' the woman in front of me said to no one in particular.

'Is something wrong?' I looked up from the grated cheese I was sprinkling on my rice. The speaker was attractive, about my age, with medium-length, honey-gold hair that flopped carelessly over her left eye.

Holding her plate in both hands, she smiled benevolently at the server – the same young woman who I'd met earlier in the discussion over the ranch dressing. Now the server wore a uniform and a badge that identified her as 'Tina.'

'Do you have any *plain* broccoli and cauliflower?' The

woman's tone was almost pleading. 'I'm a vegan and I don't eat cheese.'

Tina beamed. 'Oh, honey, don't worry.' She flapped a dismissive hand over the vegetables. 'That's not really cheese.'

I'd been about to help myself but drew back. 'What is it, then, Tina?'

Tina leaned forward over the steam tray and whispered, 'You don't want to know.' With a sideways I've-done-my-homework look at me, she added, 'It comes in a tub. I read the ingredients, though, and it doesn't have a smidgen of milk or eggs in it.'

'That's OK,' the woman said, raising her hand, palm out. 'I'll just have salad.'

'I can take the broccoli back to the kitchen and rinse it off under hot water for you.' Tina, again, trying to be helpful.

'Um, no, thank you. Salad will be fine.'

'Salad! What a good idea,' I said, laying the 'cheese'-coated serving spoon aside and moving along the buffet line behind her.

Sensing a kindred spirit and mindful of Susan's request that I mingle with the attendees, I trailed after the woman's sheer, multicolored paisley top as she headed toward a vacant table. 'Mind if I join you?' I asked just as she was sitting down.

She brightened, her blue eyes twinkling at me through rimless, almost invisible eyeglasses. 'Please.'

I set my plate on the table and glanced casually at her nametag: Leah Solat, Sacramento, CA. 'What brings you here, Leah?'

'I'm a journalist, writing an article for *The Sacramento Bee*.'

'Pro or con?'

'Hah! I try to maintain my impartiality but it's all hogwash, isn't it?'

'Well, I've never seen a Bigfoot but I'm betting more than half the people here are convinced they have. The catalog of sightings goes back for centuries, as you probably know. Can all those people be mistaken?'

While Leah pondered a response, a red-haired woman I recognized as the one who'd been standing in front me earlier at the reception desk drifted past, scanning the tables as if she were lost. 'Please, join us,' I said, taking pity. 'I'm Hannah and this is Leah.'

'Athena Davis,' the woman said, indicating her nametag. 'My husband, Jim, is around here somewhere. Ah, there he is!' She began waving frantically, as if trying to hail a cab.

As she sat down, she said, 'Jim's been fascinated with apes ever since he read Tarzan as a kid.'

'Edgar Rice Burroughs?' Leah said. 'But that's fiction, surely.'

Athena lowered her voice. 'Don't tell Jim that.'

Jim Davis, when he joined us, wore a nametag decorated with a green ribbon that said, 'Speaker.' It clashed loudly with his banana-yellow Hawaiian shirt decorated with surfboards and palm trees.

'So, what will you be talking about?' Leah asked as Jim sat down at the table opposite us.

'Surveillance,' his wife supplied.

Jim swallowed a mouthful of beef and washed it down with a gulp of iced tea. 'We used to own a Radio Shack franchise in Altoona,' he explained. 'When the company went belly up I simply closed the door. But – silver lining! – I got all this cool equipment to play with.'

'You should see our garage,' Athena grumped in a good-natured way. 'It's a disgrace.' She waved a fork at her husband. 'If you're not careful, Jimmy, you'll end up on that TV show, *Hoarders*.'

'You'll sing a different tune, Athena, my love, when the system works.'

'What does your system do, Jim?' I wanted to know.

'It's a prototype for a 360-degree remote video monitoring system.'

'Like a webcam?'

'Similar,' Jim said, 'but a webcam is usually fixed.' He drew a circle in the air with his index finger. 'My camera revolves.'

Athena bounced in her chair. 'Jimmy's a genius! It's all connected to his laptop on the Internet.' She cupped her hand and rotated it from side to side like a searchlight. 'Jimmy's goes all the way around like this, doesn't it, sweetie?'

Across the table, 'sweetie' flushed modestly and nodded. 'Twenty-four seven.'

'The cool thing,' Jim added, gesturing with a fork piled high with mashed potatoes dripping gravy, 'is that it's triggered by motion. Once the camera starts filming it sends an alarm directly to my laptop.' He demonstrated: 'Whoot, whoot, whoot!'

Athena beamed. 'I told you he was a clever boy.'

'Are you giving a demonstration here at the conference?' Leah asked.

'Better than that. I'm setting the system up in the woods out there.' He gestured again with his fork, dangerously heaped with faux-cheesy broccoli. 'Not far from the Metolius River.'

'There have been multiple sightings of Bigfoot along the river,' Athena said.

'Then tomorrow, I'll fire it up,' Jim continued as if Athena hadn't spoken. 'Demonstrate how it works.'

'It sounds expensive,' Leah said.

'Not at all, Miss Solat. Radio Shack is no longer around, of course, but you can buy all the component parts at Best Buy, or even over the Internet. Beautiful, huh? Three, four hundred dollars tops for the lot.'

'It would be worth that much to catch whatever is getting into my garbage cans at night,' Leah commented.

'Wouldn't it be amazing if Jimmy caught a Bigfoot on camera?' Athena said. 'That would show Mr Smarty Pants a thing or two.'

Jim tore a roll in half and used it to sop gravy off his plate. 'Athena means Martin Radcliffe.'

I raised an interrogatory eyebrow.

'My husband took a series of Bigfoot videos,' Athena clarified, 'and posted them on Facebook. Martin McNasty told everyone they'd been faked.'

'To be fair,' Jim said, 'the quality sucked. I was using a cheap, battery-operated wildlife camera in those days, but still, there was no need for Radcliffe to question my integrity.'

'Our new equipment is state of the art,' Athena said. 'When Bigfoot shows up we'll be ready for him.'

'So you're believers?' Leah asked, stating the obvious. I noticed that during the course of our conversation with the Davises she'd extracted a small notebook from her handbag and had begun taking notes.

'Absolutely!' Jim said. 'And I'm hoping to prove it. Right here. Right now.'

'How do you decide where to set up your camera, Jim?' Leah wanted to know.

'As Athena mentioned, there've been numerous Bigfoot sightings along the Metolius River, especially down near the rapids just below Flat Rock.'

Bears, more than likely, I thought. Bears snagging salmon. But I kept my mouth shut.

'Prairie Flower helped us pinpoint the location,' he continued.

Prairie Flower! My ears perked up. This must be the person the van driver, Scott, had cautioned us about. 'She's an expert, is she?' I asked, assuming that no self-respecting 'he' would willingly choose to name himself after a flower.

'She uses one of those . . . those . . .' Jim searched for the correct word.

'Wand pendulums,' Athena supplied. 'She dangles this crystal gizmo over a map on a string. That's how Randall Frazier decided to take the expedition to Mount Saint Helens this summer.'

Pendulums and magic crystals. Sounded more like a gypsy skill than one associated with Native Americans, but what did I know. I was thinking that I should hire Prairie Flower to help locate my grandson's lost Elmo doll when Susan Lockley caught my eye, gesturing at me from the podium. I excused myself and joined her.

Together we fiddled with the laptop and projection cables. Susan supplied me with a thumb drive that I plugged into the laptop's USB port. A few minutes after firing up the PowerPoint software Martin Radcliffe's presentation filled the screen.

I jiggled with the focus then paged through the first few slides to make sure everything was working smoothly, including his video link to the iconic fifty-nine-second Patterson-Gimlin film of a female Bigfoot strolling along a stream bed in Willow Creek, California. Satisfied, I returned to the title slide and left it up. BIGFOOT ON FILM: FACT vs FICTION?, scrawled in a spooky font I recognized as Slasher was superimposed in red over the 'look back' image of the Bigfoot nicknamed 'Patty' taken from frame number 352 of the controversial 1967 film.

'There's Martin now,' Susan whispered as a man strode purposely through the seated diners, making a beeline for the podium.

Radcliffe was younger and thinner than he looked on TV. (OK, I confess to watching his silly show from time to time.) The thirty-five-year-old entertainer had fair skin and pale hair slicked straight back and trendy. He was dressed in chinos and a light blue, long-sleeve button-down Oxford shirt with the sleeves rolled up. Your typical college-prep look, with the exception of his athletic shoes, which were lime-green Reebok Crossfit trainers. Radcliffe was famous for them, according to the tabloids. Never wore anything else, they claimed, not even to weddings and funerals. 'Thank you, ladies,' Radcliffe said as he approached. 'Looks good.'

Susan shook the man's hand and said, 'It there's anything you need, Martin, Hannah will get it for you.'

'I'd like to keep the front row clear for the cameraman,' Martin said, looking directly at me.

'That shouldn't be a problem.'

Said cameraman, a jean-clad twenty-something with a shock of shaggy, jet-black hair, sat cross-legged on the carpet near a tower of black cases, installing what I assumed was a battery pack into a shoulder-mounted camcorder. 'Brad's filming the conference for a documentary. If it's good enough I'll feature it on my fall show,' Martin explained.

'When will the show air?' I asked, just to be polite.

'September. It takes a couple of months to put it together.' He grinned. 'A *good* show, anyway.'

I cast my mind back to a sleepless night when I'd been channel surfing. 'I caught your program on poltergeists,' I confessed. 'Couldn't sleep a wink after that.' Which was certainly true, although I suspected it had more to do with the high-test cappuccino I'd drunk that night at dinner than the acid-green, white-eyed creepiness of the images staring out of my television screen.

While Martin Radcliffe rummaged through his briefcase looking for who knows what, Susan and I watched Brad fiddle with his equipment, his long legs folded stiffly beneath him. I couldn't help but notice his boots. They were pock-marked, as if the cow they'd been harvested from had suffered some horrific disease.

'You pay extra for that,' Susan said when I pointed it out.

I simply stared.

'Ostrich,' she informed me. 'Those bumps are vacant quill follicles – where the feathers used to be.'

'Ewww,' I said.

Brad shifted and a pant leg rode up, exposing more of the boot. Fancy multicolored stitching exploded over the front and sides in a pattern like angels' wings. A square toe and a sensible, one-and-a-half-inch heel completed the look. *Gen-you-wine*, handmade in Texas, thank you very much, the look said.

'I want me some of them,' I whispered to Susan.

She scowled. 'You're joking.'

'I'm serious.'

'Those?'

'Well, not those exactly. Something a little less, um, exotic. Rattlesnake, maybe.'

Susan rolled her eyes. 'No more wine for you, Hannah Ives.' And with a friendly pat to my shoulder, off she went.

Radcliffe touched a button on his Apple Watch secured high on his wrist with a bright orange band, then looked at me. 'I'll start speaking in fifteen minutes, give or take. Do you know who's introducing me?'

'According to the program it's Ron Murphy. I haven't met him yet so I'm not sure if he's here.'

'Ah, yes. I know Ron. Good, good.' And with a tip of an imaginary hat he went off to chat with his cameraman.

My work here is done, I thought. I grabbed a brownie from the buffet then wandered back to the table and rejoined my dinner companions. Jim Davis was holding forth on night-vision wireless trail cams you could get on overnight delivery from Amazon. Athena looked on adoringly. Leah was openly taking notes.

As I sat down, Jim said, 'We'll try to even up the odds a bit, though, Miss Solat.' He leaned forward, both forearms resting on the table. 'Do you know what you bait a Bigfoot trap with?'

Leah raised an eyebrow, ballpoint pen poised. 'No, tell me.'

Jim tapped his temple with an index finger. 'Tuna fish.'

You learn something new every day.

The next time I saw Nicole Baker she had abandoned her million-aire boyfriend and plopped herself down next to Martin Radcliffe who was sitting on a chair, his feet stretched out in front of him. He glanced up from the business at hand – shuffling through a

large-font printout of his talk – and caught my eye, looking
desperate.

I sashayed over. 'Just checking on the equipment, Mr Radcliffe.
Is everything working properly?'

He shot to his feet and laid the printout on the chair. 'I'll
need some help with the microphone,' he said, motioning
for me to follow him up to the podium. 'I usually use a lavalier
mike so I can walk around while I talk.' He pointed to the
microphone attached to the stand on the podium. 'Those are so
restrictive.'

Nicole, I noticed, had picked up Martin's printout and was
leafing through the pages.

'Thank you,' he whispered.

'Don't thank me until I can locate a lavalier for you,' I said
with a grin.

'Not for the mike.' He nodded in Nicole's direction. 'For saving
me from that.'

'Was she talking your ear off?'

Turning his back to the young woman, he said quietly, 'She's
angling for a job on my show.'

Remembering what he'd told us about Brad Johnson, I gestured
toward the cameraman and said, 'Isn't everyone?'

Radcliffe laughed but there was no mirth in it. 'Brad's got a
chance. He's got the talent. He gets it. Nicole Baker? Who's ever
heard of Nicole Baker? Community theater, a two-bit modeling
career in Chicago, a cringe-worthy walk-on in *Ted 2* and she
thinks she'll be the next Vanna White.'

'Nobody turns letters on your show.'

'She figures I have connections.'

'Doesn't Mr Gilchrist . . .?' I paused.

'Sure, but money doesn't buy everything. To coin a phrase.'

Martin's talk took an Equal Opportunity jab at all manner of
video fakery. Beginning with UFOs – pointing out the wires,
shadows, reflections and even flying objects made out of Lego
toys that were glaringly obvious once he directed our attention
to them – he went on to consider the Loch Ness monster. Quickly
eliminating the obvious bathtub toys, he zeroed in on the famous
1933 'Surgeon's Photo' of Nessie, revealed in 1994 as a hoax

perpetrated by Christian Spurling using a toy submarine outfitted with a sea serpent head. 'Besides,' Martin said, 'exercise your brains, people. There isn't enough food in the lake to sustain a monster as big as Nessie.'

A woman in the front row waved her hand, interrupting the presentation. 'But,' she said without waiting to be called on, 'isn't it possible that Nessie has died? Due to global warming?'

Radcliffe gave her a withering look. 'Please hold your questions until the end of my presentation, madam.' And he forged on.

One by one, he dissected historic Bigfoot videos from Russia, Poland, Manitoba and Prince Edward Island that most of the audience had seen multiple times on the Internet. Closer to home, videos from Washington, Colorado, California, Texas and Georgia were analyzed, dismantled and thoroughly debunked.

The video clip shot in Maine by a twelve-year-old boy? An admitted hoax.

The National Park Service's webcam footage of a four-member Bigfoot family stalking buffalo at Old Faithful in Yellowstone? Cross-country skiers.

The Pennsylvania trail cam? A young bear, with mange.

'Now just a darn minute!' someone shouted from behind me.

All heads swiveled in that direction.

Jim Davis was on his feet, waving a fist in the air. Athena, still seated, grabbed her husband's arm and tried to pull him back into his chair but he shook her hand off. 'I never claimed it *was* a Sasquatch!' Davis yelled. 'I said I'd been hunting in those woods for years and never seen anything like it. That it *might* be a Sasquatch.'

When I glanced back at Radcliffe, he was smirking. 'A bear,' he repeated, 'with mange.' He stabbed a button on the controller, more viciously than was necessary, I thought, and pointed it at the projector. 'For comparison,' Radcliffe continued as the next slide clicked into place, 'here is a picture of a mangy bear cub. Any idiot can see the resemblance.'

Whispering, murmuring, hissing, a quiet boo.

'That was harsh,' someone sitting next to me said.

A sudden hush. The clink of glassware from one of the bars.

We all watched Jim stalk out of the room, his back rigid and shoulders straight. Athena scooped up her handbag from under her chair and hustled after him.

'Moving on to the Pyrenees,' Radcliffe oozed, clicking forward to the next slide, a photograph of a shaggy white figure that seemed to be strolling casually down a snow-covered mountain slope, 'here we are at a ski resort in Formigal in northeast Spain, right on the border with France.' He zoomed in on the mysterious figure. 'Definitely a bear,' Radcliffe declared with certainty, 'or a hoaxster in a furry suit.'

Several minutes later, when he came to the Patterson-Gimlin film of a Bigfoot nicknamed Patty shot in 1967 alongside Bluff Creek in California by two cowboys out for a ride, Radcliffe remained uncharacteristically circumspect. 'It's been analyzed to death,' he explained, paging through slide after slide. 'If it's a man in an ape suit, as I tend to believe, it's an awfully good one. No one over the past forty years, not even the BBC with all their considerable resources, has been able to replicate the hoax, and heaven knows they've tried.

'People want to believe that such creatures exist,' he concluded. 'Like Fox Mulder in the *X-Files*, they are convinced that "The Truth is Out There."'

As he spoke, *The X-Files* logo morphed into a giant question mark, expanding until it filled the screen. 'But, remember this. It's science, and pure science alone, that examines the proof and will finally give you the answers you seek.'

FIVE

Sacket's Harbor, New York, August 30, 1818. '[I]n the vicinity of Ellisburgh, was seen on the 30th Ult. by a gentleman of unquestionable veracity, an animal resembling the Wild Man of the Woods . . . He is described as bending forward when running – hairy, and the heel of the foot narrow, spreading at the toes. Hundreds of persons have been in pursuit for several days, but nothing further is heard or seen of him . . . We wish not to impeach the veracity of this highly favored gentleman – yet,

*it is proper that such naturally improbable accounts should be
established by the mouth of at least two direct eyewitnesses
to entitle them.'*

The Exeter Watchman (Exeter, NY),
September 6, 1818

Still operating on east coast time, I awoke at five o'clock the following morning. I didn't have to report for duty until eight-thirty, so after staring at the ceiling for fifteen minutes I got up, brewed a cup of coffee in the hotel room's coffee maker, stirred in a packet of powdered cream with a plastic swizzle stick – ugh! – then took it out on the balcony to watch the sun rise. After sending a quick email to my husband to let him know I was still among the living, I showered, got dressed and went downstairs in search of a proper cup of coffee.

I was so early it was just me and a woman wearing a name tag that said 'Debbie' in the hospitality suite. While hotel staff fussed with uncooperative coffee urns, I helped Debbie arrange boxes of donuts on the table next to a tent sign that said, 'Donuts Compliments of Debbie's Donut Dugout.'

'Will twelve dozen be enough, you think?' Debbie wondered.

I took the liberty of sampling one of the glazed variety. I took a bite, closed my eyes and moaned.

'Does Krispy Kreme know about these?' I mumbled around a sweet, yeasty mouthful. While Debbie observed me silently, beaming, I polished off the donut in four bites then licked each of my fingers in turn, keen to make the goodness last. 'One hundred dozen isn't going to be enough,' I told her.

Debbie blushed, then grinned. 'Try the chocolate.'

I held up both hands defensively, palm out. 'There's only so much ecstasy I can take in a single day.'

While I stood at the urn fixing myself a cup of coffee, Leah Solat breezed in looking fresh and fit in pink yoga pants and a pale yellow top, followed by Martin Radcliffe carrying an insulated travel mug. 'If you've already been to the gym,' I told Leah as she waited her turn at the urn, 'I think I'm going to kill myself.'

Leah laughed. 'Just on my way out there now.'

'The donuts are to die for,' I said, feeling a bit wicked for even mentioning them. 'You can work the calories off on the treadmill.'

Holding her coffee, Leah wandered over to the table where Debbie stood guard over her luscious wares. 'Do you have gluten-free?'

To my surprise, Debbie reached under the table and withdrew another box, opened it and held it out. 'I make them with chickpea flour, ma'am. My specialty.'

The chickpea donut must have been every bit as delicious as the one I'd just demolished, because after Leah scarfed it down she snagged a second to take along to the gym with her.

I had to laugh. Vegan *and* gluten-free. Conference meal planning could certainly be a challenge.

'Good morning, Hannah.' It was a familiar voice, so close to my ear that I could feel his warm breath on my neck.

I stepped back then turned to face the speaker. 'Good morning, Jake. I looked for you last night at dinner, but . . .'

'Jet lag,' he explained before I could finish the thought. 'Air travel doesn't always agree with old Harley here.'

Harley, sitting patiently beside his master, looked fresh, bright-eyed and a match for any squirrel that might cross his path in the forest that day.

'Besides,' Jake continued, 'I think I've heard everything that Martin Radcliffe has to say.'

'You missed the fireworks,' I said.

'Oh?'

'Radcliffe showed a video taken by Jim Davis a couple of years ago. When Davis objected to the way it was being presented, Radcliffe kinda called him an idiot.'

Jake snorted. 'Par for the course with Radcliffe.'

'Otherwise,' I said, 'I found his talk intriguing. It didn't seem to me that he had an axe to grind. What I mean is he wasn't trying to convince the audience that *all* those videos had been faked.' I paused. 'Have you had coffee?'

'Up in the room, thanks.'

'*Proper* coffee,' I said, indicating the urns.

Jake closed his eyes for a moment and said wistfully, 'Proper coffee, ah. That would be The Angry Catfish on 28th in

Minneapolis. No frou-frou brew. A caffeine high so fine that the DEA should take notice.'

'I don't really believe in Bigfoot,' I confessed, 'but it was fascinating to hear about the lengths people go to in order to fake it. With all those fruitcakes out there crying wolf, it must make it harder for someone who has a legitimate sighting to make anyone believe them.'

'We take every sighting very seriously,' Jake said.

'We?'

'Bigfoot Field Research Organization. BFRO. Ever since I retired I've been volunteering as one of their investigators.'

'Gosh, that must involve a lot of travel.'

Jake shook his head. 'Not necessarily. Mostly I interview witnesses over the phone who have posted sightings on our website. We apply the closest scrutiny to the A-rated sightings.'

'A-rated? Are there B-, C- and D-rated sightings, too?'

'No, just A to C. The Cs are so iffy that we don't generally list them in the database, but the As, the clear sightings, are always investigated. Bs?' He rocked a hand back and forth. 'Poor visibility, footprints, sounds. Anyway . . .' He paused to take a breath, then shrugged. 'Keeps me off the streets and out of trouble.'

After a moment, he asked, 'Where are you from, Hannah?'

'Maryland,' I said, wondering why he wanted to know since it was clearly printed on my nametag. I looked down, clicked my tongue then flipped the tag over so the name side faced out and flapped it at him. 'Annapolis. The sailing capital of the eastern seaboard.'

'Ah, well, you might be surprised to learn that Maryland has had over thirty-four sightings since we started keeping track of these things. I interviewed a guy recently who had an eye-to-eye standoff with a big, hairy creature in the Pax River watershed area near Fort Meade.'

'No kidding. That's less than twenty miles from my house. Did he get any pictures?'

'Sadly, no.' Jake stared at my face so intently I wondered if I had chocolate donut icing on my chin. I was reaching for a napkin when he said, 'Can you spare a few minutes? I want to show you something.'

'Sorry, can't.' I fingered the ribbon on my badge – the one that marked me as one of the hired help. 'I'm on duty.'

'Oh.' He paused. 'Well, then. I have a complaint.'

'Sorry?'

'A customer complaint. Something I want to show you. And Harley needs to go for a walk anyway.'

'OK, but I'll need to check in with Carole first,' I said. 'Follow me.'

'No rush,' he said. 'When you're done we'll be in the lobby.'

I found Carole exactly where I thought she would be, manning the reception desk. Only a handful of registration packets remained on the table in front of her. 'You've got things well under control, right?'

'You bet.'

I indicated the remaining packets. 'Any of those folks likely to show?'

Three of the registrants' names were new to her, she told me, but Carole fully expected to see the others, with one exception. 'Homer Guthrie is a no-show,' she said. 'I should have pulled his packet, I suppose.'

'Homer Guthrie? Sounds like a character out of Mayberry, RFD.'

Carole frowned. 'It's a sad case, really. When he was two he was diagnosed with hypertrichosis. He's got hair all over his body.' She paused, leaned across the table and lowered her voice. 'Long, reddish-brown hair – even on his eyelids, for God's sake.'

'Yikes.'

'Exactly. He spent his youth in a carnival sideshow billed as "The Werewolf Boy" until around 1977.'

I puzzled over the date for a few seconds then asked, 'What happened in 1977?'

'*Star Wars* happened. Then his loathsome parents reinvented him as "Son of Chewbacca." From the photos I've seen, Homer really looked the part of a wookie, too. Hairy, six-foot-seven . . .' Her voice trailed off. 'Nowadays they'd throw parents like that in jail.'

'Was Homer going to speak?'

She shook her head. 'No, just attend. He wanted to meet Professor Cloughly. All his life people have been treating him like the missing link rather than a genetic anomaly, so he sent her a sample of his hair for DNA testing.'

'I thought Cloughly's expertise was scat.'

'Oh, shit's the name of her game, for sure, but there's a DNA lab at South Jersey Shore University where Cloughly's got tenure, so that's where all the Bigfoot hair samples got sent. Homer's was one of them. She'll be presenting the results later this afternoon,' Carole added. 'Ron scheduled it late in the day on purpose so everybody's going to be frothing at the mouth, waiting to hear.'

'How come Homer's not coming?' I asked.

'Poor guy. He had hip replacement surgery and rehab wasn't going as quickly as he'd anticipated.' Carole flapped her hand, shooing me away. 'You go on. It's just the walk-ins from now on. I'm good.'

'I plan to be back for Professor Cloughly's presentation on scat analysis,' I told her.

'I saw her a couple of years ago,' Carole said. 'She is a hoot!'

I was trying to work out what someone – other than a group of potty-mouth pre-schoolers – would find remotely humorous about poop, but made a mental note not to be late for Cloughly's talk.

'It's dead easy to put together a hoax today, technology being what it is,' Jake said a few minutes later as I trailed through the lobby behind him and his dog. 'But the same technology also makes it easier to weed out the fakes.'

I had to agree. Martin Radcliffe's talk the previous evening had made that abundantly clear. Jake opened the door that led from the lobby to the outdoor patio and held it open for me. 'It's amazing,' I said, 'that nobody, not even Radcliffe, has been able to debunk the Patterson-Gimlin film. That female Bigfoot Patterson filmed at Willow Creek looked convincing to me. I think it was the breasts that did it.'

As we weaved our way through a half-dozen conversationally-oriented clusters of patio furniture each grouped around a mini fire pit, Jake said, 'That fifty-nine-second clip has been analyzed frame by frame more often and more thoroughly than the Zapruder film of the JFK assassination. Some see a guy in a monkey suit and point out a shiny bit they say is a zipper. No, no, someone else says, it's simply matted feces. Others highlight the natural way her muscles ripple under her fur and the pendulous breasts. One guy zeroed-in so close he claims to have seen a braid dangling from Patty's head.' He stopped then turned to look at me. 'Remember the spot toward the end of the film where Patty disappears over a log?' When I nodded, Jake said, 'When you zoom in and enhance the image? Apparently, Patty has hemorrhoids.'

This made me laugh out loud. 'If what I saw last night is any indication, the film is so grainy and jumpy you could probably see Elvis in it if you had a mind to.'

We paused for a moment, waiting and watching as Harley auditioned several pine trees. After the winning tree had been sufficiently watered, the dog and I followed Jake along the path that led through the woods, away from the tennis courts. 'A number of people have tried to recreate that video with a stunning lack of success,' he continued. 'Nobody's been able to get the ape suit right. The recreations are, without exception, obvious fakes. To my mind, it beggars belief that two cowboys had the expertise to carry out such a hoax, especially using 1967 technology.'

We'd reached a scenic overlook. While Harley continued to snuffle through the pine needles at the edge of the trail, Jake and I leaned casually over the wooden railing that separated us from the river chuckling over the rocks hundreds of feet below. 'That's the Metolius River,' he said, pronouncing it carefully. Muh-*toll*-ee-us. 'It flows north from here.' He pointed. When I turned my head I could see a snow-capped mountain just to the north, too. 'Is that Mount Jefferson?' I asked. 'I saw it on a map in the room.'

'Yup.'

'Strange name for a river,' I mused. 'I keep confusing it with Grace Metalious, the woman who wrote *Peyton Place*.'

Jake snorted. 'Although it doesn't sound much like it, it's a Native American name. Means white fish, stinking water or spawning salmon, depending upon who you ask.'

'Help me out here, Jake,' I said after a moment. 'Everyone has a cell phone these days. Even my nine-year-old grandson has a cell phone. They carry them twenty-four seven. With all those built-in cameras floating around in the world, why don't we have zillions of Bigfoot videos?'

'Bigfoots are reclusive,' he explained. 'If you see one, that's usually Bigfoot being sloppy. They're not likely to bother us up here in the open but if one popped out of the woods over there, what would you actually see?'

He indicated the sun-splashed, spring-green grassy lowlands that bordered the river on the opposite bank then merged almost seamlessly into a wall of stately, dark pines.

I squinted. 'What? That dark blob?'

He nodded.

I eased my iPhone out of my handbag, entered my code, tapped the camera icon and held it up to capture the scene. 'Not much,' I admitted, studying the image on the screen, turning it sideways. 'Could be a tree stump, a bear or even a guy in a monkey suit, stooped over to tie his shoelaces.'

'And by the time you've done all that . . .' Jake gestured at my bag and my iPhone. 'Whatever it was will have been long gone.'

'I see your point.'

'But the thing that keeps me going, Hannah, is this. If you bundle all the evidence together – and there are well over three thousand reports in the BFRO database alone – how can *all* of them be hoaxes? You'd have to believe in a worldwide conspiracy going back for centuries with literally thousands of people involved.'

'Occam's razor,' I muttered, dredging up the term from the place in my brain where arcane facts are stored.

Jake shot me a lopsided grin. 'Exactly. The odds are a lot stronger that Bigfoot exists than he doesn't. Nobody'd seen a giant squid in the flesh until the Japanese first filmed one in 2004.' He paused. 'Remember the coelacanth?'

I nodded, recalling an article I'd once read in *National Geographic*. 'Thought to be extinct for some sixty-eight million years, then one of them turned up in a fisherman's net off the coast of South Africa.' Something else suddenly occurred to me, also gleaned from the stacks of the *National Geographic*s my parents hoarded, military move after military move, in their attic. 'Or take the mountain gorillas in Rwanda – those gorillas in the mist that were studied by Dian Fossey. Scientists believed they were extinct, too, until the turn of the last century when a couple of hunters shot one and dragged it down from the mountains.'

Jake grunted. 'If it takes finding a specimen as proof, I hope it's one that has died of natural causes rather than having been blasted to smithereens by some moron in the backwoods.'

'Radcliffe talked about that last night,' I said. 'There was this guy in Georgia who claimed to have a dead Bigfoot in his freezer, but it turned out to be a Halloween costume covered with roadkill.'

Jake nodded. 'I'm familiar with that one. Dyer tried the same trick again a couple of years ago, this time using foam, latex and camel hair. Sold tickets, too, before owning up to the fraud on Facebook.'

'What was he thinking?'

Jake shrugged. 'Who knows? Starved for attention, maybe?'

A splash of red caught my eye on our side of the river, several hundred yards downstream. 'What's that?'

'Where?'

I pointed. 'Up by the rapids.'

Jake shielded his eyes and squinted. 'Probably just a fly fisherman.'

'I don't think so. Don't fly fishermen wear hip boots and wade out into the water, flicking a rod back and forth?' I raised my iPhone, waited for the camera to focus then used two fingers to zoom in as closely as the app would allow. 'This guy's squatting on the ground, hacking at it with an ax, fiddling with something.'

'Maybe it's Bigfoot.' Jake's elbow nudged mine.

'Not unless Bigfoot is partial to Hawaiian shirts. My keen detecting skills tell me that we're watching Jim Davis fine tune his surveillance cameras.' I squinted. 'Yes. He's digging up the dirt and burying a cable. He told me last night he'd be demonstrating the system later today.'

The iPhone, still in my hand, began to vibrate and play a fanfare. I'd set an alarm so I wouldn't be late for the first session. 'Time's up,' I said. 'If I'm not back when I'm supposed to be Susan is bound to send out a search party.'

Jake smiled. 'Have I converted you, then?'

I dropped the phone back into my bag and scurried up the trail, calling back over my shoulder, 'As persuasive as your arguments are, Officer Cummings, the jury is still out, I'm afraid.'

'You getting paid for this?' he hollered.

I stopped and waited for him to catch up. 'No, just helping out a friend.'

His eyes caught mine, and for a moment the only sounds around us were the susurrus of the wind in the tree tops and the raucous call of a far-away bird. 'Sorry, gotta go!' I squeaked and dashed away before I could get sucked into the vortex of those dangerous, ice-blue eyes.

SIX

Gladwin, Michigan, October 26, 1891. '[Two] reputable citizens report having seen a wild man near the Tittabawassee River, in Gladwin County. The man was nude, covered with hair, and gigantic in proportions. According to their stories, he must have been at least seven feet high, his arms reaching below his knees, and with hands twice the usual size. Mr Vivian set his bulldog on the crazy man, and with one mighty stroke of his monstrous hand he felled the dog dead. His jumps were measured and found to be from 20 to 23 feet.'

The Commoner (Colfax, WA), November 6, 1891

I had intended to visit the dealers' room before the first session of the day, but after playing hooky with Jake and Harley I was too late. In fact, the doors to the William Clark Room had already closed on Professor Cloughly's session, so I eased in as quietly as I could and stood at the rear of the room, not far from the refreshment table. I didn't want to take a better spot from a true believer.

I was relieved to see that the professor's PowerPoint equipment seemed to be functioning perfectly. SCAT ANALYSIS!

ADVENTURES ALONG THE DUNG TRAIL filled the screen standing just to the left of the podium. The dot on the exclamation point had been replaced with the emoji I recognized as the wide-eyed, smiling pile of poo. My grandddaugther, Chloe, had once pointed out that, except for the color, the poo emoji was identical to the one used for soft-serve ice cream. I smiled, remembering. It was hard to un-see that.

The presentation was ready, but unless Professor Cecelia Cloughly, PhD, Mzool, MusB was a six-foot-four guy wearing a blue baseball cap with the Ford logo embroidered on it, her session had not yet begun. This had to be Ron Murphy, I thought, the car dealer Carole Pulaski told me had sponsored the conference. He wasn't listed on the program so he must be preparing to introduce the scientist.

Perched on a chair to the right of the podium, sporting a blonde mop of Orphan Annie-style curls, was a woman I took to be Cloughly. Although her hands remained demurely folded in her lap, she seemed to be shooting daggers at Ron through a pair of round, oversized eyeglasses. Cloughly couldn't have been more than five feet tall because, even in heels, her feet barely touched the floor.

As Ron droned on – 'How many of you here have had a Bigfoot experience?' – I stood at the rear of the room surveying the crowd, or rather the back of their heads. It was astonishing how many men wore hats while indoors – ball caps were well-represented, of course, as well as a half-dozen visors and a bandana or two – but the proliferation of cowboy hats caught me by surprise. The guy sitting directly in front of me was hatless, though. He sported a comb-over that defied the laws of gravity, a prize-winning effort that began an inch above the nape of his neck and swept upward, a comb-over so elaborate that even Donald Trump's hairdresser would have taken three steps backward and fallen to his knees in awe of it.

The big coverup. So many bald spots to disguise. So little hair to do it with.

At the refreshment table nearby, the server I recognized as Tina was fussing with a plastic tub of ice and cans of soda – Pepsi products, not Coke, I noticed, feeling annoyed – but when Ron's question boomed out she set down the can of Mountain

Dew she was holding and, like at least fifty others in the room, tentatively raised her hand.

'You have?' I whispered.

Tina sucked in her lips and nodded, her hand still aloft.

'You! In the back!'

Tina jumped as if she'd been shot, immediately withdrew her hand and took two steps back. Her pale face flushed red, as bright as bad sunburn. 'Not me,' she croaked.

'Yes, you!' Ron waved Tina forward, twisting the mic out of its stand as he did so.

Professor Cloughly, scowling, made a production of checking her watch. Ron Murphy was hijacking her session. If he didn't relinquish the mic soon, someone – probably me – was going to have to make a dash for the stage and wrestle it out of his beefy hands.

Meanwhile, Tina was dragging herself up the side aisle as slowly as a reluctant bride – one step, then another, staring at her feet as if she had forgotten how they worked. Tina might have had a story to tell, and a good one, too, but this didn't seem like the time. According to the schedule, Friday and Saturday evenings were set aside for audience participation, sitting around-the-camp-fire-style sessions on personal Bigfoot encounters. Didn't anyone remember we were supposed to be analyzing shit here today?

As Ron urged Tina forward – 'Come on, young lady, don't be nervous. We're all family here, aren't we folks?' – among the bobbing heads and murmurs of approval there was a lone dissenter. Professor Cloughly leapt to her feet, her voice infused with exasperation. '*Mister* Murphy! This is my program, I believe. The microphone, *please*. Or I'm leaving.'

You go, girl, I thought, suppressing the urge to applaud.

At that moment, the screaming began.

The sudden silence that followed Professor Cloughly's ultimatum was filled not with a long, drawn-out, *Friday the Thirteenth* slasher-in-the-woods shriek of terror but staccato whoops of excitement, as if someone's come-from-behind team had just scored a winning touchdown.

I had been leaning against the door so I nearly stumbled into the hallway when someone wrenched it open behind me. 'Oh my God, oh my God, oh my God!' Athena Davis appeared, her face flushed as red as her hair. She paused to draw a deep breath and gulped it in.

I touched her arm. 'What's happened? Are you all right? Where's Jim?'

Athena pressed a hand flat against her chest as if trying to keep her heart from leaping out of it. She gulped again. 'It's finally happened! Something triggered Jim's camera!'

All heads in the audience swiveled in our direction, turning to focus on what Athena was telling them. 'He set it up this morning!' Another gasp. 'Then we went to breakfast. Oh my God, why did we go to breakfast? I wasn't even all that hungry!' Another deep, ragged breath. 'When we came back to the conference room just now, it was recording.' She grasped the back of a chair, steadying herself. 'Proof! We finally have proof! Martin Radcliffe can eat his snotty words. You have to come see. Hurry!'

With an elaborate, follow-me sweep of her arm, she dashed out of the room.

Half the audience were already on their feet, scrambling for the aisles.

'People! People!' Ron shouted into the mic, but after Professor Cloughly and Athena's announcements the man could exercise his outdoor, just-who-do-you-think's-in-charge-here sort of voice until his throat grew sore but he'd never regain control.

Hopelessly entangled in the surge of humanity hot-footing it out of the room, I found myself in the hallway, swept along with the tide. In order to reach the Meriwether Lewis Conference Room before they did – the last thing we needed was for someone to be crushed to death in a stampede – I swam through the crowd doing the breaststroke. When I reached the doors I hastily propped them both open then stood to one side as people poured into the room.

Projected on a large screen pulled down from the ceiling at the front of the room was an image I recognized: a view of the banks of the Metolius River, its lush marshlands and tall pines. In the center of the image someone had erected a tee-pee of sticks, as if preparing a campfire. To the right, the river raged over the rocks that Jake and I had seen earlier.

A live picture, then.

But, other than the rapids, everything seemed still.

People clogged the aisles, moving clumsily, their eyes glued to the screen. 'Do you see anything?' 'What's going on?' 'Ouch! Watch where you're going! That's my toe you're stepping on.'

Athena had beaten everyone there. She stood up front, next to the projector, but although I looked for him, I couldn't find her husband, Jim.

'Sit down, everyone, please.' Athena leaned into the mic, her lips almost touching it.

I remained at the door, directing traffic, taking wanderers gently by the arm and shoving them in the direction of the first available chair. Everyone wanted to sit in the front row – no surprise.

The screen suddenly went blank, replaced by an intense white light. I suppressed an insane urge to fill the screen with hand shadows – I had a good bunny rabbit, a so-so eagle and an amazing camel in my repertoire – which was a wise move, because Susan Lockley chose that precise moment to explode into the room and make a beeline for me. 'Where's the fire?' she whispered hoarsely.

'Something activated Jim's camera so Athena's gone to general quarters. If she'd been on a ship all the horns would be going *ooo-ga, ooo-ga, ooo-ga.*'

Susan cast her eyes toward the ceiling. Her mouth moved in silent prayer. 'This better be freaking worth it,' she muttered at last, her eyes drilling into mine. 'Honestly, this is the biggest bunch of kooks I have ever worked with. Ever.'

'Sit down, please, everyone.' Athena again. 'Jim's queuing up the recording now.'

With an exasperated sigh, Susan made her way toward the front of the room. I figured she planned to help expedite the queuing-up process, whatever that entailed.

'What the hell's going on?'

I wasn't expecting to see him, so Jake's voice directly behind me made me jump.

'I was heading into the scat session,' Jake said, 'when the doors flew open and all hell broke loose. Somebody set a bomb off in there or something?'

'You can't roller skate in a buffalo herd,' I said.

'What?'

I flapped a hand. 'Never mind.' I managed a wan grin and quickly explained what I thought was going on. Jim had apparently finished with his set up because he climbed up onto the low dais and took the microphone from his wife. Susan, looking somewhat relieved, came back to stand with Jake, Harley and me near the rear door.

With the mic in one hand and a remote in the other, Jim, dressed in the same bright red Hawaiian shirt we'd seen him in earlier, began the show. He pointed a remote at the projector and the screen filled with a static image of the clearing and the over-sized, campfire-like structure. 'As most of you know, Bigfoot often builds structures like this, so that is where we put the bait.'

I leaned closer to Susan and whispered, 'Tuna fish. Just so you know.'

On the screen, nothing was happening, except that the river continued to babble and the bushes stirred in the breeze. We waited, holding our collective breaths.

A creature stepped out of the trees.

'Oooooh . . . ah!'

Tall, covered in reddish-brown fur, the animal sloped toward the water's edge with loose, man-like strides. Its arms were long, its hands – or paws? – swinging just shy of the creature's knees. Its feet seemed large and hairy. When it reached the river it turned and stared directly at Jim's camera as if it knew exactly where the camera was. A face like a gorilla, I thought. Too far away to see the eyes.

'Jesus, Mary and Joseph!' someone in the crowd muttered.

Perhaps the creature heard. It turned and ran, faster than I believed possible for such a large animal. As it fled, the marsh grass lashed its fur like corn stalks until it reached the safety of the tree line and was swallowed up again by the forest.

SEVEN

Winsted, Connecticut, August 30, 1895. 'The Connecticut wild man, that has divided honors with the sea serpent, is a full-grown gorilla. John G. Hall runs a stage between here and Sandisfield, Mass. While he was passing through Colebrook a large animal crossed the highway on all fours and leaped a stone wall . . . The animal, when the stage approached, stood erect. Hall drew a revolver. The beast did not stir. Hall stopped his horses and was getting a good aim at the brute when off it sped on four feet . . . uttering awful cries . . . They say that it has large white teeth, black hair, a muscular form and is about 6 ½ feet tall. It is thought the gorilla made its escape from some circus, and has since made its home among the Litchfield hills.'

The North Adams Transcript (North Adams, MA),
August 30, 1895

'**S**hit,' Jake said. 'What was that?'

Jim replayed the clip two, three times. He ran it backward, then forward. At the moment where the creature first emerged from the trees he froze the image. Zoomed in.

'Looks like Caesar from *Planet of the Apes*,' Susan muttered. 'Although it's a bit fuzzy.'

It had been a long time since I'd seen the classic movie but I had to agree. 'Except Caesar and his clan walked like chimps,' I said, 'mostly on all fours.'

'That's because they were chimps,' Jake said. 'This creature is something entirely different.'

Jim pressed the remote and the creature moved in slow motion toward the river, turned then stared at the camera. Jim looped the film back, running it over and over, freezing it on the last frame, zeroing in on the creature's departing backside. 'Just like Patty,' I muttered.

'I think Jim Davis just blew Patterson and Gimlin clean out of the water, don't you?' Jake said. 'The video will have to be authenticated, of course, but who better for the job than Martin Radcliffe.' Jake seemed be to surveying the room. 'Where the hell is he, anyway? You'd think he'd be all over this thing like a duck on a junebug.'

I shrugged. 'I spotted him earlier this morning, getting coffee. Maybe he's not that much into scat.' I sent Jake a crooked grin. 'People don't usually fake poop, do they?'

Jake seemed miles away. He didn't answer.

When I tuned in again, Jim was saying, 'I know we could

watch this clip for hours – and it will be up on YouTube before the end of the day, I guarantee you – but in order to understand it I think it's important for you to see how my system works.'

He aimed his remote and the screen went blank again before returning to what I presumed was the live image of the stick teepee. 'When the alarm was triggered,' Jim explained, 'the camera started rolling. It's motion sensitive so it actually follows the object that triggered the alarm. And at that point, too, it starts recording.'

As he spoke, the camera began to pan. 'We're live again, now,' Jim told us, 'but this time I'm in control.' He panned first to the left, then to the right, then back again, putting the camera through its paces like an oscillating fan. 'The range is 360 degrees,' he continued as the camera began another rotation to the right.

Now we were viewing the river again – the marshland grasses, the pines, the flat ledge higher up where Jake and I had been enjoying the view earlier that morning.

Suddenly the camera jittered to a stop. 'What the blue blazes?' Jim muttered into the mic. 'Ooooh, have you come back again, you tricky devil?' Under his control, the camera stalled then zoomed in closer and closer on some anomaly in the forest landscape. A fallen log, perhaps? A bag of trash? Whatever it was, the camera had to be positioned between it and the makeshift teepee.

Jim thumbed the control and zoomed in, still closer.

I stifled a gasp.

'Shit,' I muttered, just loud enough for Jake to hear. 'A trash bag doesn't wear lime-green track shoes.'

Jake grabbed my hand and dragged me toward the door. As he passed Susan, he hissed, 'I don't care how you do it but keep these people here. Don't let them out of this room.'

Susan opened her mouth to protest but Jake silenced her with, 'I'm a cop. And if you've got a cell phone with you, I'd call nine-one-one.'

'*Hier!*' he commanded. Harley and I followed.

A minute later, Jake, Harley and I were racing down the path we'd taken earlier. Before we reached the overlook, however, Jake veered off to the left on a hiking trail I hadn't noticed before. A carved wooden National Park Service sign read, 'Riverwalk Trail, 0.3 miles.'

'These shoes aren't designed for hiking,' I complained as I scrambled, slipping and sliding on wet pine needles down the steep trail behind him. 'What do you need me for, anyway?' I panted as I stumbled over an exposed root.

'You have a cell-phone camera. It's with you, right?'

Oh, ugh. I didn't relish the idea of taking pictures of whatever lay in that sad, dark heap. I prayed it was simply Martin Radcliffe's trademark shoes that had found their way into a trash bag and not the rest of him.

When we finally reached the clearing I had to pause, bend over and rest my hands on my knees, gasping, trying to catch my breath.

'*Bleib!*' Jake said. Stay. I figured it applied to both me and the dog.

While waiting for my heartbeat to return to normal, I kept my eyes on Jake as he approached the mound we had spotted on Jim's camera. Even from my position some ten yards away, I could see it was covered with something in a camouflage pattern. A tarp?

Jake lifted a corner of the fabric, pulled it back then squatted beside whatever was underneath. He reached out, touched it, paused for a moment then shook his head, just like cops do on TV. Still squatting, with his forearms resting on his thighs and hands dangling between them, he said, 'It's Radcliffe, I'm afraid. And he's not been dead long; the body's still warm.'

My heart began to race again. Bile rose in my throat. Breathe in, Hannah. Breathe out. In with the good air, out with the bad.

Almost before I noticed, Jake was at my side, a comforting hand on my shoulder. 'You OK?'

I wasn't but I nodded, swallowing hard. 'I've seen dead bodies before.'

I thought nothing could be as horrific as the woman I'd once discovered savagely bludgeoned to death in her Eastport home. Now I stood a good distance away from the flesh and bones that had once been Martin Radcliffe, and yet, somehow, it felt worse. Someone had savaged the man's face – broken his neck, too, if the unnatural angle of his head in relation to his shoulders was any indication.

'Let me have your jacket,' Jake said gently.

I must have looked puzzled because he jerked his head in the direction of Jim's camera which, I realized, must still be transmitting away, feeding everything we were doing into that conference room back at Flat Rock Lodge, zero point three miles away.

I slipped out of my jacket – a quilted denim one from Chicos – and handed it over. Holding the jacket open in front of him like a matador, Jake approached the camera and draped it ceremoniously over the camera lens. He patted it almost fondly. 'Nighty night.'

When he returned, and before he could ask again, I handed over my iPhone, too. Sitting on a log at the edge of the forest, feeling ill, I watched as Jake moved carefully around Radcliffe's body, taking photos. When he was done he joined me on the log where I sat, shivering.

'What do you think, Jake?'

'As a professional?'

'Of course.'

'Looks like someone whacked him on the head then broke his neck,' Jake said. 'Someone or something.'

I turned sideways to look at him. 'Bigfoot? You're joking. Surely you don't really believe . . .?'

'Don't you?'

I shook my head. 'No.'

Jake snorted. 'Been at the conference for only one day and already a skeptic. If you stay till the end your eyes may be opened.'

'This may *be* the end,' I said.

'I doubt it, Hannah. Too much time and money has already been laid out. Besides, nobody's going to be allowed to leave until the cops are finished with their interviews.' He checked his watch. 'They should be here shortly.'

Thinking of the staff and hundreds of attendees, I said, 'That could take until the Fourth of July.'

Jake laughed grimly. 'Oh, they'll narrow it down to a few persons of interest fairly quickly.'

While we talked, he used his thumb to scroll quickly through the images he'd just taken. 'Will those photos help?' I asked, indicating my cell phone. 'Did you notice any evidence? Footprints, maybe, or tufts of hair?'

'Nope. Pine needles mostly. Leaves, twigs, ferns. A few rocks. The ground was kicked up a bit but nothing obvious.'

When he was done reviewing the photos I expected Jake to return my cell phone, but he surprised me by tucking it into the back pocket of his jeans. 'A pity your iPhone has been lost,' he said, smiling crookedly. 'Perhaps you'll find it again in an hour or so?'

I wasn't worried about losing the pictures he'd just taken. Even as we stared each other down in the forest, I knew the photos were being uploaded automatically, one by one, to Apple iCloud. They would be waiting for me to view, full size, on my computer when I got back to my room. But I couldn't imagine a situation where I'd ever want to look at them.

'Aren't you forgetting something?' I asked.

'Like what?'

'A password.'

'I watched you type it in.'

This guy was as clever as my seven-year-old grandson. Timmy had used the same technique to bypass parental controls while playing *The Simpsons* on his Kindle Fire. By the time my daughter caught up with the little rascal he'd bought more than a thousand dollars' worth of virtual donuts with his mother's real world credit card. 'I thought you weren't familiar with iPhones,' I said.

He smiled sheepishly. 'I said I didn't own one, not that I didn't know how to use one. It's an iPad in miniature, and I've got one of those.'

Hugging myself for warmth, I nodded.

'It won't take long for the cops to get here from Sisters,' he said. 'I'd like you to stay here while I . . .' His voice trailed off. 'Harley, *hier*!'

Harley, who had been lying at my feet, shot to attention. '*Geh voraus*,' Jake ordered.

Slowly, deliberately, man and dog circled Radcliffe's body. '*Such!*' Jake ordered, and Harley, nose down, head sweeping from side to side, trotted into the forest.

'Stay here, please,' Jake said. 'Tell the Sisters police where we've gone.'

'But . . .' I began. How dare the man leave me all alone when a savage killer was on the loose!

As if reading my mind, Jake said, 'You'll be fine. According to Harley, whatever it was went that-a-way.' He turned and trotted after his dog.

I was sitting on the log, still sulking when Jake reappeared less than five minutes later. Jake led Harley to the body and said, '*Wache.*'

Harley dutifully stood guard.

'Where did it go, the trail?' I asked when Jake rejoined me.

'Up a path of sorts. Ends at the parking lot. That's where Harley lost the scent.'

'Does that mean that whoever it was got into his car and drove away?'

'Possibly.'

'Someone who left the conference?'

'It doesn't have to have been someone attending the conference at all, Hannah. It could have been an outsider, a complete stranger to us.'

'But probably not to Martin Radcliffe.'

'No.'

I sat up straighter as a thought occurred to me. 'Security cameras! Hotel security keeps an eye on the parking lot, surely, in case someone decides to break into our cars at night.'

'That would be bears, mostly. No matter how many times they are warned, people continue to leave food in their cars.' He paused for a moment. 'To a bear, a car looks like a cookie jar. They'll even tear through a rear seat if they smell food in the trunk. I wasn't doing a thorough search, of course, but if there were any security cameras covering that end of the parking lot I didn't see them. Something for the cops from Sisters to sort out, in any case. I've overstepped myself already. Oregon is totally out of my jurisdiction.'

'What don't you understand about "retired," Jake?'

'Old habits die hard.'

I shivered, growing chillier by the minute without my jacket. 'I wonder if Martin was lying dead over there all the time we were gabbing away up on the overlook?'

Jake shook his head. 'Not likely. A semi-educated guess, of course, but as I said, I don't think he'd been dead all that long.'

'But we saw Jim Davis down here earlier!'

'Correction. We saw someone wearing a bright red shirt down here earlier.'

'Jim was wearing a red Hawaiian shirt at his presentation this morning.'

'True. But I own a red shirt. You probably do, too.'

'Oh,' I said, feeling deflated.

'What puzzles me is why Radcliffe was dressed in camouflage gear.'

So it wasn't a tarp. 'Obviously he didn't want to be seen by someone.' I paused. 'Or some*thing*.'

'You're right. Now that I think about it, it's likely he was staking out the camera site, hoping to catch someone trying to pull a stunt,' Jake said. 'Somebody he could later "out" on his TV show.' After a thoughtful moment, he added: 'Jim Davis springs immediately to mind, considering the bad blood between them. Radcliffe made a fool of Jim once – you saw it yourself last night. I can imagine him rubbing his hands together and cackling over the possibility of embarrassing the poor guy again.'

'You think Jim Davis caught Martin spying on him and snapped?'

'It's certainly possible. How well do you know the Davises?'

The question caught me a bit off guard. 'Hardly at all. I talked to Jim and his wife last night at dinner. They don't seem like devious types to me. Jim really believes that Bigfoot exists and that it's just a matter of time before he or someone else captures one – dead, alive or on film. You should have seen the look on his face this morning, Jake. The man was over the moon when his alarm went off. I don't think he's that good an actor. And Athena?' I paused. 'She was positively levitating.'

Jake leaned against a tree trunk, deep in thought. When he didn't comment, I said, 'You told me you're a believer. Tell me about the time you saw Bigfoot.'

'I was around twelve,' he replied. 'It was winter and I was out duck-hunting with my dad and my uncle. We were riding snowmobiles through a track in the forest going maybe twenty, twenty-five miles an hour. Uncle Joe's vehicle turned left ahead of us . . .' he demonstrated with his hand, '. . . and as we banked into the turn, too, I happened to look to my right and there, staring at me from behind a tree was a hairy, ape-like creature. About eight feet tall, I reckoned. Widow's peak, wrinkly leather-like face, the whole nine yards. He looked at me, I looked at him, then he took off running.'

'Did your dad see it, too?'

Jake shook his head. 'I was too scared to ask. Kept the story to myself for years.' He smiled. 'You're only about the second person in the world I've told.'

The silence between us was shattered by a ringing phone, causing me to jump.

'Sorry, mine,' Jake said, fishing in his breast pocket.

I scowled. 'If you have a phone, why'd you need to borrow mine?'

He showed me his phone then flipped it open. A basic, no-frills clam shell. 'I'm a low-tech kind of guy. No camera.' He put the phone to his ear. 'Cummings.'

As I waited, listening in, Jake gave someone directions to our location then snapped the phone shut without saying goodbye. 'Sheriff's on the way,' he said. 'Just rounding up her posse.'

Thinking about a monster that could still be running loose in the woods around us, I asked, 'Do you carry a gun, Jake?'

'No. Do you?'

'Lord, no. I have grandkids at home.'

'Wise,' he said. 'I've seen too many kids . . .' His voice trailed off. 'Not going there.'

That was when a parade of five individuals in uniforms approached, three in khaki and two in dark blue, snaking single file through the trees and down the Riverwalk Trail. Every one of them was packing heat.

'Sheriff's department from Sisters,' Jake told me as the officers drew nearer. 'Headquarters in Bend.'

A female officer, hatless, her medium-length dark brown hair twisted into a no-nonsense knot at the nape of her neck, took a quick look at the body then approached us and introduced herself. Detective Lieutenant Barbara Cook wore a shiny badge, a star patch on her sleeve and a frown. 'We don't get many murders here, Cummings. Mostly speeding, hazmat and animal control.' She jerked her head backward, indicating the two deputies who were pounding metal stakes into the ground and stringing yellow crime scene Do Not Cross tape between them. 'What does it look like to you?'

'Early days yet,' Jake said. He took a moment to explain how

Harley had picked up a scent and followed it up to the parking lot where the trail had gone cold.

Lieutenant Cook nodded. Glancing with approval at her team who were busily securing the crime scene, she asked, 'Reckon it was a grizzly?'

Jake shrugged. 'Nothing would surprise me but I like to leave those things up to the ME.'

Barbara Cook was solidly built, like she might have played women's soccer in college and been very good at it. Like she kept herself in shape at the gym. 'Right,' she said. 'Someone from the ME will be here shortly.'

Jake introduced me and explained briefly how we'd come to be there.

'So, you're one of the organizers of this Sasquatch do?' she asked, turning to me.

'Yes, ma'am.'

'Good. When we're done here I'll need you to go up to the lodge and organize an interview room for us. Board room, conference room, something like that. If someone's already in it you have my permission to boot 'em out. How many people are attending this conference, anyway?'

'Two hundred, more or less. I don't know how many are on the hotel staff.'

'Jimminy.' She took a deep breath. 'Oh, well, it is what it is. We'll need bottled water, ice and soft drinks. Talk to the kitchen and see if you can round up some sandwiches. Nothing fancy. I figure we're in this for the long haul.'

While she dealt with us, two crime-scene technicians – one with a camera – were dealing with the late Martin Radcliffe. 'Who was he, anyway, the victim?'

'He's a TV star from LA,' I said. 'His job is to make people look either dishonest or stupid. I imagine he has lots of enemies.'

'But who in *this* bunch might have had it out for the guy?'

'Nobody's going to be wearing a black armband,' I said.

Cook frowned. 'An insider, then. I'm going to assume that nobody's going to be making a fun trip up to Oregon when they could just as easily bump the guy off in LA.'

'They might,' I said. 'Particularly if they wanted to pin it on Sasquatch.'

Cook's eyebrows disappeared under her bangs. 'Don't tell me you're one of them, too.'

'A Squatcher? Not really. Just doing a job. Helping out a friend.'

Cook made a flapping motion with her hand. 'Better get the show on the road, I guess.' Meaning me.

With a nod to Jake, I made a wide circle to avoid the crime-scene tape then headed up the hill. When I was about halfway up the path, Cook called after me. 'And I'll need a complete list of attendees!'

I waved, indicating that I'd heard.

EIGHT

9 December 1882. 'A few days ago I saw one of these strange creatures . . . on the coast between Bateman's Bay and Ulladulla. I should think that if it were standing perfectly upright it would be nearly 5 feet high. It was tailless and covered with very long black hair, which was of a dirty red or snuff-colour about the throat and breast. Its eyes, which were small and restless, were partly hidden by matted hair that covered its head.'

H. J. M'Cooey, 'The Naturalist: Australian Apes.'
Australian Town and Country Journal,
December 9, 1882, p. 23

When I emerged from the woods I found three official vehicles blocking the trail head, two white cruisers labeled SHERIFF – the blue letters leaning back as though facing into a high wind – and the Sisters/Camp Sherman Fire Medic ambulance. If the vehicles were not already a dead giveaway (so to speak), when I caught up with Susan a few minutes later I learned that the bad news had spread through the lodge faster than rumors of an increase in the minimum wage.

With the possible exception of a quiet heart attack by some septuagenarian on a weekend canoodle with his 'secretary,' the staff at the lodge were not used to dealing with sudden, violent death investigations. They lived, after all, in Flat Rock Freaking Oregon.

It had been impossible to keep everyone in the conference room, as Susan had been instructed.

Tina, the server, had fled almost immediately, getting those in the kitchen stirred up: 'The conference will have to be cancelled, the temp staff let go! Everyone is under suspicion!'

Susan Lockley had been cornered by a worried group of attendees in the hallway outside the Meriwether Lewis Room.

'I paid good money to attend this conference!'

'If it's cancelled, will I get my money back?'

'My tickets are non-refundable, in case you didn't know!'

Meanwhile, Ron Murphy, who was seeing the prospect of two years of planning swirl down the drain, could be seen wringing his ball cap in his gnarled mechanic's hands while enduring a spectacular E. Gregory Gilchrist tongue-lashing where every sentence was prefaced by the words: 'My attorney . . .'

Sensing defeat, Susan had given Ron Murphy the task of juggling the ruined program and escaped to find the hotel manager. After a quick consult with the front desk, that's where I found her.

The manager, Jared Tucker, had the clean-cut good looks of a young man fresh from a two-year stint as a Mormon missionary. When I barged in, he and Susan were in the midst of a heated discussion that my arrival did nothing to cool.

Susan turned on me. 'What the hell did Jake Cummings want *you* for, anyway? Leaving me to deal with all this . . . this . . .' She flapped her hand.

'A witness, I think.'

She narrowed her eyes. 'Why didn't you answer my texts?'

I decided not to mention my 'lost' iPhone. 'I have a message from Lieutenant Cook,' I said. 'She's the officer in charge. From what I can tell, she plans to interview everybody and they'll need a conference room to do it in.'

'Everyone? You have got to be kidding!' Susan sputtered. 'That'll take forever. People have planes to catch, miles to drive, jobs to get back to.'

I held up both hands, palms out. 'Don't shoot the messenger, Susan. I'm just telling you what Lieutenant Cook said. Maybe she exaggerates.'

Susan took a deep, calming breath. 'This is a disaster. From day one, it's been a disaster.'

'More of a disaster for the victim, I think, don't you?' I said reasonably.

Susan collapsed backward into a chair, her arms dangling limply to each side. She looked as exhausted as I felt. 'Of course. I'm sorry. It's just that I'm so stressed. It *was* Martin Radcliffe, wasn't it? The green shoes? They were his trademark, apparently, so everyone says.'

I squeezed my friend's shoulder. 'I'm afraid so.'

'I'm probably the only one in the world who hasn't seen this morning's video,' Jared said. 'Can you fill me in on what happened, please?'

I summarized what I'd seen then added: 'I didn't get all that close to Martin's body but I think, uh, maybe someone broke his neck?' No need to go into the gory details, I thought. Martin Radcliffe would be just as dead no matter how simple or elaborate the tale.

'Susan, the police want a complete list of conference attendees,' I added, 'presumably with contact information.'

'That's not a problem,' Susan said, sounding relieved. This was something she could easily provide. 'Jared, can we print it out here?'

'Of course. And I'll provide the sheriff's office with a staff list, too.' He managed a tight-lipped smile. 'Although I can't imagine that any among our staff would be involved. With very few exceptions, they've worked here for years.' He checked his watch. 'Ouch! It's forty-five minutes until lunch. Do you want me to tell the kitchen to delay it?'

Susan sat up straight and adjusted her straight black skirt which had ridden halfway up her thighs. 'No, no. The sponsors and I agree that everything needs to go on more or less as scheduled. Besides, it'll give folks something to do – something to talk about other than poor Martin.'

'Is there a conference room the police can use, Jared?' I asked.

Jared nodded. 'There's a board room adjacent to the dealers' room. We've been using it to store the cardboard boxes their stuff came in but I can get that cleared away, moved temporarily to the furniture storage area in the basement. We can have it ready by noon, I should think. What else do the police need?'

'Coffee, tea, bottled water, sandwiches.' I paused then dared to wink. 'And some of your chocolate-chip cookies?'

Jared managed a smile. 'Sure.' With a slight bow, and a 'Ladies, if you'll excuse me,' he went off to see to it.

When we were alone, I asked, 'Susan, what do we do about the programs? Everything's all screwed up.'

'Ron and I worked it out. We'll announce the changes at lunch and hand out copies of the revised schedule.'

Thinking about how quickly the three talks on that morning's agenda had simply evaporated, I asked, 'How on earth did you manage that?'

'If we shorten the lunch hour from an hour and a half to an hour and eliminate the mid-afternoon coffee break . . .' She paused. 'Don't look so crushed! We'll still have the coffee but people will just have to wander in and out of the sessions to get it.'

'OK by me,' I said. I was already running on an adrenaline high. I didn't need to escalate it with caffeine.

'We're trying again with Professor Cloughly,' she said. 'Slotting her in just after lunch.'

'Scat or hair?'

'What?' Susan looked puzzled, her mind already elsewhere. 'Oh, right. Both. Scat *and* hair. We've still got the PowerPoint program queued up for her talk on scat analysis. The hair bit is simply an announcement of the results of the university's DNA analysis of the samples. She says it will take ten minutes, max.'

'Everyone's been waiting for those results, especially Leah Solat,' I said, thinking that the results might not turn out to be all that 'simple.'

'Who?'

'Leah Solat. A reporter for *The Sacramento Bee*. One of the samples came from a sighting near Strawberry, California. Leah told me that somebody with ties to the paper had a summer cabin up there. When they returned for the season something had broken into the cabin and ransacked the place. They found fifteen-inch footprints in the snow outside one of the windows and tufts of fur on what was left of the back door.'

'Makes me glad I live in a condo,' Susan said, rising wearily from the chair. 'On the seventh floor.'

'There's a bit of time left before lunch,' I said. 'Is there anything in particular you'd like me to do?'

'Yes, please. After you help get the conference room set up, could you cruise through the dealers' room and let everyone know what's going on? As far as I know, they were all busy at their booths when Jim's camera alarm went off. If they're worried, please explain that nobody's going to cancel anything. We're in it for the long haul.'

'I'd been wanting to visit the dealers anyway. Catch you at lunch?'

'Not much of an appetite, I'm afraid, but yes.'

For some reason, the events of the morning had sharpened my appetite rather than killed it, but I wasn't about to announce that fact. 'I'm not all that hungry either,' I lied.

After giving my old friend a reassuring hug, I trotted off to take care of arrangements for Detective Lieutenant Cook and her staff and, after that, to check out the exhibits in the dealers' room.

NINE

'. . . The DEC does not recognize the occurrence of Big Foot in [New York] state, therefore it is not addressed directly in our hunting regulations. Because it is not addressed there is no open season on Big Foot and they may not be taken. We are confident that the current laws and regulations afford adequate protection for Big Foot if one were to be found in NY.'

Mark Kandel, Regional Wildlife Manager, New York
State Department of Environmental Conservation,
August 13, 2012

After running several laps between the lobby and the Sacajawea Board Room by taking a shortcut through the dealers' room, I finally slowed down long enough to take in my surroundings.

Fifteen vendors had paid the two-hundred-and-fifty dollar fee for the privilege of exhibiting at the Flat Rock Sasquatch Sesquicentennial. A combination of modest tables and more elaborate booths lined the walls of the room, while a four-sided, free-standing display featuring an electronic device called the FLIR One occupied the center.

Among all the booths, however, Prairie Flower's Trading Company made the biggest splash. Native American art covered the wall just behind the booth and her tables – three long ones arranged end to end – displayed a variety of merchandise. Books, T-shirts, calendars, glassware, mugs, keychains, jewelry. A bumper sticker proclaimed 'I Brake 4 Bigfoot.' From Prairie Flower I could buy a cutting board shaped like a footprint carved out of Oregon myrtle wood, or if that was too expensive, a bathmat. For the children in my life, a Sasquatch doll – 'Squeeze the Squatch' – or a 'L'il Squatch' onesie. For my husband, Bigfoot playing cards. Clearly, Bigfoot was a star. His image appeared on more T-shirts and hats than Blitz, the Seattle Seahawk. You'd think he was the mascot of the Northwest.

I was tempted to browse but first I had a job to do.

With my back to the FLIR display, I used my loudest outdoor voice to get everyone's attention, introduce myself, explain what little I knew about Martin's tragic death and the ongoing investigation and announce, as Susan had instructed, that in good, old-fashioned 'the show must go on' tradition, the show would, well, go on.

It may have been my imagination but a collective sigh of relief rippled around the room, setting the table skirts aflutter. From a booth somewhere behind me, someone began to applaud.

Poor Martin, I thought. Gone and so quickly forgotten. But perhaps he was destined to live on forever through syndicated late-night re-runs.

FLIR, I learned, when I turned in the direction of the applause, stood for forward-looking infrared. FLIR One was a clever gizmo that instantly converted your smart phone into a thermal imaging camera. 'It works by detecting heat energy,' the salesman told me when I asked him, holding one up. 'It gives you the ability to see and measure minute temperature variances. You can use it to detect energy leaks, empty propane canisters, hidden moisture and other problems around your home.'

'That would come in handy,' I said, thinking about the drafts that plagued us, particularly in the basement office of our centuries-old house in historic downtown Annapolis. The $200 price tag seemed like a good investment.

'But the most important thing for us here,' he said, lowering his voice mysteriously, 'is that the FLIR One enables you to see in pitch-black darkness so you can detect intruders and observe wildlife at night.'

'Ah, ha,' I said. 'Wildlife. Tell me more.'

'Check this out,' he said, aiming the device at me. I heard the familiar click of a shutter closing. The next thing I knew, I was looking at an infrared photograph of myself, apparently warm and healthy in psychedelic shades of fuchsia, gold and yellow.

He handed the device to me. 'See for yourself,' he said. 'FLIR won a MAC World Best in Show a couple of years ago,' he added, waiting and watching as I panned the room with the demo device. Multicolored images undulated across the screen like a seriously good marijuana high during the Summer of Love. Vendors and their computer screens pulsated, glowing yellow against a colder, deep blue background. A bookstall vendor had vacated his chair, I noticed. Red patches smoldered on the seat and back cushions where he'd so recently been sitting.

'Cool,' I said, meaning it. 'Do you have any in stock?'

The salesman beamed. 'I do. We take credit cards,' he hastily added.

I handed the device back to him. 'Will it fit an iPhone 6?'

'Absolutely.'

'Sold,' I said. I was eager to try it out on my own phone, if I ever got it back from Jake, that is.

Earlier that morning, optimistically thinking I'd have time to duck into the lodge's gift shop to look for souvenirs for the grandkids, I'd tucked my Visa card into the pocket of my badge holder, along with my room key and some emergency cash. I fished the card out and watched while he swiped it through the portable credit card reader plugged into the top of his iPad. I used my index finger to sign directly on the screen. 'Thanks for solving the question of what to get my husband for his birthday,' I said as he handed me my new FLIR One in a small plastic bag with the company logo on it. 'Maybe it'll help turn the do-it-himself-list into a done-it-himself list.'

'Absolutely,' he said. 'It's almost like having a sixth sense, you know. Is your oven energy efficient? Has the dog been lying on the sofa? Are there rats in the walls?'

I had no doubt that Paul's new toy would make rats nests look as pretty as rats nests possibly could, but I didn't want to think about it. 'The grandkids will have fun with it, too, I imagine.'

He laughed. 'There's a Zombie Vision app you can get. Gives everyone green skin and red eyes. Costs two bucks. My kids are crazy about it.'

Turning people into zombies. What next? Thanks to my grandchildren I already had Talking Tom, Hair Salon and Plumbers Crack installed on my iPhone. Games like Candy Crush and Minecraft were also popular. Zombie Vision? Some app developers had entirely too much time on their hands. I promised to look the program up in the App Store, thanked the salesman again then wandered over to a small table near the door.

Monique Deschamps sat behind a colorful banner that read 'Support America's Only Great Ape,' babysitting her petition and a pile of her books – *Bigfoot: Fact, Fiction and Fable* – on sale at the conference special price of thirty dollars. I didn't have to ask Monique if she was a believer. The proof lay on the table before me.

Through the FLIR One, Monique had been a warm core with sharp, cold edges. After a few minutes chatting with her, I had to agree with the device's state-of-the-art technology. 'Hannah Ives,' I said when she stared at me blankly. 'Randall Frazier introduced us last night.'

'Oh, yes,' she said, her eyes flicking from my badge to my face. 'Sorry, but I've met so many people since yesterday.' She managed a tight smile. 'Thank God for nametags.'

'I've been pretty busy myself,' I said. 'Or I would have stopped by sooner.'

'Poor Martin,' she said, wagging her head sadly.

'Did you know him well?' I asked.

'Oh, no. I think everyone knows *of* Martin Radcliffe but nobody really *knew* him, if you know what I mean. We'd see him at conferences but he was always so aloof.' She pursed her lips and aimed her nose at the ceiling. 'Big TV star and all that. Doesn't have time to hobnob with ordinary mortals.' She leaned forward and gave a half-smile, quickly suppressed. 'How ironic if he were to be killed by a creature he spent a lifetime debunking.'

Thinking the customer is always right, I decided to smile, ignore the remark and move on. I picked up a copy of her book and opened it to the front flap. It didn't tell me anything I hadn't already gleaned from the title, except that Monique's excursion into the fact, fiction and fable of Bigfoot promised to be 'fascinating and comprehensive.'

Reviewers tended to agree. Printed on the back of the jacket were blurbs from people I'd never heard of but I figured were experts in the field. 'Skillfully weaves history, legend and honest research together . . .' said one. 'Readable and informative . . .' stated another. 'If you think monsters aren't real, think again . . .' claimed a third.

But one name was glaringly missing. 'Did Martin Radcliffe read your book, Monique?'

The question seemed to take her by surprise. 'What?'

'I was just wondering if you asked Martin Radcliffe for an endorsement?' I said.

She snorted. 'My publisher sent him an ARC, of course, but Radcliffe didn't even deign to acknowledge it.'

'What's an ARC?'

'Advance Reading Copy. It's what they send out to reviewers.'

'You must have been disappointed,' I said, laying the book back down on the stack I'd taken it from.

Monique grimaced. 'He probably would have trashed it anyway. He's not a particularly nice man. Can we change the subject?'

'Sure,' I said. 'Why don't you tell me about your petition, Monique.'

Her face brightened; FLIR would have colored it white hot. 'We believe that Bigfoot descended from *Gigantopithecus blacki*, an ancient ape that migrated from southeast Asia to the Americas over the Bering land bridge more than ten thousand years ago.' She shoved a laminated card across the table. It showed the silhouette of an enormous ape, nearly three meters tall. Standing next to the creature for comparison was the silhouette of an average human male, one point eight meters high.

'This bad boy weighed over one thousand pounds,' she told me. 'And we don't believe for a minute that's he's extinct.'

The petition, addressed to Daniel M. Ashe, director of the US Fish and Wildlife Service, was attached to a clipboard lying on the table in front of me. Each page had space for fifty signatures and the page on top was nearly full.

'Our model is the state of Washington,' she informed me. 'Skamania County passed a law in 1969 declaring that any willful, wanton slaying of creatures such as Bigfoot would be deemed a felony subject to a substantial fine and/or imprisonment. And . . .' she raced on, nearly breathless, as if she were just getting warmed up, 'Whatcom County has actually been declared a Sasquatch Protection and Refuge area.'

'No kidding,' I said.

She nodded. 'In Washington state, killing Bigfoot is homicide.'

'Doesn't every state already have laws on the books to protect newly discovered species of wildlife?' I asked.

'Yeah. Unless, of course, you're in Texas where you're allowed to hunt any "unprotected, non-game wildlife."' She drew quote marks in the air. 'In Texas, unless an animal is specifically listed as protected, you can hunt it on private property as long as you have permission from the landowner. And you can hunt it by any means, at any time and there is no bag limit or possession limit.'

'Any means? Really?'

'Any. Even rocket-propelled grenade launchers, if you've got one.'

I grunted. 'Texas. Why am I not surprised? So,' I continued after a moment's thought, 'if I want to see Bigfoot in his natural habitat I need to make my way over to Washington state. But if I feel more inclined to shoot one, I should head to Texas.'

I meant it as a joke but Monique didn't smile. 'Some people think that current laws already protect all non-game species, including undocumented ones, but we believe the federal government needs to follow the lead of Washington state.'

I had the clipboard in my hand by then. A ballpoint pen was attached to it by a red string. I must have looked like a fence-sitter because Monique suddenly chirped, 'Think about what would happen if a Bigfoot actually turned up, Hannah. If whatever showed up on Jim's camera this morning was real, not some trickster wearing a monkey suit. If we had positive proof CNN would have reporters on the scene in two-and-a-half seconds and the discovery would flash around the world in minutes, fueled by Facebook and Twitter. Within days, throngs of curiosity seekers and would-be captors would turn up in this area, creating chaos for the local residents and quite possibly threatening the Bigfoot itself. You might even have to call out the National Guard!'

'Right,' I said, fingering the pen. I wasn't buying into her doomsday scenario, not exactly, but in my desire to help protect Bigfoot from crazy cryptozoologists packing high-powered rifles, I signed.

Monique sighed with satisfaction then sat back in her chair. 'Thank you!' She reached into a small plastic box and handed me a sticker, bright green and in the shape of Bigfoot. 'I Signed,' it said.

I peeled it off and stuck it to the front of my badge. A team player, that's me.

TEN

Big Run, Jefferson County, Pennsylvania, November 1888.
'People in this vicinity are considerably exercised over the discovery in the woods of tracks about eighteen inches long, which, being unlike those of any known animal, give rise to the belief that they are those of a wild man.'

The Olean Democrat (Olean, NY), November 8, 1888

The woman sitting behind the table wore her black hair in a single plait, long enough to drape over the shoulder of a plain, long-sleeve denim shirt. She was a born saleswoman, too. Once Prairie Flower's dark brown eyes caught mine and she motioned me over, I figured my goose was cooked. I would end up buying something from her booth before the day was over, for sure.

'I thought you were one of the organizers when I saw you running in and out, back and forth like a maniac,' she said.

'Is there something I can do to help you?'

She grinned, revealing oddly uniform teeth, evenly spaced like cemetery tombstones behind full, unpolished lips. 'No problem, really. It's just that I've been watching you and I thought maybe you could use a break.'

'Me? How about you?' I indicated the array of items displayed on the table directly in front of me. Kachina figures, dream catchers, shell necklaces, silver and turquoise jewelry, pendulums fashioned of crystal and of glass and piles of CDs and books. 'How do you even work in a bathroom break?'

She bobbed her head in the direction of the booth next door where a bearded gentleman, presumably the 'Marty' of Marty's Mountain Gear & More was showing a Coleman nine-can cooler to a customer. 'Marty and me. We look out for each other.' Then, 'Is it true?' she asked after a moment.

'Is what true?' I said.

'Marty says that *Don't You Believe It!* guy was attacked by a Bigfoot.'

'Something certainly beat him to death,' I blurted. 'Did you make these?' I asked, indicating the jewelry, eager to change the subject.

'The dream catchers, yes, but the rest came from my aunt down in Taos.'

Taos. I wracked my brain, trying to think what Native American tribes lived in that area. 'Pueblo?' I asked.

She raised a single unruly eyebrow. 'I'm impressed.'

For the first time since the day began, I managed a genuine smile. 'The shell necklaces are gorgeous.' From among the assortment of single, double and triple-strand necklaces she had artfully displayed on the table, I selected one crafted of blue and coral shells.

'Hee-she,' Prairie Flower said.

'I beg your pardon?'

'H-e-i-s-h-i.' She spelled the word out for me. 'In our language, it means, quite literally, shell necklace.'

'How much is this one?' I asked, thinking it would go beauti-
fully with the sundress I'd bought several years ago in the
Bahamas, an off-the-shoulder number made out of teal-blue
Androsia batik strewn with white hibiscus blossoms.

'Forty-five dollars. It's a nice one, Hannah. Fine quality coral
and amazonite.' She watched me examine the clasp, then added:
'Don't just touch it. Pull it gently through your fingers. That's how
you tell the quality. It should feel smooth, like a snake's skin.'

I'd never touched a snake before – eew! – but if that was what
snakeskin felt like I wouldn't mind so much. As I dug around
in my badge holder fishing for the fifty-dollar bill I'd folded in
along with my credit card, I asked, 'Prairie Flower. Is that your
given name?'

'It's what I go by now. When I was little they named me
Cha'Kwaina which means "One Who Cries."' She snorted. 'Can
you imagine? By the time I reached my teens it no longer seemed
appropriate, so on my sixteenth birthday everyone started calling
me Leotie, Flower of the Prairie.' She handed me a five-dollar
bill in change. 'Do you want a bag for that?'

'No, I'll just wear it. Thanks.'

One of the books offered for sale, I noticed as Prairie Flower
stood and leaned across the table to help me hook the clasp
around my neck, had the most recent version of her name on it.
It featured a garish cover in passionate purple and a pendulum
superimposed over a full moon. The letters of the title – *Secrets
of the Pendulum: A Divining Guide* – sprawled across the top in
a spidery, practically unreadable neon-yellow font. 'You write
this?' I asked stupidly.

She beamed.

'That's what you do then?' I tapped the title. 'Divining?'

I'd once worked as a counselor in a summer camp in Vermont
where a succession of plumbers had been hired to locate the
source of a water leak. One by one, they had failed. In a last-
ditch attempt to stem the flow, a diviner was called in. Holding
two L-shaped metal rods, he isolated the leak to an underground
pipe running between the kitchen and the camp doctor's cabin.
I'd been mightily impressed. 'Like a water witch?' I asked,
remembering.

'I don't have that gift,' Prairie Flower said. She selected one of the pendants and held it aloft by its chain. 'Just divining. I use a wand pendulum to help answer people's questions.'

'Will my baby be a boy or a girl? Like that?'

'Hah! Sonograms put me completely out of the baby business,' she said.

'What brings you to this conference?' I asked, wondering what divining had to do with Bigfoot.

'Oh, I've been fascinated for years! When I was a little girl I saw what the Zuni people call an Atahsaia – a cannibal demon – up in the Sangre de Cristos.' She looked both ways as if crossing the street, leaned forward and lowered her voice. 'Scared me so bad I wet my pants. He was enormous, with long gray hair and fangs. My aunt told me that if I were disobedient Atahsaia would catch me and make me into soup.'

'I'll bet you did your chores without being asked after that.' I picked up a pair of earrings attached to a paper card labeled in a flowery script. I tried them out, tilting the card and holding it up to my ear.

'I've got a mirror,' Prairie Flower said, handing it to me.

'How much are these?' I asked.

'Thirty-five, but I'll give them to you for thirty.'

'Thanks,' I said, admiring the way the polished stones caught the light.

'Have you heard about the Mount Saint Helens expedition?' Prairie Flower asked.

I nodded. 'Randall Frazier mentioned it at dinner last night.'

Her eyes flashed as bright as her crystals. 'He's invited me to go!'

I wasn't sure whether to congratulate her or sympathize. 'You must be over the moon,' I said, deciding against the earrings and hooking them back on the display rack.

She pressed both hands flat against her bosom. 'Are you kidding? I feel like I've just been asked to the prom by the captain of the football team. There isn't anything Randall Frazier doesn't know about Bigfoot, but he asked my advice. Me! Praise the goddess! I nearly passed out. Here, let me show you something.'

Prairie Flower bent down, reached under the table and withdrew an oversized mailing tube. As I watched she popped the lid, inserted two fingers into the opening and eased out a rolled-up document. She shoved some of her merchandise aside, clearing a space, then smoothed the document out on the table. I could see it was a large-scale typographical map of Washington and Oregon states.

She stabbed an index finger on an area in the southeast corner of Washington near the border with Oregon.

I leaned in. Mount St Helens.

'There!' she said, tapping. 'Lava caves. That's where I told him we'd find Bigfoot.'

Ah. Prairie Flower must be the 'local Indian gal' that Frazier told me had pinpointed the spot.

'And you figured that out using one of these?' I fingered one of her bejeweled pendulums.

She nodded. 'He was so excited, Hannah. He squeezed my hand and said, "I knew it!"' She paused to take a deep, calming breath. 'I didn't know anything about lava caves, truly. I always thought Bigfoot built nests in the woods, you know. Who would want to live in a drippy, rocky cul-de-sac with no light?' She shivered. 'But you know what he told me?'

'No, what?' I said, genuinely curious, too.

'The temperature in one of those caves is forty-four degrees Fahrenheit, year round. Where better to camp out in winter, huh? Or to stash the babies while you're out hunting?'

Where indeed?

'How does this thing work?' I asked, lifting the pendulum off the arm of the display rack. She took it from me, held the chain between her right thumb and forefinger and dangled the pendulum over the map where it calmly rotated. Keeping everything steady, she waited patiently as the pendulum spun in circles of increasingly smaller diameter.

'You can ask yes or no questions,' she told me. 'Go on. Ask me something.'

'Like a Ouija board?'

'Sorta. Divining is guided by intuition, you know. Everyone has intuition – I'm just able to focus it.' She moved the map to one side where it curled up obediently, clearing a space on the tablecloth. 'Make your question specific, Hannah.'

My big opportunity and my mind drew a complete blank.

Will I marry someone tall and handsome? Got that. Live long

enough to spoil my grandchildren? Managed that, too. Win the lottery? Ha ha ha. You gotta play to win.

My mind inevitably wandered to the question that must have been on everyone's mind that morning: who, or what, had killed Martin Radcliffe? I took a deep breath. Yes or no, she'd said. 'Was Martin Radcliffe's death an accident?'

Prairie Flower didn't even blink. Her face remained calm, serene. The pendulum began circling, eventually swinging from side to side. 'No,' she said.

'Did Bigfoot kill him?'

Side to side, the pendulum swung again. 'No.'

Somehow, I wasn't surprised. I tried again. 'Was Martin killed by someone attending this conference?'

As I watched, holding my breath, the pendulum circled then gradually changed direction, swinging first toward me, then toward Prairie Flower and back again to me.

'Yes.'

'Whoa,' I said.

Spelling out the killer's name would have been helpful, too, but that, sadly, wasn't a yes or no question. Should I start at the top of the list of conference attendees? Was it Aaronson, yes or no? Was it Barton? Was it Collins? We could go through the whole roster, all the way down to Yasinsky, but we'd simply be banking on Prairie Flower's intuition, focused or not.

Prairie Flower opened her mouth to say something but just then Susan breezed by, hooked her thumb toward the doors and said, 'Catering office. No rush.'

'Sorry, but I have to get back to work,' I apologized after Susan had trundled on.

Prairie Flower began rolling up her map. 'Stop by again, any time. Or visit my shop in Sisters. It's on North Fir Street.'

'I will,' I said. 'Who knows, I might need to buy that statue of Bigfoot over there.' The garden statue, nearly thirty inches high, was – according to its sign – made out of 'quality designer resin.' It could me mine, all mine, for a mere $195.

'Ships in five to seven business days,' Prairie Flower assured me.

I pictured Bigfoot in my Annapolis garden, in the far corner near the wall, emerging from the rhododendron. I managed to escape into the hallway before doubling over with an attack of the giggles.

'Hannah! Are you all right?' Someone had come out of the dealer's room just behind me.

I felt my face flush. I was embarrassed to be caught laughing, this day of all days. I coughed, cleared my throat and coughed again, flapping my hand in a just-a-minute way. 'I'm fine, Jake. Something went down the wrong way, is all.' I straightened and leaned back against the wall. 'After visiting the vendors, it seems to me that the best tool for finding Bigfoot is a credit card.'

'Ha!' he snorted. 'Seeing Jim Davis's video, half the people here think Bigfoot's wandering around the woods just outside this hotel.'

'With murder on his mind?'

'Bigfoot are notoriously shy,' Jake said. 'There may have been a Bigfoot out there today but I very much doubt that it did Radcliffe in.' He reached into his shirt pocket and came up with my iPhone. 'Thanks for this, Hannah. Do what you want with the pictures.' He pressed it into my hand. It was still warm from riding so close to his chest.

'I doubt they'll be much use to me, Jake. Just thinking about them kind of creeps me out.'

'I wasn't sure where to find you so I left your jacket with the concierge. Hope you don't mind.'

In all the excitement I'd actually forgotten about my jacket. 'No, no. That's perfect. Thank you.'

It was then I noticed Jake was carrying a seven-pound bucket of UltraCal30 gypsum cement. The last time I'd seen it, the bucket had been sitting on Marty's table between a pair of hiking boots and a backpack, some of the 'more' among the rugged 'mountain gear' that Marty offered for sale.

My heart flipped over. 'You found footprints, didn't you? You're making a cast!'

Jake beamed. 'Remember the marshy area near the riverbank?'

I did. Jim's video had shown the creature walking on two legs toward the river, then turning around before hightailing it into the woods. 'What do the prints look like in your professional opinion? Ape or man in a monkey suit?'

Jake's eyes shone like a child's on Christmas morning. 'Fifteen and a half inches long, according to the techs.'

I spread my hands, estimating the size. 'Big,' I said. 'That guy should play basketball for the New York Knicks.' I thought for a moment. 'Do you suppose there are living humans with feet that big?'

Jake, it turns out, was an expert on that, too. 'The largest feet in the world belong to a twenty-year-old from Venezuela. Sixteen inches. He's over seven feet tall and wears a size twenty-six shoe specially made in Germany. But I can't believe that anyone featured in the Guinness Book of World Records is going to hike all the way from Venezuela to Oregon just in order to stomp around the woods in a monkey suit. And where would you find a monkey suit to fit a guy that big?' Jake shifted the bucket from his right hand to his left. 'This stuff's heavy. Better get a move on.'

As he stepped away, I followed. 'Have you been deputized or something?'

'There are enough footprints to go around.' He hefted the bucket. 'I'm saving the locals a trip back into town.'

'Do you think the footprints belong to the murderer, Jake?'

'Could be, but as I told you earlier, there were no footprints around the body. When we found Radcliffe he was lying on the forest floor in a bed of pine needles, twigs and bark. Once the creature reached the edge of the forest, the footprints disappear. He could have gone anywhere after that.'

I halted, grabbed Jake gently by the elbow and pulled him back. 'It all depends on the timing, doesn't it? If the creature everyone saw on Jim's video made those footprints, he couldn't be the murderer because Martin was already dead.'

'Precisely. What I plan to determine . . .' he hefted the bucket to illustrate his point, 'is whether the footprints belong to an ape or to a man pretending to be an ape. If we're dealing with a man, he may be able to tell us something.'

'Aren't you dissing the local talent?'

'Lieutenant Cook seems comfortable with my kibitzing. It's not like I don't have experience with crime scenes, Hannah.'

'Speaking of crime scenes, where's Harley?'

'He's resting up in the room, watching *Judge Judy*.'

I laughed out loud. 'You're making that up.'

'I am not. It's Harley's favorite show. That and *Storage Wars*, especially when the bidders break out in brawls.' With his free hand, he tipped an imaginary hat. 'Hope to make it back in time for the afternoon sessions. If the casting goes well I should have something for show and tell. The toes are well-defined in these prints, indicating flexible midtarsal joints. That's not the usual case with fakes.'

Leaving me to ponder the significance of flexible midtarsals, he straight-armed it through a side door market 'exit' and hustled away.

ELEVEN

Boonville, Indiana, August 18, 1937. 'A stranger who declined to identify himself strolled into the newspaper office here today and declared that the weird, mysterious beast whose screams and prowlings have terrified residents of the Ohio river valley is simply a giant sloth. The man said he and his uncle were returning home from Mexico two years ago with the sloth, which they had captured on a game hunting expedition. He said they lost it near Evansville and never had found a trace of it since.'

Hammond Times (Hammond, IN), August 18, 1937

Leah sidled up to me in the hallway. 'You have photos of Martin Radcliffe?'

Damn! Where had she been hiding?

'I'm sorry you overheard that, Leah,' I said as I tucked the iPhone into my pocket, as if shoving it down deep might get rid of the evidence.

'Would you be willing to share them with me?' she asked.

'You're kidding me, right?'

'The newspaper would pay you for them.'

'Leah, I'm sorry, but I just can't.' When she didn't say anything for a moment, I added, 'Besides, Jake says they're too graphic for publication.'

'Nothing is too graphic these days, Hannah. You know that. Once somebody posted the autopsy photos of JFK online all pretense of decency flew straight out the window.'

While I knew that was true, and worse – what ghoul thought post-mortem photos of a five-year-old beauty queen belonged online? – I still didn't feel the photos were mine to share.

'You'll have to ask Jake.' Tap dancing as fast as I could, I added, 'He used my camera phone because it was handy. I told him to erase the photos after he was done with them.'

She frowned, clearly disappointed. 'He's a cop, right?'

I nodded.

'Active duty?'

'Retired.'

'Then why is he sticking his nose into Martin's murder? Won't he be stepping on local law enforcement's toes?'

'Probably, but that's Jake's problem, not mine.' I thought for a moment. 'If the locals are smart they'll listen to what he has to say. He's been tracking Bigfoot for years. It's kind of a hobby.'

While we talked, I moseyed in the direction of the catering office. Just outside it, I paused with my hand on the ornate brass handle and said, 'Sorry, but I've got a meeting. See you later?'

She wagged a finger. 'Count on it.'

I had the feeling Leah didn't believe my story about the pictures. She'd come back to the topic later, I felt sure, sailing in on a different tack.

Susan, it turns out, simply wanted to make sure the conference room was ready for the police who would be arriving, she'd been informed by the hotel manager, promptly after lunch. After I confirmed the arrangements she sent me off to mingle with the masses. Chat to them. Keep everyone happy.

By the time the doors opened on the dining room at noon, in spite of any official word on the subject, it seemed to be common knowledge that Martin Radcliffe had been murdered by Bigfoot. They'd all seen Jim Davis's video – some of them many more times than once. Jim had uploaded a copy to his website – the original having been turned over to Detective Lieutenant Barbara Cook – where it had been playing in an infinite loop for anyone who bothered to click on it. Jim's website traffic was up one thousand percent, Athena reported proudly as I waited in line behind her at the salad bar, and KGW Channel 8, the Portland NBC affiliate, had picked up the story for the five, six *and* seven o'clock news.

Bigfoot had definitely been at the scene of the crime. No doubt about that, people were saying. But so had Athena's husband, Jim, I wanted to shout. And so had Jake and I. Not to mention the dog.

As I ladled some thick, country mushroom soup into my bowl, I thanked my lucky stars that I was thoroughly alibied. I'd been in the company of someone ever since I took my first bite of donut that morning, and one of those someones was a retired Minneapolis cop.

Nobody I knew was eating lunch that early, so I sat down next to a young couple who were tucking enthusiastically into their cheeseburgers and fries. 'What brings you to Flat Rock?' I asked. 'Have you had an experience?'

'Gosh, no!' the woman said. 'We just come for the stories. They're so interesting! Who cares if Sasquatch is real or not.'

'We even brought the kids,' her husband added. 'They have all these cool activities for children.' He grinned at his wife. 'It's a mini-vacation for Carla and me.'

'How old are they?' I asked. 'The kids, I mean.'

'Seven and nine.'

'Same age as two of my grandchildren,' I said. 'Maybe I'll bring them along next time. What kind of activities?' I asked a few seconds later, genuinely curious about how anyone kept youngsters busy in a hotel primarily designed for grownups. You couldn't exactly send a seven-year-old off to the spa for an all-day mani-pedi and an oil and hot rock special.

'Yesterday morning they told Sasquatch stories,' the husband said. 'The kids thought they were kind of scary but in a good way.'

In my opinion, nothing could be scarier than the fairy tales I'd grown up on before Disney sanitized them. Cinderella's sisters chopped off their toes trying to fit into the glass slipper, as I recall, and Rapunzel's prince had his eyes scratched out by thorns. In the original Sleeping Beauty the besotted prince had sex with her while she slept. After a blissful hundred-year nap, the princess wakes up as a rape victim and the mother of twins. Don't you hate it when that happens?

I had scooped the last of the soup out of my bowl when a child raced up to the table dressed in jeans and a 'Bigfoot Doesn't Believe in You Either' T-shirt. The face she turned to her parents had been painted white like a cartoon cat, complete with a tidy, pink Hello Kitty bow over her left eyebrow. The girl clutched a piece of paper and waved it in her mother's face. 'I have to find a plastic fork!' Hello Kitty cried, sounding desperate.

Her mother grinned at me. 'They're on a scavenger hunt today,' she explained, patting her daughter's pigtailed head. 'You'll probably see all the little rug rats wandering around the lodge.' She smiled down at the girl who was bouncing impatiently on tiptoes. 'Have you tried the snack bar, Kylie? The place Daddy bought you ice cream yesterday?'

'Do they let seven-year-olds loose in the hotel all by themselves?' I wondered aloud.

The girl's mother bobbed her head in the direction of the doorway where a young woman dressed in jeans and a shirt identical to Kylie's, but several sizes larger, stood holding the hands of two even more juvenile rug rats. 'That's Shannon. One of the Bigfoot Camp counselors. There's another counselor, too. Colin. He usually takes the boys.'

After Kylie raced off to join her campmates, I asked, 'How many children are attending the conference, do you know?'

'Around ten, I think. Wasn't the face-painting amazing? You should see Kylie's big brother, Jason. Shannon turned him into lizard man, all green and scaly. She painted scary red eyes right on Jason's closed eyelids. Spooky as hell. Now I'll never get that kid into a bathtub.'

After a bit, I excused myself and made a brief circuit of the room so I could truthfully tell Susan I'd looked after business, then slipped out of the hotel in search of a quiet spot to check my email for a message from Paul. I had a lounge chair by the swimming pool in mind, but surprisingly four people were using the pool and three were already sunning themselves in said loungers. I recognized Randall Frazier – his bare, fur-covered midrift was not, in my opinion, ready for prime time. His mentor, a fully-clad E. Gregory Gilchrist, occupied the adjacent chair. As Gilchrist shouted at the cell phone held in his outstretched hand, there couldn't be anyone within a five-mile radius who didn't know the details of his multi-million dollar negotiations to add Mining Amerika-Mexico to his considerable portfolio. Propped up on one elbow in the lounger next door to Gilchrist's, wearing a cut-out tankini, her fair complexion protected by a broad-brimmed floppy hat, Jackie-O sunglasses and a smear of white sunscreen, was Nicole Baker. As her boyfriend talked she toyed with his tie.

I scooted past the pool area, hoping not to be noticed. A woman waved from the diving board and called cheerfully, 'Come on in, Hannah! The water's great!'

Carole Pulaski.

I stopped, smiled, leaned down and tested the water with my hand. Except for polar bears – and Canadians – the water was far too cold for me. 'It isn't heated!' I called back. 'Barbaric!'

'Sissy!' Carole laughed, bounced once on the end of the diving board and executed a perfect, ten-point, one-and-a-half somersault in the pike position. By the time her head popped up in the shallow end I was well away from the pool, hurrying along a path that led past the snack bar (Opening July 4! Make Your Reservations Now!), past the adjoining spa and fitness center and toward an area marked on the map of the hotel grounds as 'Meditation Garden.'

Long before I reached the garden, however, I heard what sounded like the call of an alpine horn. Maybe the lodge was getting to me – the bear rugs, the colorfully painted woodwork, the mounted deer heads with lanterns hanging from their antlers. I followed the sound, expecting at any moment to encounter a guy in *lederhosen* standing in a field of *edelweiss*, tooting his horn. As I got closer, I recognized the tune: Siegfried's horn call from Wagner's *Götterdämmerung*.

Do doo-doo-doo, do, do.

Do doo-doo-doo, do, do.

Auditory hallucinations. Stress can do that to you, I'd heard.

A sign at the side of the path directed me to the right. When I made the turn I nearly collapsed with relief. I wasn't losing my mind after all.

On a park bench at the far end of the garden, her hair a nimbus of gold in the midday sun, sat Professor Cecelia Cloughly, looking like a dandelion in full bloom. She held a French horn to her lips. I froze for a moment, breathing through my mouth. Was it a mirage? Cloughly played the familiar horn call once, twice and a third time. I waited until she had finished and lowered the horn.

'Doctor Cloughly. I'm sorry. I didn't mean to interrupt.'

'Call me Cecelia, please.' She patted a spot on the bench next to her. 'You're probably wondering what I'm doing out here with this.' With her right hand still inside the bell, she raised the horn.

'Just a little, although nothing would surprise me when it comes to this particular conference. Jim and Athena Davis were abducted by space aliens, somebody had told me, and Sasquatch is probably a time traveler from the future. That's why they leave no bodies, but you probably knew that.' I sat down. 'Makes playing a French horn in the middle of a garden seem positively normal.'

'Relieves the tension,' she explained. As I watched, she removed the mouthpiece from the instrument, pulled off two of the slides, turned the horn to the right as if it were a steering wheel and shook spit out onto the grass.

'Wagner, right?' I said.

She nodded. 'In my spare time I play with the New Jersey Philharmonic. We're doing a night at the opera in a couple of weeks and I've got to master that solo.'

'If it looked like I was gaping . . . well, I've only known you as a scientific expert on scat analysis, so hearing the horn took me a bit by surprise.'

'You'd be amazed how many scientists are also musicians,' she said as she began to disassemble the horn, laying the pieces out on her neon-blue slacks. 'According to the ancient Greeks, music *was* math.' She bent over and started arranging the pieces in the black carrying case that lay at her feet.

I'd worked part-time at Saint John's College in Annapolis, some-times known as the Great Books School, so I knew all about the *quadrivium*: geometry, arithmetic, astronomy and music. 'My husband teaches math at the Naval Academy,' I told her. 'There's a ton of musical talent there, too. The academy's annual production of *Messiah* would knock your socks off.'

'My point exactly.'

'I'm looking forward to hearing your talk,' I said after a moment. 'You got the schedule change?'

'I did. Poor Martin.'

'You knew him?'

She made a rocking motion with her hand. 'Sort of.' Cecelia took off her eyeglasses and wiped the lenses with the hem of her white silk blouse. 'I guess I shouldn't be surprised, though.'

'Why not?'

'Well, he made a lot of enemies, didn't he? Some of them are here, attending this conference.'

'You?' I asked.

'Not at all.' Cecelia paused, checked her eyeglass lenses for any remaining specks of lint, then put them back on. 'Like me, Radcliffe was just doing his job.' She swiveled on the bench slightly so that she was looking directly at me. 'If I've heard it once I've heard it a thousand times from these people. "Science has rejected us; they don't listen!" It couldn't be further from the truth. Professional scientists, of which I am one, don't accept or reject anything offhand. We simply study the evidence and draw conclusions from that. If the evidence doesn't go along with somebody's pre-conceived notions . . .' She shrugged. 'We can't be responsible for hard-headed stupidity.'

'But who here had it in for Martin? Who specifically?' I asked.

'It's not my job to speculate,' she said.

I nudged her with my elbow. 'You're no fun.'

Cecelia laughed. 'Have you ever watched his show?'

'Once or twice,' I admitted.

'Then you already know. Radcliffe can be brutal.' She paused then corrected herself. '*Could* be brutal. Some folks are less resilient than others.'

A bee dive-bombed Cecelia's hair, perhaps mistaking her for a flower. She brushed it away impatiently. 'I watched Radcliffe take down a Pentecostal faith healer once. It was pretty ugly.'

'I missed that show,' I said.

'When Radcliffe insisted that there was no historical evidence that Jesus Christ ever existed, I thought the guy's head was going to explode,' she said. 'Fortunately they cut to an ad before the preacher forgot all about keeping the Sixth Commandment.'

'Thou shalt not . . .' I paused, mentally running down the list I'd had to memorize as a kid in Vacation Bible School. 'Hah! Thou shalt not kill.'

'He provokes people just for the ratings.'

'I was impressed by Martin's talk last night,' I said. 'He could have dismissed the Patterson-Gimlin film out of hand like a lot of people but he didn't.'

'He wouldn't,' Cecelia said. 'It could be a hoax, of course, but conclusive evidence that it was faked simply doesn't exist.'

'Speaking of hoaxes, what did you find out when you analyzed the hair samples?' I asked. 'Were they legit?'

She grinned. 'Ah, for that you'll just have to wait like everyone else.'

I stood up and smiled down at her. 'If you aren't going to give me a sneak preview then I guess I better be getting back to work.'

'I'll come with you,' she said, picking up her horn.

'Have you had lunch?'

'Grabbed a salad before I came out here.' She patted her blouse where it strained slightly over her stomach. 'Watching my waist-line. It's here somewhere, I feel sure.'

I chuckled, as she probably intended.

'What would Sasquatch scat look like, anyway?' I asked as we headed back toward the lodge, walking side by side along the winding path. 'If it exists, I mean.'

'Picture this: a two-ton bear after a bout of chronic constipation.'

For the second time that day I dissolved into totally inappropriate laughter.

Professor Cloughly said, 'I saw you earlier talking to Jake Cummings. Outside the dealers' room.'

I wondered if my laughter had triggered the memory. I felt my face flush. 'He's found some footprints down by the river,' I told the doctor. 'He tells me they have flexible midtarsals, whatever that means. It seemed important.'

'The midtarsal joint is formed by the articulation of the calcaneus with the cuboid and the articulation of the talus with the navicular.'

I grinned. 'Well, thanks for clearing that up!'

'Simply put, the toes have knuckles.'

'Ah.'

Resting one hand in the palm of the other, she demonstrated by flexing her fingers like a spider doing pushups. 'Because of the way hominids walk, the toe impressions would be slightly deeper than the heel,' she explained. 'This can be faked, too, of course, but a footprint with that characteristic would be worth looking into.'

'They were big, Jake said. Almost sixteen inches long.'

'Interesting.'

'He's making plaster casts,' I continued as we made our way across the patio and into the lodge.

'Hmmm.' Cecelia seemed distracted. A case of nerves, perhaps? Worrying about her talk?

'See you in ten minutes.' I needed to give myself time to text my husband before heading to the conference room. 'I'm sure your PowerPoint is ready to go but no harm in double-checking.'

'Thanks, Hannah,' she said and chugged down the hallway as fast as one can go on short legs while lugging a French horn.

Where was she going? The elevators were off the lobby behind me, the restrooms just to my right and Professor Cloughly's conference room was in the opposite direction.

An absent-minded professor, perhaps? I shrugged. Everyone was a little distracted these days.

TWELVE

Londonderry, Ireland, 1800. 'There is now in the River an astonishing large Hairy Wild Man, caught 400 miles from the Cape of Good Hope, brought over in the Rambler, South Sea Whaler; he is of astonishing muscular strength, a specimen of which had nearly proved fatal to one of the custom-house officers, who inadvertently went too near him; he seized hold of the man, twirled him about two or three times with the greatest velocity, and then threw him over the side. Luckily the man escaped with a horrid fright and a sound ducking.'

Glasgow Advertiser, September 7, 1800

'When it comes to scat analysis,' Professor Cloughly began, 'the fresher the better.' On the screen, a pony-tailed, khaki-clad volunteer squatted over a mound of dung, holding a brown paper bag – the kind my mother used to use to pack school lunches. 'Shoo away the flies and examine it closely,' Cloughly instructed.

Sitting in the back row on the chair next to me, Leah Solat mumbled, 'No, thank you.'

'Are we having fun yet?' I asked.

'Better than hanging around California to investigate why the Elk Grove school district is buying canned peaches from China to serve in their cafeterias despite federal Buy America guidelines,' she said.

'Glad this comes after lunch rather than before,' I whispered back as the next photograph slid sideways onto the screen: a row of paper bags neatly labeled with a date, elevation and GPS location in bold black letters.

The bags dissolved into a photograph entitled 'Cat Scat,' showing a snow leopard beautifully posed on a snow-dusted rocky ledge. 'Because of their rarity and the human inaccessibility of their habitat,' Cloughly continued, 'snow leopards in Mongolia and the Himalayas are rarely seen, but we know that they exist and can estimate population numbers because of their scat. To my knowledge,' she continued, 'no one has yet collected any suspected Sasquatch scat that cannot be conclusively linked to an existing mammal – primarily bears.' The snow leopard dissolved, replaced by a grizzly bear reared up menacingly on its hind legs and captioned, 'Bears Do *What* in the Woods?'

Someone in the audience sniggered.

The bear on the screen dissolved, revealing the next slide. 'That's an imposing pile of poo,' I said softly. A ruler placed next to the mound of scat measured an impressive ten inches.

'Very moving,' Leah muttered.

Bathroom humor. Always good for a laugh.

Cloughly went on to illustrate how frozen fecal samples are air dried, transferred to nylon stockings, washed and then air dried again before the indigestible remains – bones, feathers and hair – are examined using a light microscope. 'This sample,' she continued, moving to the next slide, 'is from an American black bear, collected in the spring. It consists primarily of big-tooth Aspen catkins.'

Before Cloughly could move on to the next slide, a woman wearing a dark green hoodie interrupted: 'But what does what bears eat have to do with Squatch?'

'It's just an illustration,' Cloughly explained with patience. 'Because of the color, size, shape, consistency and content of this particular sample, we can say it's definitely bear. That's because we have other samples, also from bears, to compare it to.'

Even from where I sat, I could see the lightbulb go off over the woman's head. 'And we don't have any Sasquatch poop that we know of, do we? Poop to compare it to?'

'Exactly. And that's why hair analysis is so important. Which brings me to my next slide. Over the past several decades,' Professor Cloughly continued, 'the science of identifying animal species by studying hair samples has been well-developed. You've all watched *CSI*, haven't you?'

Nodding all around.

'The serial killer caught by distinctive cat hairs on the carpet the body was rolled up in. The extortionist who overlooked the hairs from his pit bull, Bruno, when he supplied the canvas bag to put the money in.'

'Dumb and dumber,' somebody muttered.

Cloughly smiled, as if she heard and agreed. 'Under a microscope,' she continued, 'human hair is especially easy to distinguish from that of an animal. Animal hair medullas – by that I mean the centers – are quite structured, as in these samples.'

On the screen, photographs of lab slides labeled 'cat' and 'rabbit' reminded me of a necklace and an ear of corn respectively. The sample labeled 'bat' resembled a row of miniature shark's teeth. 'The medulla of human hair, on the other hand,' she went on, forwarding to the next slide, 'is typically thin, broken or not even present, as in the sample pictured here. Note that there is no medulla. The strand is a uniform color throughout.'

More nodding. Everyone was following the professor so far.

'I should explain that this particular sample is from a subject who is known to some of you: Homer Guthrie.'

A photograph of Homer filled the screen.

I stifled a gasp. Every inch of the poor man's face was covered with long, reddish-brown hair. Blue eyes, brimming with all the sadness in the world, stared out from under the fringe that on anyone else would have been eyebrows. Homer looked more like a werewolf than a Sasquatch, I thought, wondering if he'd ever tried depilatories, or if electrolysis would do the trick.

'Homer had hoped to be with us today,' the professor said, 'but circumstances prevented it. Fortunately he's generously agreed to let me share the results of our DNA analysis of his hair sample with you.'

'Cut to the chase, Doc,' somebody muttered.

I was sure she heard but Cloughly ignored the heckler and forged on. 'I'd like you to note the uniform, reddish color of this sample taken from Homer's head. It has all the characteristics of being human. But could Sasquatch hair have similar, human-like characteristics? Or is it more like an animal's? Impossible to tell until we have hair from a Sasquatch for comparison.

'Mister Guthrie has been led, all his life, to believe that he is a missing link – half human, half Sasquatch,' she continued. 'But is he? We can't tell by simply looking at Homer, or at his hair, so we move on to the next step: DNA analysis. We thought, and Homer agreed, that his sample should be included among the hairs presumptive for North American Sasquatch that have been supplied to us for examination.

'From the samples provided to our laboratory, we selected hair shafts approximately four centimeters in length and thoroughly cleaned them to remove all surface contamination. Then we ground them up in a buffer solution which was incubated for two hours at 135 degrees Fahrenheit in a solution containing proteinase K.'

Her eyes went on scan, studying the audience, some of whom were scribbling madly in notebooks or on the blank 'Notes' pages at the back of their conference programs. A dazzling smile. 'Am I going too fast for you?'

She gave the scribblers time to catch up before moving on. 'In the next step, we extracted the DNA and performed PCR – that's polymerase chain reaction amplification – of the ribosomal mitochondrial DNA 12S fragment corresponding to bps 1093-1196 of the human mitochondrial genome . . .' She paused. 'Are you still with me?' Then laughed. 'I thought not. It's all rather complicated.'

The image on the screen of a rubber-gloved hand holding a rocket-shaped test tube evaporated to be replaced by a diagram featuring photos of lab equipment connected by lines, circles and arrows. 'In simpler terms,' she explained, highlighting one of the images with a laser pointer, 'we isolated one or more of the DNA fragments carried by the hair.'

As she spoke, most eyes in the room followed the red laser dot, with the exception of one lonesome cowboy who'd fallen asleep, chin on chest, in the back row. 'We amplified the fragment, mapped the sequence and then compared it with the DNA sequences of known mammals that are on file in the GenBank at the National Library of Medicine outside of Washington, DC.

'Sadly, two of the samples were too degraded to recover any DNA, but in spite of the age and condition of some of the hairs – one sample had been in a museum for over forty years, imagine that – we were able to obtain DNA and match them with one hundred percent certainty.'

The next slide showed columns of seemingly random letters – g's, c's, t's and a's – arranged in six groups of ten, row after row after row. The screen was full, thick with them. 'This is a GenBank record for *bos taurus*, otherwise known as a cow,' she said.

The face of a black-and-white cow slowly materialized, pixel by pixel, superimposing itself over the dense columns of letters. 'When we compared the results of hair sample number one taken from a barbed wire fence in Arizona,' the professor continued, 'this was the result. Cow.'

'Shee-it,' someone in the audience muttered, possibly the donor from Arizona.

The dozing cowboy awoke with a snort and glanced around in confusion. Somebody tittered.

'The next slide is a table showing our results. Don't worry about trying to copy it all down. I'll have handouts for you at the back of the room after the session. Please note that each sample is listed by location, to what creature – yeti, Bigfoot, almasty, yeren and so on – the sample was attributed, the GenBank match and the common name of that match.'

Professor Cloughly paused, giving the audience time to scan the table of results.

My eyes strayed immediately to the 'common name' column: brown bear, horse, black bear, wolf, raccoon, porcupine, sheep . . .

Deep silence filled the room as the significance of the professor's results sank in. All of the samples matched up with a known mammal. Without exception. Even Homer Guthrie. *Homo sapiens.* Human.

Next to me, Leah had her iPad open to a document in Pages. After Professor Cloughly announced the findings, Leah's fingers flew over the virtual keys and tapped a few icons.

'There!' she whispered in an aside. 'Story filed.'

'What story is that?' I whispered back.

'Remember that hair sample I told you about – the one from Strawberry, California?'

'The guy connected with your newspaper?'

She tipped her head toward the screen where the official table of results from the lab at South Jersey Shore University was still displayed. 'Porcupine. How embarrassing is that?'

I grinned. 'Could have been worse, I suppose, like the hair of the wild Dacron.'

She waggled her fingers. 'Ooooh . . . I saw a giant Orlon once. The teeth, the claws!'

I nudged her with my elbow. 'Shhhh. Have some respect.'

We both watched as, from the second row, a tattooed arm shot up and waved to attract Professor Cloughly's attention. When she called on him, the man stood. 'With all due respect,' he began, which in my experience usually prefaced a remark that would be anything but respectful, 'this is total bullshit.'

On the stage, Cloughly waited, smiling indulgently. Clearly, she had been expecting criticism. I prayed she was prepared for it.

The guy leaned so far over the woman sitting directly in front of him that she had to duck sideways to avoid being smacked by one of the arms he began thrashing around to emphasize his point.

'I seen that critter! We was eyeball to eyeball for, like, two minutes, neither of us saying nothing. After he skedaddled I picked that hair off the tree he was standing behind. You think I don't know the difference 'tween a Bigfoot and a goddam deer?'

Speech delivered, he fell back in his chair, arms wrapped around himself, sulking like a petulant child.

'You may very well have encountered a Bigfoot, sir,' Cloughly said gently, 'and he may very well have been standing behind that tree, as you said, but a white-tailed deer rubbed up against the tree first.'

From the rigidity of his back, the guy didn't seem convinced.

'Professor?' This from a young woman, a bronze-colored ponytail protruding from the opening in the back of her navy blue ball cap.

'Yes?'

'I'm new to this so I'll probably sound stupid, but there's some words up there I don't understand. What's an almas? What's a yeren?'

'*Almas* is the Mongolian word for "wildman,"' the professor explained, 'and *yeren* quite literally means "wild man" in Chinese. 'Bigfoot is a relatively new term, dating to 1958, I believe. As long as there have been campfires there have been as many words to describe these mysterious creatures as there are cultures,' she continued. While cradling the laser pointer in her left hand, she ticked them off on her fingers. 'In Kenya, it's the *Chemosit* or Nandi Bear.' She leaned forward conversationally. 'It eats the brains of its victims. There's the *hibagon* in Japan, which is smaller and cuter than Bigfoot, and a creature called *mapinguari* in Brazil. *Mapinguari* means either roaring animal or fetid beast – take your pick, although hunters in the Amazon report that the animal reeks of feces and rotting flesh so I'd plump for the latter. In Sumatra it's the *orang pendek*, or *short person,* and in Australia they're referred to as *Yowies*.' She smiled and surveyed the audience. 'Have I forgotten anything?'

'Skunk ape,' someone volunteered.

Cloughly smiled. 'Yes, primarily in the Everglades. Recently photographed. Anyone else?'

'Hairy Bill!' someone shouted.

'Jacko!' A woman's voice, from the back and to my right.

'Nuk luk!'

'Wooly booger!'

The woman with the ponytail, her head studiously bowed, scribbled frantically in her notebook.

Someone else shouted, 'Tsiatko!' and the woman looked up, wondering, I suspect, how to spell the word.

Professor Cloughly raised a hand. 'Thank you all! You've made my point, I think. Many centuries, many cultures, many names. That's what makes this study so fascinating to scientists like me.'

She clicked forward to the next slide, a huge, stylized question mark. 'How can all these people be wrong?'

A murmur of agreement swept the room like a wave.

'Remember, the absence of evidence we found here does not mean that such creatures do not exist. What it means is we do not yet have the evidence to prove it.'

The tattooed guy in front chose that moment to stand, make his way clumsily along the row, stepping on toes, and into the aisle. I caught the distinct odor of hops as he stomped past me and out the door, muttering, 'Bullshit.'

On stage, Professor Cloughly waited, calmly observing his departure. When the last of his blue jean-clad butt had disappeared into the hallway, she smiled indulgently and continued the thought. 'The analysis techniques scientists have developed here and elsewhere are rigid, accurate, definitive.' She spread her arms wide, taking in the entire audience. 'You, people like you, are the key. Keep bringing us samples. Perhaps one of you will discover something new, a sample that produces a genomic sequence that GenBank has never heard of. Now that would be something to write home about!'

With a modest, my-job-here-is-done bow, Professor Cloughly unclipped the microphone from her lapel and left the stage.

The audience sat quietly for a moment, as if in shock. Then someone to my right began to clap. I joined in (figuring it went with the job description, although the woman certainly deserved it) and before long the room erupted in applause, heads turning toward the back of the room to acknowledge the speaker. 'That's a slick way to avoid the Q and A,' I whispered to the professor, who had come to stand in the aisle next to my chair.

She smiled and bobbed her head, acknowledging the applause. 'It's show business, ladies,' she whispered back. 'Always leave them wanting more.'

THIRTEEN

*'In the Tian Shan mountains themselves live a wild people,
who have nothing in common with other human beings. A pelt
covers the entire body of these creatures except the hands and
face. They run around in the hills like animals and eat leaves
and grass and whatever else they can find.'*

Johann Schiltberger, *The Bondage and Travel of Johann
Schiltberger, a Native of Bavaria, in Europe, Asia and
Africa, 1396–1427*, London, Hakluyt Society, 1879, p. 35

Even A-type personalities like me who'd be lost without
their to-do lists need a little down time. My chance for a
break came after I'd thanked Cecelia for her research,
funded, she told me when I asked, not by the state of New Jersey
but by the seemingly bottomless pockets of E. Gregory Gilchrist,
the mining magnate and billionaire banker I'd met at the opening
reception the night before. While I chatted with Cecelia, Leah
Solat loitered nearby. I figured she would attempt another run at
me, twisting my arm about sharing Jake's crime-scene photographs, but by walking Cecelia to the elevators I managed to
escape to my room without incident.

Once there, I kicked off my shoes and flopped down on the
bed, plumping all five of the pillows – soft, hard and decorative
– behind my back. I closed my eyes for a few minutes, hoping
for a cat nap, but my iPhone, still tucked deep down in my
handbag, kept calling to me:

I have some photographs you want to see!

Sorry, no. I really don't.

C'mon, Hannah. You know that you do!

Be quiet! I have a trash icon and I know how to use it.

It can't hurt to look, can it?

I'm not listening to you!

How silly you are. Photographs don't bite.

After five minutes, I caved and dug out my phone.

Staring at the screensaver – a photograph of my grandchildren taken at Thanksgiving – I wavered. I could text my husband. I could watch *Cosmos* on Netflix. I could play Solitaire.

Go on, just do it!

I sighed, swiped the phone on and entered my password.

There were no messages from Paul. Just as well, I thought. It wouldn't matter if it took him a few more days to find out that his wife had turned up, once again, in the general vicinity of a dead body. The last time that happened he'd been downright grumpy about it.

On my home screen, the rainbow-colored rosette that was the Photos icon seemed almost to pulsate: *Tap me! Tap me!*

So I did.

While I had sat a safe distance away like a mushroom on a log, Jake had photographed the victim from all sides. There were twenty-four photos in all. The first two made me cringe. The close-ups of Martin's injuries made me wish my camera weren't quite so robust, megapixel-wise. I groaned and paged on. By the time I got to five and six, I'd overcome my revulsion. Photos eight, nine and ten, from a forensic point of view, were fascinating. By the time I got to fifteen, I knew what had killed Martin Radcliffe, and what's more, I knew that Jake did, too.

Among the pine needles and moss-covered rocks not far from the mess that had been Martin Radcliffe's head lay a broken tree limb the size of a man's arm. Jake had zoomed in on the ragged end where the branch had been ripped away from the trunk of the tree. I was no expert, but in the clarity provided by the iPhone's retina display, the dark smear on the pale, raw wood certainly looked like blood. There was no doubt in my mind, however, about the clump of blond hair that clung to the jagged tree fibers.

Unless bears had evolved to use tree limbs as weapons, no *gigantopithecus blacki* had done the deed. Martin Radcliffe had been murdered by homo sapiens.

I picked up the bedside phone and dialed the hotel operator, asking to be put through to Jake Cummings. After four rings, he picked up.

'Cummings.'

'This is Hannah. Do you have a minute?'

'Sure,' he said. 'Harley and I are just watching *America's Funniest Home Videos*. What's up?'

'I looked at the photographs.'

'Ah.'

'When you borrowed my iPhone, Jake, before you returned it, did you share the photos with the local cops?'

'No, why?' he said. 'They have their own cameras and much better quality, too.'

'Then why on earth did you take those awful pictures?'

Jake snorted. 'You think I was taking pictures of my victim as souvenirs like some homicidal maniac?'

'No, of course not,' I said, 'but you must have had a good reason, other than morbid fascination.'

'I wanted time to study them, Hannah. You know what they say: use it or lose it. It's been a couple of years. I don't want my investigative skills to get rusty.'

'You should apply for a license as a private investigator then,' I suggested quite seriously.

'As soon as I get the money together, Hannah. It's not exactly free.'

I sat quietly for a moment, staring at the last picture displayed on my screen, a closeup of the branch. 'So, Officer Cummings, what do you think?'

'You saw the branch?'

'I'm looking at it now. Hard to miss.'

'OK. From the damage to Martin's skull, I figure he was struck from behind with a tremendous amount of force by a right-handed person. Picture a batter, warming up at home plate then knocking the ball clear out of the park.'

I shivered. *Let's not and say we did*, as my late mother was fond of saying.

'Whoever it was dropped Martin where he stood,' Jake continued. 'I don't think the poor guy saw it coming.'

'So we agree it wasn't a bear.'

'No. Primates use tools. Grizzly bears, not so much.'

'Or Bigfoot.'

Jake paused thoughtfully. 'Primates generally use tools to get food, not as weapons. We know three cases of gorillas in the Cameroon, however, who threw clumps of grass and tree branches at humans, so I don't think Bigfoot can be entirely ruled out. But I think it unlikely.'

'A human, then? You agree?'

'Sadly,' he said.

'Disappointing in a way,' I mused.

'What on earth do you mean?'

'I was thinking about something that Monique Deschamps said when I met her in the dealers' room. How ironic would it be if Martin Radcliffe, the great debunker, had been killed by a creature he spent a lifetime denying existed.'

If we had figured it out, the police probably had, too. They'd been at the scene, taken photographs and examined Jim Davis's video and the tapes from the security cameras. Even as Jake and I chatted, an autopsy was being performed.

As if reading my thoughts, Jake said, 'Soon the whole world will know what you and I know. But in the meantime, it can work to our advantage.'

'Our? You think we're some sort of crime-solving team?'

'Aren't we, Hannah?'

'I'm not a detective – I only play one on television,' I said with a laugh. I thanked Jake for his professional opinion, said I'd probably see him at dinner and hung up.

Then I deleted the photographs, one by one, from my iPhone. Those photos were the last thing I wanted my grandchildren to stumble over whenever they got bored playing Minecraft or Candy Crush.

And I certainly didn't need any *aide mémoire*. The sooner I replaced those graphic images in my brain with something more benign – like Facebook kittens decked out in Halloween costumes – the better.

FOURTEEN

Walker County, Georgia, 1889. 'The wild man has again made his appearance . . . [He] was about 7 or 7 ½ feet high, hairy as an old bear and would weigh from his looks, 400 pounds; had a pole in one hand that looked to be ten foot long which he handled as easy as a stout, healthy man would a pipestem. His name was asked and the answer came in the shape of a large stone, which weighed at least 100 pounds, which was hurled at the inquisitive gentleman.'

The Atlanta Constitution (Atlanta, GA),
February 4, 1889

Susan had asked to go over the following day's program with me. After dinner, while almost everyone – including Jake and Harley – clustered on the patio around one of the fire pits drinking mulled cider and sharing Bigfoot encounter stories in a no-shame zone, I wandered into the lodge's White Horse bar where Susan and I had agreed to meet. But either I was running early or she was running late.

I skirted the bar, sat down at a small, round table for two and picked up the plasticized tent card that described the specialty drinks of the house. Adventurous whisky drinkers could order a Mountain Man-Hattan or a Fool's Gold. Gin aficionados could drown their sorrows with a Silver Bullet; animal lovers with a Bighorn Cocktail or a One Good Buck. On Top of Old Smokey sounded a lot like Kentucky moonshine to me, but the Suspender-Free Zone, a blend of whiskey, lime and soda water, held promise. Tempting, I had to admit, but just to be on the safe side I sighed and ordered an alcohol-free spicy tomato juice concoction called A Bloody Shame.

While I checked my iPhone for messages and waited for my drink, a couple wandered in and sat down at the table next to me.

'Hi, Shannon,' I said after they'd gotten settled.

She looked up at me, her brow slightly furrowed.

'We met at lunch. You were wrangling Kylie and a couple of other youngsters.' I turned to the young man sitting across from her. 'And you must be Colin.'

He raised a dark eyebrow and looked concerned. 'How did you know?'

'Kylie's mother mentioned it. Carla Somebody or Other? She said you looked after the boys and she happens to have one of those.'

He grinned. 'Ah, yes, the irrepressible Jason.' Colin ran a hand over his head, ruffling his tight blond curls. 'Any gray you see here, it's because of Jason.'

'I'm Hannah, by the way,' I said. 'I help wrangle the presenters.'

'Poor you,' Shannon said. 'Anybody giving you trouble?'

I shrugged. 'It's not too bad.'

'What brings you two here?' I said after a moment. 'Excuse me for saying so but camp counselors of my experience tend to be more, uh, college age.'

Shannon laughed, a bubbly, contagious sound. Even Colin seemed to relax and be drawn into it. 'Brad Johnson got us the gig,' Colin explained. 'Shannon met him at a party in LA and we got to be friends.'

'We were all "between jobs,"' Shannon added, drawing quote marks in the air. 'Colin starts at Sony in a couple of weeks but I'm still looking.'

'What do you do?' I asked Colin, genuinely curious about anything smacking of Hollywood, like most folks who devour *People* magazine while waiting for their hair to change color at the beauty parlor.

'I'm a researcher for *Jeopardy*,' he explained. 'Every clue the writers come up with has to be backed up by two independent sources.'

'You have to take a test to get the job,' Shannon told me. 'Just like the contestants do.'

Jeopardy had been on the air since I was a kid in elementary school. I was going to ask Colin what Alex Trebek, the quiz show's longtime host, was *really* like, but remembered he hadn't started to work at Sony yet.

Across from her, Colin was blushing modestly. 'You'll never guess in a million years what Shannon did.'

I turned to Shannon, whose sly smile was daring me to take a stab at guessing anyway. 'You *must* be an artist,' I said. 'I was super impressed by your face-painting talent. Did you hire out for parties?'

'On the side,' she said, 'with BoomBoom the Clown, the Amazing Stefanini and a stripper named Tanqueray. But that wasn't my real job.'

'But you are an artist, right?'

'Right.'

'Did you work for Disney? Pixar?' I guessed.

Shannon laughed. 'I wish!'

The waitress delivered my Bloody Shame. After she went away with Colin's order for two Midnight Snowstorms, he took pity on me. 'Ever watched *Naked and Afraid*?'

I had to admit that I had wasted more time than I cared to think about on that silly television show, kind of a nude *Survivor*. Two naked strangers are dropped into a remote wilderness area with no food, no water and no clothes and have to survive for twenty-one days. Other than drawing clothing on the contestants, I couldn't imagine what an artist could do for a show like that. It turns out I was half right.

'I worked for the Blur Man Group,' Shannon said. 'It's OK to show butts and butt cracks on the Discovery Channel but you have to blur out the boobs and the naughty bits.'

I nearly choked on my drink, laughing. 'It's a family show, I take it?'

'Go figure,' Shannon said.

'Isn't it weird looking at naked people all day?' I asked.

Shannon shrugged. 'Doctors do it. You get used to it.'

'Shannon makes light of it, Hannah, but it's painstaking work,' Colin said. 'They have to go frame by frame by frame, using computers and a stylus. You have to blur out the boob but keep the braid dangling down in front of it.'

'It's totally weird,' Shannon said. 'It's the only job I know of where you can say, "Oh my gawd, look at that penis!" and not get fired for it.'

'Blurred boobs have turned me into the sex fiend I am today,' Colin said, patting her hand.

'They're gateway boobs.' Shannon laughed. 'Anyway, if I do

my job right, everyone ends up with anatomy that's as smooth as Barbie and Ken.'

'I keep telling Shannon, she's got a marketable skill. Who else can spot a bug on a nipple at five hundred paces?'

'And ticks on dicks. It's a glamorous job.'

'So why did you leave?' I asked. 'Is the show going off the air?'

'Are you kidding? There's *Buying Naked* and *Dating Naked*. Next thing you know there'll be *Here Comes the Naked Bride and Groom*.' She sighed. 'Two of the shows, *Naked Vegas* and *Skin Wars* actually use body painters but I'm aiming higher than that. You said it a few minutes ago, Hannah. Pixar, Disney, Dreamworks. Or Illumination Entertainment. They did *Despicable Me*.'

'There you are!' caroled Susan, waving at me from the entrance to the bar. She hustled over. 'Sorry I'm late. Got tied up with someone who left his Lopresor at home. Had to find a pharmacy that was still open and get the guy taken care of before he blew a gasket.'

'Nice talking to you,' I said, nodding at Shannon and Colin in turn.

Susan and I excused ourselves and tucked into a far corner of the bar where I nursed my Bloody Shame and Susan hunched over an ice-cold glass of Sauvignon blanc.

Robin Burcell, the forensic sketch artist, a former policewoman who worked closely with local authorities and the FBI, would be first up in the morning, Susan confirmed. Just as she had done for the Feds, Robin would draw sketches of Bigfoot based on eyewitness descriptions. 'She's only got time to do two sketches, so we'll have to draw numbers out of a hat or something,' Susan said.

'Or something?'

Susan, calmer than I had seen her all day, sipped her wine. 'You'll figure it out.'

I flashed forward to a late evening in my room, snuggled under the duvet, television tuned to Jimmy Fallon as I cut bits of hotel stationery into squares using cuticle scissors from my toiletry bag.

After the morning coffee break, the forensic artist would be followed by a former navy linguist who worked with transcriptions of Bigfoot vocalizations. I'd heard about the Sierra Sounds

from Leah Solat who wrote for the same newspaper as the late
Al Berry, one of the two men who'd recorded the vocalizations
during the early seventies, but I'd never heard the recordings and
had no idea they'd been transcribed. 'Don't tell me that Bigfoots
have a language,' I said.

'Apparently,' Susan said. 'This guy, Larry Mack, works with
the linguist who actually invented UHPA.'

I must have looked puzzled.

'Unclassified Hominid Phonetic Alphabet,' she explained.
'They use it to write the sounds down.'

As I kid, I'd always been fascinated by codes; somewhere in
my jewelry box I still had the Captain Midnight Plane Decoder
pin to prove it. Later, I'd studied Latin and French. What is
learning a foreign language, after all, if not breaking a code?
You sit in a Paris restaurant, say to the waiter, *Comme plat principal, je vais prendre le bifteck à point*, and a short time later,
voila! A steak, medium rare, arrives at your table. It's magic.
Assuming my presence wasn't required elsewhere, I decided to
give the UHPA session high priority.

The afternoon session, I learned from the updated schedule
Susan provided, was a lecture by Monique Deschamps. 'Zana:
the Last Neanderthal?' Zana, I remembered from a special I'd
seen on television, was thought to be a female almasty, captured
in 1850 by hunters in the mountains between Georgia and Russia.
Caged, domesticated and kept as a slave by a local landowner,
the poor creature had eventually died in 1890, but not before
giving birth to several children. 'Was she?' I asked Susan.

'Was who what?' she said, her mind clearly elsewhere.

'Zana. A Neanderthal?'

Susan laughed. 'You think that because I organize a conference
I have intimate knowledge of the subject? I organized a heavy
duty truck convention once but I still can't tell an alternator from
a flux capacitor.'

It was my turn to laugh. 'A flux capacitor is imaginary – you
know that, don't you? It's what turned the DeLorean from *Back
to the Future* into a time machine.'

Susan shrugged. 'See? What do I know?'

Susan and I had been leaning close, talking just loud enough
so we could hear each other over the buzz of conversation and

the *whump-whump-whump*, *squeep-squeep-squeep* of a basketball game showing on one of the two television screens mounted over the bar. 'Getting back to Zana,' I said in a normal tone that boomed into the sudden silence around us.

I clamped my lips shut.

All eyes seemed to be focused on the television where a KGW8 reporter had launched into the seven o'clock news.

'. . . Radcliffe's widow, Sonya Jovanka, a former Miss Maine, arrived late this afternoon from Los Angeles. Accompanied by family friend and attorney, Gordon Parker, she is seen here leaving the office of the Oregon state medical examiner in Clackamas where the body of her late husband has been taken for autopsy.'

'Whoa, that was fast,' I muttered.

'Maybe she had to identify the body?'

'Ugh,' I said, hoping Susan was wrong. I'd seen the photographs. I wouldn't wish seeing the real thing on my worst enemy.

As we watched, the pair emerged from a modern glass and concrete building, then paused for a moment under one of four contemporary glass-globed post lamps. Parker's arm snaked comfortingly around Miss Jovanka's shoulders as she sobbed into the reporter's microphone, 'They don't know what happened to Martin, they . . . they . . .'

'We're waiting to hear from the medical examiner.' Parker took over for his stricken client. 'It looks as if Martin may have been attacked by a bear, most likely a grizzly, but it's early days yet.' He took a step forward, putting an end to the interview by steering the grieving widow in the direction of the nearby parking lot.

The reporter, a blonde ingénue wearing a purple windbreaker, faced the camera. 'KGW has reached out to network executives at the History Channel, who expressed shock at the tragic loss of one of their most popular stars. There is no word about the future of Radcliffe's show, *Don't You Believe It!*, which had been renewed for a seventh season. New episodes had been scheduled to air in the fall. Back to you, Scott.'

'Thank you, Belinda. Earlier today, Tyree Smith was on the scene at Flat Rock Lodge near Sisters, Oregon, where the tragic incident took place. Here's what Tyree had to say.'

Tyree, it was soon apparent, had been reporting from the foot

of the drive that led to the lodge, being prevented from proceeding
further up it by a Deschutes County patrol car and a long, white
hearse. 'Behind me is the custom Toyota Prius from Holloway-
Johnson Funeral Home that will carry the body of Martin
Radcliffe to the office of the Oregon state medical examiner,
where it will be determined what caused his death. Witnesses
tell us that Radcliffe was last seen at breakfast. His body was
discovered in the woods several hours later by a retired policeman
from Minneapolis who was walking his dog. Radcliffe was one
of several hundred people who are in Sisters this weekend
attending the Sasquatch Sesquicentennial. He had addressed the
group just the evening before.'

'No mention of a retired grandmother from Maryland, thank
goodness,' I whispered to Susan.

'Yet,' she said.

'Is Jake sure it wasn't a bear?' Susan asked.

'Positive.'

In a voiceover, Scott said, 'Sasquatch is taken very seriously
here in Oregon, isn't it, Tyree?'

'Yes, indeed, Scott. I've talked to several of the conference
attendees and some of them are even speculating that Martin
Radcliffe was attacked by a Bigfoot. I should point out that a
sheriff's officer who agreed to talk to me dismissed that scenario.
It's far more likely to have been a bear, he said, but cautioned
that we needed to wait for the medical examiner's report.'

Scott thanked Tyree, then segued to an interview with a
National Park Service employee, ranger hat tucked under his
arm, who offered helpful tips on how hikers could protect themselves from bear attacks. 'Be Bear Aware!' proclaimed the crawl.
If I had to summarize the ranger's advice, it would be this: do
not look like prey. Just to be on the safe side, I decided to pick
up a spray can of EPA-approved bear repellant at the earliest
opportunity, possibly from Marty in the dealers' room. If it
worked against bears it was probably good against homicidal
maniacs, too.

FIFTEEN

Martins Ferry, Ohio, August 27, 1891. 'The farmers near Negree, this county, have organized to hunt down the wild man or animal that has been killing and devouring sheep, hogs, chickens, etc. . . . The wild man . . . is covered with dark reddish hair, has large ears, small eyes, teeth like those of a wild boar, huge mouth and paws, measures about five feet in height, and weighs 200 pounds. It is said that the animal walks and runs as well on two as four legs, can climb a tree or hill very quickly, and is seen only in the morning and evening.'

The Salem Daily News (Salem, OH), August 27, 1891

K nowing what I did about the bloody branch, it didn't surprise me when the police returned to the lodge early the following morning. I watched the first patrol car arrive around eight-fifteen while I was lounging on my balcony, sipping a lackluster cup of watery hotel-room coffee. The second car arrived five minutes later and Detective Lieutenant Barbara Cook stepped out.

The evening before, I'd made sure the conference room she'd been using for interviews was good to go so I didn't feel the need to rush downstairs. By eight forty-five I was still dilly-dallying around the coffee urns in a futile attempt to avoid the siren call of Debbie's Donut Dugout. I failed. Carrying a Styrofoam cup, I marched over and helped myself to a little bit of heaven with white frosting and confetti sprinkles.

In mid-bite, my phone began to chirp. It was tucked so deep down in my bag that I nearly missed the text message from Jared summoning me to the manager's office.

I wrapped my donut in a napkin and headed for the office.

Susan and I arrived at his door almost simultaneously.

'The police want to see you both in the conference room,' Jared explained. 'They have stills from the surveillance tapes and need your help identifying the people who are in them. I've already identified the staff members they were curious about.'

Susan and I exchanged glances. 'We're just organizers,' Susan said. 'Except for a few people we've met so far, we don't have a clue who most of the attendees are. They need to talk to the sponsor, Ron Murphy.'

'Carole Pulaski should know just about everyone,' I added. 'She's attended the two previous conferences and, besides, she manned the registration desk. I helped out at registration too for a while, but the people came in so fast and furious that it's all kind of a blur.'

While I was speaking there was a brisk shave-and-a-haircut on the office door. Before Jared could acknowledge the knock, the door opened and Detective Lieutenant Cook eased into the room. 'Sorry to bother you, but . . .' Seeing us, she paused. 'Ah, Hannah Ives. We may need to talk to you again.'

Susan frowned.

I explained about Ron Murphy and Carole Pulaski. When asked to do so by the police officer, Jared had them paged.

While we waited for Ron and Carole to arrive, Cook pulled a smart phone out of the breast pocket of her uniform and tapped a few keys. She seemed to be puzzling over something for a moment, then addressed me. 'I know you have responsibilities here at the conference, but will you be free later this morning?'

'I can make time,' I said.

Her smile was so disarming it made me nervous. 'Just a few questions,' she said. 'Won't take a minute. After we finish with Mr Murphy and Miss Pulaski, we'll have you paged.'

I smiled back. 'As long as Susan doesn't need me.'

Susan, still frowning, said, 'No, that's fine,' although it was clear that it wasn't.

Thirty minutes later, the summons came. I swore quietly, hoping that whatever was bothering Detective Cook wouldn't make me late for that morning's Sierra Sounds session.

'You rang?' I chirped as I entered the room.

Detective Cook was no longer smiling. 'Sit down, please.'

Cook wasn't alone. A second officer sat in a chair slightly behind her, holding a ballpoint pen and a small notebook. She introduced him as Sergeant Edwards.

'I was going to suggest coffee but I see you've already taken care of that,' Cook said.

I set my coffee and donut on the tabletop, figuring it wouldn't be polite to eat and talk at the same time. 'How can I help?'

She launched right into it. 'You were less than forthcoming with us yesterday.'

I sat back in the chair, hard. 'I was?'

'We've gone over all the security tapes,' she said.

I was still puzzled. 'I don't understand.'

'Let me clarify it for you, then. About the time the medical examiner estimates someone was murdering Martin Radcliffe, you and Jake Cummings were seen leaving the lodge and heading in that direction.'

My heart did a quick rat-a-tat-tat. Now it was out there. Official. No bear. No Bigfoot, for that matter. Jake and I were right. Cook believed that Martin Radcliffe had been murdered by a flesh and blood human being.

'So?' I said cautiously, drawing out the word. 'Surely you don't suspect me. What beef would a last-minute substitute organizer from Maryland have against Martin Radcliffe? I'd never seen the man before, except on late-night TV.'

'After you left the lodge, what were you doing?'

The answer seemed simple. 'Walking the dog.'

Detective Cook arched a dark, neatly-groomed eyebrow. 'Cummings needed your help to walk his dog, did he?'

'No, of course not, but he was showing me around. Like a tour guide, really.'

I suddenly realized how stupid that sounded, as if Jake knew the Sisters area well. 'What I mean is, I'm new to this Sasquatch business and he was filling me in on various topics, giving me pointers.'

'Would it surprise you to learn that Jake Cummings has been to the lodge before? Several times, in fact.'

'Not really. But, I wouldn't know. The subject never came up.'

Cook began playing with a ballpoint pen, twirling it between her fingers like a cheerleader's baton. 'There was a conference here five years ago, and another one five years before that. Jake Cummings is somewhat of a regular.'

I shrugged. 'He told me he's an investigator for the Bigfoot

Field Researchers something-or-other, so I don't find that surprising. He probably attends lots of conferences.'

'Lots of conferences,' she repeated. She seemed to be doodling circles on the official lodge notepad, the one that I'd so helpfully laid out for her yesterday. The promotional pen, too. After a moment, she stopped doodling and leaned forward. 'Do these conferences you refer to tend to invite the same speakers?'

After I'd agreed to help Susan, one hundred years ago back in Ohio, I'd done some research on Bigfoot conventions. In the previous year alone, according to Google, there'd been confabs of like-minded Squatchers in Ohio, Oklahoma, Florida, Texas, Washington and even upstate New York. In Chautauqua, no less, at a family-run camp that rejoiced in the name We Wan Chu Cottages. None of the participants had been familiar to me at the time so I couldn't recall a single name now, but I suspected where Cook was going with her question. 'Are you suggesting that Jake knew Martin Radcliffe?'

'You'd have to ask him. I can't possibly say.'

A red shirt suddenly swam into my brain. Jim Davis had been there, too. Or somebody wearing a red shirt, anyway, fiddling with Jim's cameras. Should I mention it? Looking at her sullen face across the table, I decided not to. Why should I do the woman's work for her? Besides, I reasoned, she probably already knew.

In the silence that followed, waves of troubling whys and what-ifs washed over me. Why did Jake insist I walk Harley with him yesterday morning? About the time Martin Radcliffe was being beaten to death with a tree limb, we were . . . I took a deep breath then let it out slowly, stalling for time. Was Jake setting me up as *his* alibi? With Martin freshly dead, had Jake invited me out for a friendly stroll to a scenic overlook as if we were casual tourists? I only had Jake's word that Martin had been dead for a short time when we found his body. What if . . .?

Cook continued to stare.

I knew the trick. Sit quietly, say nothing, wait the suspect out. I wasn't playing that game. I stared back, hands tightly clasped under the table so she couldn't see them shaking.

Finally Cook broke the silence that lay like a wedge between us. 'Tell me again what you did.'

I took a deep, steadying breath. 'We walked Harley to the over-look, waited for him to do his business then walked back. End of story. I had to get back in time for the opening session at nine.'

'And were you?'

'If you saw the surveillance tapes, you know that I was.'

My brain was spinning, fast and furious. Everything depended on exactly what time Martin was murdered, I thought. Until eight o'clock I'd been with Debbie. After that, with Carole. From then until nine, I'd been with Jake. But where had Jake been before he met up with me?

A knot, cold and hard as ice, formed in my gut. Just last night Jake had said, 'Do you think I was taking pictures of my victim like some homicidal maniac?'

My iPhone. His pictures.

Had Jake set me up?

SIXTEEN

Logansport, Indiana, October 2, 1886. '[T]he people in the vicinity of Kouts . . . are living in terror of a strange apparition . . . Some describe the strange being as a man covered with hair over a foot long, and when he travels he strides along at a wonderful pace. He steps or jumps . . . over ten feet, and with apparently no effort. He is described further . . . as a sort of half man and animal, having a tail which drags the ground behind him when he is on the run . . . [H]e has been seen at a house in the vicinity of the marsh sitting down near the barn, tearing and eating a chicken from which life had scarcely departed. His mouth and fingers were covered with the feathers and blood of the chicken, and when aroused he darted off with a low shriek.'

Pharos – Tribune (Logansport, IN), October 2, 1886

I checked my watch and was stunned to see that the interview – or interrogation, depending upon your point of view – had taken only fifteen minutes. By the time Detective Cook waved me out of the room I felt tired, defeated. My first impulse was to

find Jake Cummings and demand an explanation. My second was
to order a good, stiff shot of brandy at the Wild Horse Bar, except
that it was only nine-fifteen and the bar didn't open until eleven.

I know. I checked.

To avoid having to make small talk with the folks who were
undoubtedly milling around the coffee urns in the hospitality
suite, I found a quiet spot in the hotel's coffee shop and ordered
a small cappuccino. I tapped a bit of cinnamon on top of the
foam, worrying that I'd allowed Jake's easygoing charm to over-
ride my common sense. I had Paul Newman at home. Why would
I need to go out for George Clooney?

Jake had charmed my socks off, to be sure, but so had a lot
of other guys and I'd never leaped into anything more than a
friendly relationship with any of them. Not even that hottie at a
library convention in Austin, Texas, who'd cornered me in the
hotel sauna and explained how 'understanding' his wife was
about his *ménage a trois*. Had I allowed Jake's charm to blind
me to his possible involvement in Martin Radcliffe's murder?

Motive, means and opportunity.

Opportunity, for sure. Until Jake hooked up with me around
eight-fifteen, only Harley knew where the man was.

Means? Those biceps could rip a branch off a tree any day of
the week and twice on Sundays. Effortlessly.

But motive? I didn't get it.

Jake seemed very much the once-a-policeman-always-a-
policeman type to me. A believer, sure, but open-minded
about it.

So what if he'd attended conferences with Martin Radcliffe
before? Considering his interest in the subject and his involvement
with BFRO, I'd be astonished if he hadn't. Didn't mean he knew
the guy. I'd been to rallies for Barack Obama, and once shook his
hand, but I didn't know the president. I've never been invited to
the White House for dinner.

Jake thought we were a crime-solving team, did he? If so,
he'd have to answer a few questions.

Thinking I might corner Jake at the morning session, I slipped
into the conference room just as the forensic artist, Robin Burcell,
was wrapping up. Displayed on the overhead projector, her

drawing in progress looked only vaguely like the creature I'd seen on Jim Davis's video, although that's what I gathered it was supposed to be.

I leaned against the wall at the back of the room and listened as two witnesses argued about the size and shape of the creature's nose. When consensus on the final drawing was reached by a show of hands, Burcell threw an enlargement of one of the stills from the Davis film up on the screen. She paused, letting the audience compare the film to the drawing now that they were displayed side by side.

Two different critters.

Burcell's sketch, based on witness feedback, looked like a creature from *Planet of the Apes*. The photo, more like Homer Guthrie. 'This illustrates how fallible eyewitness accounts can be,' she said.

I was surprised, frankly, by the fuzziness of the right-hand photo. Where were Randall Frazier's high-end cameras when you needed them, the ones that could 'freeze a cheetah running flat out?' That's what you get, I guess, when you buy your video equipment at WalMart.

'The Innocence Project,' the artist continued, 'determined that more than seventy percent of the 337 DNA exoneration cases they've handled to date had occurred due to inaccurate witness testimony.'

An astonished *ooooh* from the audience.

'And they have three hundred cases currently on their docket. If that percentage holds, that means that two hundred and ten of those individuals have been unjustly imprisoned.'

Burcell offered her drawings to the two audience members who had travelled the farthest to attend the conference – Key West and Mexico City won out. After the drawings had been collected by their new owners, she opened the session up for questions.

Surprisingly, nobody seemed particularly interested in Bigfoot. They wanted career advice. Just like any professional, Burcell explained to an eager young woman who asked, you took courses, put together a portfolio. You had to prove proficiency in composite imaging, as she'd demonstrated today, as well as facial reconstruction and age progression. There would be tests, both written and practical.

At the mention of tests, the young woman's enthusiasm seemed to evaporate. 'Oh,' she said, slumping in her chair.

The session wrapped up, the audience began to file out. I scanned the room, looking for Jake, but didn't see him.

Robin knew Jake – he'd worked with her before on a missing person's case – so I waited until she finished packing up her materials. 'Have you seen Jake Cummings this morning?'

'Oh, hi, Hannah. Yeah. He was in the dealers' room, showing off that footprint of his.'

'Ah.' I'd almost forgotten about the Bigfoot casts Jake had taken. 'What did they look like to you – the footprints, I mean?'

Robin tightened the strap on her oversized briefcase. 'Big.'

I laughed. 'Thanks for your professional opinion.'

She grinned back. 'Seriously, they're humongous. So either they were made by a basketball player on steroids or someone wearing funny clown shoes.'

'Sounds like you don't take this Sasquatch business very seriously.'

'I take my job seriously, Hannah. You describe it. I draw it. Doesn't matter if it's Ted Bundy or a figment of your imagination.'

'What's next for you, Robin?'

'Home, thank goodness. Leaving after lunch today, in fact. No gigs until August when I'm off to Cincinnati for the IAI conference. A while back I sketched a baby Bigfoot for the production company that produced a show for the BBC and NatGeo called *Bigfoot: The New Evidence*. I'll be talking about that.'

'A Bigfoot baby?' I said.

'Yeah. The witness allegedly shot the baby's mama up near Tahoe.' She leaned closer and lowered her voice. 'The guy was nuts, by the way. Probably drunk off his ass, shooting at bears or something.'

I had to laugh.

'The kid was in his twenties,' she continued as we walked down the aisle side by side. 'Had a cell phone in his pocket. Even the producers thought it was odd he didn't pull it out and snap a photo.'

'Why use a camera when you've got a gun?'

Robin laughed. 'Cynic.'

I held the door open for her. 'This job will do it to you.'

SEVENTEEN

Long Island, New York, November 12, 1886. 'An escaped gorilla from the dime museum is making life miserable for Long Island farmers whose flocks of sheep have been killed by the animal.'

The Semi-Weekly Age (Coshocton, OH),
November 12, 1886

I found Jake where Robin said he would be, in the dealers' room, capturing the undivided attention of Prairie Flower who had, apparently, agreed to display the cast of his Bigfoot footprint alongside several others in a glass case on one of her tables. After making a show of my admiration for the amazing artifact, I dragged Jake over to the only corner of the room that wasn't occupied by dealers, shoppers or gawkers – next to the recycling bins.

I got straight to the point. 'I need to know. Can I trust you?'

'What's brought this on?'

'Have you talked to Detective Cook yet?'

'Of course. We've had several conversations since yesterday morning.' Jake smiled disarmingly. 'She seemed interested in Harley, too. Wanted to know his specialty.'

'Which is?'

'Didn't I tell you? Harley's a multipurpose dog, so to speak. He's trained to detect drugs and explosives but his most recent experience before retirement was in ground-based tracking. A lot of what we did was wildlife detection, out in the field looking for game violators. Harley can sniff out venison, bear, turkey, trout, bass, perch . . . and wildlife parts, if it comes to that. Gut piles and residual blood.'

Picturing the gut piles, I was sorry I asked.

'But you didn't track me down in order to talk to me about wildlife parts, did you? What's bothering you, Hannah?'

The way Jake said 'Hannah' – gently, almost tenderly – set

off alarm bells deep within my danger zone. I took a step back.
'Cook implied that either you, or I, or both of us together had
something to do with Martin Radcliffe's murder. She has us on
the security tape, walking with Harley to the lookout.'

As I spoke, Jake's eyes never left my face. 'She's pulling your
chain, Hannah. Wants to get you talking, hoping something useful
comes out of it.' For a moment, I thought he was going to touch
my arm, but he drew back, dropping both arms to his sides,
taking me seriously. 'I'm a cop. I know the drill.'

'OK, I get it, but why did you ask *me* to walk with you
yesterday morning? Was it because you needed an alibi?'

The laugh rumbled out of him. Clearly, that was the funniest
thing he'd ever heard.

I felt like punching the man, knocking him cold. 'I'm serious!'

Jake wiped his eyes, still grinning. 'I don't need an alibi,
Hannah. I just wanted your company.'

Uh-oh, I thought. I took a deep breath and plunged. 'I'm
married, Jake.'

'And I have a partner.'

'Partner? You mean . . .?'

He smiled, nodded. 'Thad and I were married in August of
2013 shortly after same-sex marriage was made legal in
Minnesota.'

'Thank God,' I said.

'Thank God for what?' he asked, looking slightly puzzled.
'That I'm gay, or that gay marriage is now the law of the land?'

I chuckled. 'Both, I think.'

'So, are we good? You and me?'

'Of course we're good. Somewhere in the archives of the
Baltimore *Sun* there's a picture of me standing on the steps of
the Maryland State House holding a picket sign that says "Vote
Yes for 6."' I fixed him with a death ray. 'Stop trying to change
the subject. What do you mean, you don't need an alibi?'

'I have one,' he said.

'The way I see it, I alibi you and you alibi me. But when I
met with Cook she didn't seem to be buying it.'

'Look, she's not going to tell you this, but Cook knows exactly
when Radcliffe was murdered. 8:23 yesterday morning.'

I cast my mind back. Shortly after eight I'd been resisting the temptation to eat another donut courtesy of Debbie and her diabolical Donut Dugout. That's where Jake had found me. 'So Debbie can alibi for both of us,' I said, feeling relieved.

'You bet'cha. And has.'

That got my attention. 'Who told you that?'

'Barbara Cook isn't as hard-assed as she seems, Hannah. We had a little pow-wow this morning after she talked with you. I'm officially "assisting the police with their inquiries" now, but in a good way.'

I felt limp with relief. 'But, wait just a minute! How can the ME pinpoint the time of death so precisely?'

'Did you see that watch Martin wore, the one with the bright orange band?'

I nodded. 'The Apple watch?'

'No. It was a Fitbit Surge. One of the new ones that not only tracks your every move but monitors your heart rate. Continuously.'

The significance of this suddenly dawned on me. 'Jeesh.'

'Exactly. It was all graphed out for them, Hannah. Radcliffe put his Fitbit on at 7:12 and was walking around pretty constantly from then until 7:43 when he stopped walking. Probably standing still. We know where. His pulse beat slow and steady until 8:22, then the rate spiked dramatically. At 8:24? Nothing.'

I shivered. 'You are creeping me out.' After a moment, I asked, 'Fitbits have GPS tracking, don't they? Did it say where Martin went when he was walking around yesterday morning?'

'It did. He stuck around the hotel, walked out to the meditation garden briefly then headed straight to the woods, roughly to the spot where we found him.'

I took all that in and did the math. '7:43 to 8:22. Almost forty minutes. You were right, Jake. Martin *was* staking out Jim's video setup.'

'It would seem so.'

'Brave new world,' I muttered. 'Pretty soon we'll have micro-chips implanted at birth.'

'Listen,' Jake said, 'the sheriff wants to keep the Fitbit business quiet. So you didn't hear anything from me.'

I grinned. 'Hear what from you?'

EIGHTEEN

Jones County, Georgia, August 1889. '. . . The bear had stolen the planter's fence rails, had built the pen upon the secluded hammock, had stolen his hogs, and then selecting his best shoats had penned them up and was fattening them up for winter use upon Mr Beal's roasting ears. The hogs were recovered, taken to Albany and sold readily for from seven to eight dollars each to a local butcher . . . [T]he butcher's customers were so delighted . . . that they clamored for more of the same kind, but hogs fattened by bears upon roasting ears were an uncommon commodity, and the meat could not be duplicated.'

The Lafayette Advertiser (Lafayette, LA),
August 21, 1889

'**W**hy is it never easy?' my husband is fond of saying. Too true. I'd just helped a tearful woman find a local veterinarian for her listless, purse-sized Pomeranian – *if Barkley turns up his nose at Blue Buffalo Chicken Delights I know there is something seriously wrong!* – and was heading for a quiet spot to check my email, when Susan texted.

Interview Rm. STAT.

Coffee emergency? I texted back.

Srsl.

It was obvious from the minute I entered the room, however, that coffee had nothing to do with my summons. The urn was full, for one thing. Cook had already drawn a cup for herself and was tapping the contents of a pink paper packet into it.

'What can I do for you?' I asked.

'Sit down,' Cook said as she tossed a wooden stirrer into the basket set out on the table for debris. 'And close the door.'

I closed the door. I sat.

'Who is Ruth Hutchinson?' she said without preamble.

'If you're asking me that question,' I said, straight-faced, 'you already know the answer. She's my sister.'

My older sister was a superannuated flower child who owned Mother Earth, a New-Age shop on Main Street in downtown Annapolis. I couldn't imagine what had brought her name into the conversation, and I said so. 'Why do you ask?'

'Do you know where she is right now?'

'Ruth? Home, I imagine.'

'Are you sure?'

'Lieutenant, I can't be one-hundred-percent certain, but I know she's not *here*. If Ruth had taken it into her head to join me here in Oregon I think she would have let me know, don't you?'

As Barbara Cook kept me locked in a steely, unwavering gaze, saying nothing, I wracked my brain, trying to remember if I'd even told my sister where I was going. The last time we'd talked I was heading for my college reunion. The side trip to Oregon had been a spur-of-the-moment thing. For all Ruth knew, I was still in Ohio.

'What possible connection can my sister have to this investigation?' I asked.

'Do you Tweet?' she said.

I shook my head. 'I had a Twitter account once but I never got into it.'

'So you don't follow your sister?'

'On Facebook, yes, but not Twitter.' I paused. 'I didn't even know Ruth had a Twitter account.'

As we talked, Cook had been idly fingering a stack of pages on the table in front of her. She picked up the top sheet and seemed to be consulting it. 'Are you aware that your sister, Ruth, was engaged in a Twitter war with Martin Radcliffe?'

Her question hit me like a blow to the solar plexus. I'd had plenty of caffeine already that morning but I needed time to organize my thoughts. 'Do you mind if I get myself some coffee?'

Cook waved her hand in a Lady Bountiful, be-my-guest sort of way.

I stuck a coffee mug under the spigot and watched as the cup gradually filled, thinking furiously. What on earth would lead Ruth, a mild-mannered Maryland shopkeeper, into a war of words with Martin Radcliffe? Ruth was a child of the seventies, true,

but the most radical thing she had ever done was protest against
Richard Nixon and the war in Vietnam. She grew marijuana in
a flowerpot on the fire escape of her student apartment building,
too, but back then, who hadn't?

'A Twitter war?' I said as I sat down again. 'I'm not sure what
you mean.'

Cook's grimace told me she wasn't buying my ignorance for
a minute, but she must have decided to humor me. 'Hurling
insults back and forth over the Internet.'

'I see. No.'

'That she threatened his life?'

I took a deep breath then let it out slowly, trying to remain
calm. 'I don't believe it.'

Cook held the printout closer to her face and read, '"I don't
hate you, exactly, but if you were on fire, and I had water, I'd
drink it." What does that sound like to you, Mrs Ives?'

It sounded exactly like Ruth, I thought, suppressing a smile
with difficulty. 'It sounds like a lame joke, not a serious threat.'

'Or, "If we shot everyone who hates you, it wouldn't be murder,
it would be genocide."'

Oh, Ruth, Ruth, Ruth, I silently begged. When will you ever
learn to keep your mouth shut?

Keeping my voice steady, I said, 'People get death threats over
the Internet for everything from allowing transgender people in public
restrooms to posing for photos with big guns and dead animals.'

Cook nodded. 'True, but since Radcliffe is dead, we would
feel uncomfortable letting words like these go unchecked.'

'My sister identified herself, right? She wasn't using some
kind of alias and sending her emails from a Starbucks around
the corner?'

'True.'

'You mentioned a war. What did Martin Radcliffe say that
started it?'

'You'll have to ask your sister.'

'Trust me, I intend to. And in the meantime, I presume you've
checked Ruth's whereabouts, and whether she has an alibi.'

Cook's glance ping-ponged between me and Sergeant Edwards,
her second in command, but she didn't comment. Something was
apparently on her mind, and after several moments of silence, I

guessed what it might be. 'Surely you don't think that *I* bumped off Martin Radcliffe as a favor to my sister?'

Cook's laugh rang hollow. 'It seems unlikely but stranger things have happened.'

'And I have an alibi, Lieutenant. At the time of Martin's murder I was with Jake Cummings.'

'I've made a note of that.'

'Are we done here, then?' I asked, rising to my feet.

'We're done. For now.'

'Is there anything else I can do for you Lieutenant? Sergeant?'

Cook slid the printout into a black plastic folder and smiled. 'We'll be sure to let you know.'

I escaped into the hallway before she could think of something else to ask me.

Just outside the door, I leaned against the wall, trying to decide what to do. Talking with my sister had just jumped to first place on my to-do list, which was already full.

It was nearly one o'clock in Annapolis but I hoped I would reach Ruth during her lunch hour, often eaten in the office at the back of her shop while Cornelia Gibbs, our father's steady girl-friend, filled in at the cash register.

Conference attendees to'd and fro'd around me, indicating that the morning coffee break had already begun, so I nipped up to my room, plopped down on the bed and tapped in my sister's number.

Ruth answered right away, recognizing my caller ID. 'Hannah! What's up?'

I decided to leap in with both feet. 'Tell me about Martin Radcliffe.'

Ruth was silent for a moment, then chuckled. 'He has a nice tan. Orange is my favorite color.'

'*Had* a nice tan,' I corrected. 'Don't you watch the news? Radcliffe was murdered yesterday.'

Ruth gasped. 'Gosh, no! Where did it happen? In Oregon?'

'How did you know I was in Oregon?'

'Emily told me you went there on some boondoggle with an old college friend.'

'Not exactly a boondoggle,' I told her. 'I'm working a Bigfoot convention. Lots of craziness going on even before someone decided to bump off Martin Radcliffe.'

'Can't say that I'm sorry,' Ruth said. 'Radcliffe's a third-rate talent. Was, I mean. Worst series on TV.'

'Ruth, be serious. The police investigating his death called me in this morning to ask about *you*. About your Twitter exchanges.'

'That?' She puffed air into the receiver. 'Nobody takes Twitter wars seriously these days. Besides, he started it.'

'Ruth!'

'Well, he did. Have you ever watched his show?'

'Once or twice,' I admitted. 'The one on ghostbusters was kind of interesting.'

'A fluke,' Ruth snorted. 'Did you see the one on feng shui?' Before I could answer, she rattled on. 'Total garbage!'

Ruth was a feng shui practitioner. She sold all kinds of feng shui accessories in her shop. After my cancer diagnosis, she'd feng shuied my house up one side and down the other, installing (among other things) a mirror over my stove and a big, leafy ficus plant in the living room to help revive my *chi*. That I remained cancer-free since certainly earned my sister points.

'In what way was it garbage?' I asked.

'His shows are up on Netflix so you can judge for yourself, but because I love you, I'll save you the trouble. Radcliffe invited three feng shui consultants one at a time into a house and he totally set them up,' Ruth said. 'Just because they all came up with different ways to rearrange the furniture, he claimed they were phonies. Feng shui isn't a science, for Pete's sake! It's an art. It goes back thousands and thousands of years!' She took a deep breath. 'So I Tweeted Radcliffe and told him he was an idiot.'

'Sounds like you started it, Ruth.'

'Well, I never expected he'd get back to me. Who am I, after all? Just some pissant viewer. But he Tweeted right back. Said something like, "Don't let your mind wander. It's too small to be out on its own."'

'Nice,' I said.

'Well, yeah! So I Tweeted back, "Your insults need work, but don't feel bad. A lot of people lack talent."'

'Ruth!'

'You sounded just like Mom there for a moment.'

'You're giving me a massive headache.'

'Seriously, why would anyone listen to this loser? He's a total puppet of the network. He'll say anything just for the ratings. They pay him ridiculous amounts of money, too. He gets a hundred and fifty thousand an episode for this crap. I Tweeted about that too, and Radcliffe replied, "She forgot to mention my phenomenal Neilsen ratings. 7.8 percent for that show, with over eleven million households."'

I sighed. 'So who's reading all this stuff?'

'Everybody following hashtag dontyoubelieveit.'

'Tens, hundreds, thousands?'

'Who knows? Everybody in the Twitterverse for all I know. And we were getting re-Tweeted left, right and center.'

'So, I have to ask. Where were you yesterday morning?'

Ruth laughed. 'Right here, minding my own business.'

Of course she was.

I told Ruth I had to get back to the conference, promised I'd keep her up to date on what was happening and wound up to say goodbye.

'Hannah?'

'Yes?'

'I'm sorry that Radcliffe is dead, I really am. But if it means his terrible show will go off the air, well . . .' She paused. 'Always look on the bright side!'

I decided to skip lunch.

I wandered over to the desk, sat down and opened my laptop. Following Ruth's advice, I logged on to Netflix and quickly learned that *Don't You Believe It!* had been running for six seasons, ten episodes each. Sixty shows. I felt defeated just browsing through the listings.

Martin Radcliffe and his accomplices had set up elaborate stings to unmask fake psychics, embarrass chiropractors and humiliate both reflexology and reiki practitioners, lumping such tricksters in with street-corner performance artists.

He'd debunked the 'science' of feng shui, homeopathic medicine, dietary supplements and acupuncture, an episode (I found out later) that had set Ruth off on another Twitter rant.

If you were a believer in the 9/11 or JFK assassination conspiracies, in UFOs or in Area 51, Radcliffe was out to rain on your parade. He dared to tackle faith healers, creationism and even the Church of Scientology, but when he presumed to question the historical accuracy of the Holy Bible, the fur really began to fly. Faith groups on the far right organized boycotts of his sponsors – a car manufacturer and a popular soft drink – but the entertainer remained unfazed. With a minimum of fanfare, the network signed up other advertisers and the show chugged on to ever higher ratings.

But it was Radcliffe's expose on cryptozoology that really caught my eye. While everyone else was in the dining room of the lodge noshing down on Mexican food with all the trimmings, I clicked play and watched *Cryptozoology: The Monster Files* all the way through. Five minutes into the thirty-minute episode, I saw the first person I recognized: Monique Deschamps, stoically taking a licking from the head of the US Department of Interior over her broad interpretation of the Endangered Species Act. After the second ad, Randall Frazier appeared. The explorer's Bigfoot research, Radcliffe snidely reported, had been published in such well-respected scientific journals as *The National Enquirer*, a supermarket tabloid. In a short, four-minute segment near the end, Cecelia Cloughly, who, as a scientist, should have been on Radcliffe's A-List, was ridiculed for 'only' having a degree in zoology, and for sitting on her butt in a classroom when she should have been out in the field getting her hands dirty. Cecelia, dressed in a white lab coat and surrounded by test tubes, centrifuges and neatly packaged samples of scat stared morosely into the camera lens, apparently on the verge of tears.

I sat back, my gears spinning as Radcliffe wrapped up with a preview of the following week's episode. 'We are awash in the pseudosciences,' Radcliffe was saying as I reached for the phone-side notepad and pen. 'Astrology, biorhythms, divining, graphology, numerology, phrenology . . . the list goes on and on.'

I, too, was making a list.

'Pseudoscience is like pornography, my friends,' Radcliffe continued, but I was only half listening as I jotted down Monique, Cecelia and Randall's names, all three of whom I'd just watched be humiliated on national TV.

Jake and I, thank goodness, were no longer suspects, but I couldn't say the same for Jim and Athena. I added them to my list. While I stared out the window, considering their motives, I listened to Radcliffe tell his audience, 'We cannot define it, but we know it when we see it. Voodoo science! Grab your tin foil hats and join me next week for "Good Science, Bad Science and Just Plain Bunk" on *Don't You Believe It!*'

The video faded to black. 'Long-standing rival?' I wrote after the Davises' names. Thinking about the affair of the mangy bear, I added, 'Revenge?'

I got up from my chair to stretch my legs, grab a glass of water and use the bathroom. When I returned to my desk the next episode in the queue, Radcliffe's promised take on the pseudosciences, had automatically begun playing.

'I've had enough of your vitriol,' I snarled at Radcliffe's smirking image. I grabbed my mouse, prepared to click him off in mid-bombast, then froze.

The face of Prairie Flower filled my computer screen.

It was like watching a train wreck. Prairie Flower had agreed to appear on Radcliffe's show thinking he would showcase her unique talent. Instead, the loathsome entertainer used a series of trick questions to convince his viewers that pendulum divination was hogwash. Then, as if disparagement weren't enough, he stabbed Prairie Flower in the back. He twisted the knife. Although she had steeped herself in Indian customs and lore, Radcliffe informed the nation, Prairie Flower's real name was Wendy Walker, she came from Calgary and had not a single drop of Native American blood.

Poor Prairie Flower. I felt like weeping.

As I added Prairie Flower's name to my suspects list, it occurred to me that Radcliffe's show was a Who's Who of the Flat Rock Sasquatch Sesquicentennial, and none of the participants were there to pick up one of those coveted Emmy statuettes.

Was there anybody in the world who didn't wish Martin Radcliffe dead? After watching only two episodes, I wanted to kill him myself.

NINETEEN

Sandy Point, Texas, September 20, 1889. 'Some twenty months ago
a woman living on the banks of the Brazos missed her 8-month-old
baby from the pallet where she had left it lying during an absence
of a few minutes . . . [N]o trace of it could be discovered . . . until
a few days ago when [a riding party of gentlemen] were . . .
startled by seeing a strange object run across the road . . .
They could see that it had a human face, though the brown body
was covered with long, tangled hair, and the nails of the feet and
hands so long and curved as to be claws . . . [It was finally]
lassoed and half dragged, half led home with the lariat about its
neck, howling and yelping like a wolf . . . It is kept tied up in
[his mother's] cabin, suffering no one to lay hands upon it, and is
fed on raw meat as it refused to touch any other food. The woman
has hopes that she may yet reawaken the human in it, but in the
meantime she is reaping a harvest from the crowds who come daily
from all parts of the country to inspect the strange creature.'

The Decatur Daily Dispatch (Decatur, IL),
September 20, 1889

I telephoned Jake and, by some miracle, he actually answered his prehistoric clam shell. He and Harley were sharing a taco platter in the dining room, he told me, while seated at a table with Jim and Athena Davis. I summarized what I'd learned from the Netflix videos, and we agreed to meet in fifteen minutes on the patio.

In the meantime, I went looking for Brad.

After Martin Radcliffe's body had been hauled away in the long, white Taurus, Brad Johnson appeared to have evaporated, too. While I was accustomed to seeing him and his camera on the periphery of the room, so ubiquitous that we didn't even notice him any more, it took me a while to realize that he might actually be gone.

I checked with the reception desk and learned that he hadn't checked out. The maid pushing a hospitality cart on the second floor assured me that Brad had slept in his bed the night before. He'd even left a note wrapped around a two-dollar tip requesting extra bottles of the lodge's signature body scrub. When I asked Tina about it, and learned he hadn't showed up for lunch either, I grew seriously worried. Brad was Martin Radcliffe's protégé. They worked closely together. Did Brad know something that had put his life in danger, too?

I needn't have worried.

When I hit the patio, Jake was waiting for me, sitting on the smooth rock ledge of one of the fire pits. Harley lay at his feet, muzzle on paws. Brad Johnson sat poolside at a round table, deep in conversation with two men. Brad was dressed in his signature black but both of his companions wore khakis and polo shirts as if heading out shortly for a round of golf. The three seemed to be enjoying club sandwiches and French fries washed down by Rainier long necks.

I whispered to Jake, 'That guy in the yellow shirt? I recognize him. He's Martin Radcliffe's lawyer. I saw him on the news yesterday, coming out of the medical examiner's office with Martin's wife.' I scowled. 'Martin's body's not even cold, and . . .'

'Yes, it is,' Jake interrupted.

I gave him a withering look. 'You know what I mean.' I grabbed Jake firmly by the elbow and dragged him to a table not too far away from the trio.

I pulled out a chair and sat down on it. 'Sit,' I said.

He grinned. 'Me or Harley?'

'Who's the other guy, the one in green?' Jake asked once we'd gotten settled.

I shrugged. 'Don't know.'

I'd missed lunch, so no wonder the smell of salty, hot French fries wafting downwind was driving me mad. When the server came to check on the men, Jake waved her over and ordered nachos and a couple of beers for the two of us.

While we waited for our order, I strained my ears, managing to pick up only snatches of their conversation. Hoping that Jake's hearing might be better than mine, I whispered, 'What are they saying?'

He held up a hand. 'Shhhh.' His ears, too, were on scan.

At first, the men kept their voices low. I could make out every third word – options, pilot, green light, credits.

The server brought our nachos and beer, and more beer for the gentlemen. She was an efficient soul, dammit, promptly whisking away their empties, so I couldn't keep count. I suspected that was at least their third round, however, when I heard raised voices.

'Davis is on board,' Brad said, speaking to the guy I didn't know. 'He's signed a release.'

I shot Jake a look, but he wagged his head and tapped a finger against his lips.

On board. Release. That could only mean that Jim Davis had licensed Brad to use his Bigfoot tape in some way. I wondered, vaguely, how much someone would pay me for Jake's photographs. They were still floating around, as far as I knew, in the iCloud ether.

'How many shows are in the can?' Brad wanted to know.

'Two,' the green shirt said. 'We'll air them and lead in with reruns.'

Brad, it soon became apparent, was taking the lemon life had handed Martin Radcliffe and making lemonade out of it. I missed a few sentences but then Brad sat up straight, gestured with his beer and crowed, 'Think of it! All his life insisting that they didn't exist then he gets knocked off by one of them!'

The attorney – what was his name? – brought Brad up short. 'That's not what the police think.'

Brad snorted. 'What does it matter what the police think, Gordie? The audience can watch the video and judge for themselves.'

Ah. Gordon Parker, that was the attorney's name, and Brad was already on a first-name basis with the guy.

The man in the green shirt shook his head. 'What makes you think you can just step into Martin's shoes, Johnson? You think the network rubber stamps everything I propose?'

'Leo, Leo, Leo. Look at me. I was Martin's protégé. I've been working with him for a while. I know where he's coming from.'

'You'll need to pitch it to me in writing,' Leo said.

'No problem. It'll be on your desk by Friday.'

'No guarantees.'

Guarantees or not, Brad's grin signaled he'd scored a point. 'None expected.'

Brad leaned back, propped a white New Balance tennis shoe up on the table and adjusted the shoelace, a neon shade of blue.

'So,' he drawled after he'd tied it off. 'What's the latest from the cops, Gordie?'

Gordie polished off his beer and wiped his lips with a cocktail napkin. 'They've eliminated the possibility that it was a bear and they don't believe in Sasquatch.'

Brad frowned. 'So?'

'So, we all better be dusting off our alibis, Johnson.'

I kept my head low then whispered in an aside to Jake, 'What do you bet Brad killed Martin in order to take over his TV show?'

Jake sucked air through his teeth. 'Too much of a long shot. Johnson's young, a total unknown. He's naïve if he thinks he can break into the business this early in his career.'

'But he is, what's the term? Mediagenic? Good looking in a Tom Cruise sort of way.' I paused. 'Not to my taste, but what do I know?'

Jake grunted. 'He's just an opportunistic son of a bitch.'

'If not Brad, then who?' I scrabbled in my handbag for the list I'd begun up in my room and smoothed it out on the glass tabletop. 'Do you have a pen?'

Jake produced a Bic from his pocket and handed it over.

'I've started a list,' I said. 'I'd appreciate your two-cents.'

'Could be any one of the folks he skewered on *Don't You Believe It!*,' Jake said.

'You just had lunch with Jim and Athena, right?'

Jake nodded.

'Jim was visibly upset over the mangy bear video on Friday night,' I said. 'Do you think he was mad enough about it to kill the guy?'

'Frankly, no. Both Jim and Athena were hell-bent on capturing Bigfoot on video, on making "that ass hat" – Jim's words, not mine – eat his words. For maximum embarrassment, the Davises needed Radcliffe alive, not dead. They wanted to watch the man squirm.'

'So let's eliminate Jim and Athena, at least for the time being.'

'Have you written down Prairie Flower?' Jake asked. 'You told me that Radcliffe outed her as non-Native American. He destroyed her carefully constructed persona.'

Even though I had a soft spot in my heart for Prairie Flower, I surprised myself by defending her. 'Yes, but I think she's so immersed in Native American culture that she truly believes she's part of the Pueblo people. She has an aunt down in Taos, she told me.' I glanced up. 'Besides, it doesn't seem to have hurt

Prairie Flower's business or her reputation, although I could be wrong about that. These are her peeps, after all.'

'How about Randall Frazier?' Jake asked.

'He's number three on my list. For motive, I wrote "Belittled research," although that seems a wee bit thin, even to me.'

'Add "pre-emptive strike,"' Jake suggested. 'I heard rumors that Radcliffe was planning to tag along on Frazier's expedition to the lava tubes at Mount Saint Helens in August. Might have cramped his style to have Radcliffe hanging over his shoulder.'

I rolled my eyes and added the note.

'As much as I like her, I had to put Cecelia Cloughly on the list,' I said, looking at the numeral 2 in front of the scientist's name. 'Radcliffe didn't call Cecelia a fraud exactly but he implied that's she's lazy and likes to take credit for other people's work. She's pretty resilient but I imagine everyone has their limits.'

Jake nodded in agreement. 'How about Gregory Gilchrist?' he asked.

'Gilchrist? Why?'

'Jealousy would be my guess. His girlfriend was flirting outrageously with Radcliffe at the opening reception. After Radcliffe's presentation they wandered off to the bar together. I saw them there, heads together.'

'Nicole Baker,' I said, putting Gilchrist's name at number five on the list. 'I met her at the reception just before Radcliffe's presentation. He was complaining about the woman, said she was angling for a job. Wished she would get lost.'

'Perhaps Nicole decided to go the casting couch route and Radcliffe bought into it,' Jake said. 'He seemed to be plying her with martinis.'

I looked up. 'Ugh.'

'Exactly. If there was any hanky-panky, Gilchrist is unlikely to have approved.'

'Or,' I said, as a thought suddenly occurred to me, 'maybe Gilchrist was pissed off because Martin refused to give his honey a job?'

Jake shook his head. 'Gilchrist could buy Radcliffe's show ten times over. Hell, he could afford to buy the whole network. Anyone else on your shortlist?' Jake wanted to know.

'Wait a minute!' I said, glancing up from my scribbling. 'How about the no-show? Homer Guthrie? Who better to impersonate

Bigfoot than someone who actually looks like Bigfoot? You saw Homer's pictures, right?'

'I'm ahead of you there, Hannah. Checked with my sources down in New Mexico and Guthrie is exactly where he said he was – Lovelace Rehabilitation Hospital in Albuquerque. After the hip replacement he's re-learning to walk. Poor man's not going anywhere.'

'The only one left is Monique Deschamps, but it seems to me that her gripe would be against that guy from the US Department of the Interior and not Radcliffe.' I folded the oblong of paper into quarters and tucked it into my handbag. 'Not that it matters, I suppose. The conference is over tomorrow lunchtime. We're all leaving. By Sunday night I'll be home in Annapolis, you and Harley will be back in Minneapolis and everyone on our shortlist will be scattered to all points of the compass.'

'The local authorities know what they're doing,' Jake reassured me. 'They have a ninety-percent solve rate. I'm in touch. After everyone leaves, I'll keep you informed.'

TWENTY

Damascas, New York, 1877. 'Two citizens while looking for a lost cow in a swamp in this township came upon a bareheaded, ragged and bare-footed man, with short-cropped gray hair and a beard. He ran away when discovered, but was captured after a long chase. It was evident that he had been in the forest for some time. He talked wildly, in a language that no one in the neighborhood understood. He was finally taken to the county seat and placed in jail. There it was found his strange language was French.'

The Evening Gazette (Port Jervis, NY),
November 20, 1879

I'd been looking forward to 'Sasquatch Speaks: Sierra Sounds' ever since I'd read about it in the program booklet, so I arrived at the conference room a bit early. After having played hooky for most of the morning, I was pleased to see that Brad Johnson had made an appearance and that he apparently planned to tape the session. I waited quietly at the back of the room until he'd finished installing a fresh battery pack and had lowered his camera to the carpet before approaching, eager to ask him a few questions.

'How are you doing, Brad?' I asked. Of all the people attending the conference, Brad had to have been the one who knew Martin best. Even if he did seem to be after his former mentor's job, Radcliffe's death must still be taking an emotional toll.

Sure enough, Brad's face looked drawn and solemn. 'Thought about hanging it all up after Martin, uh, you know, but until they find out what happened to him, this is all part of the story, right?'

'Right.'

As I watched Brad check out his equipment, I wondered if it were common knowledge that no bear had been involved in Martin's death – that he'd probably been murdered by somebody we all knew. I decided to test the water. 'What do you think happened, Brad?'

He swiped an unruly lock of dark hair away from his eyes. 'It wasn't Sasquatch, that's for sure.' He wrinkled his nose as if the very notion stank. 'And I'm betting it wasn't a bear, either. That leaves some joker in a monkey suit.'

'Have you studied Jim's tape?' I asked.

Brad ignored my question. 'It's tough, you know. Really tough. Martin wasn't just my mentor; he was my friend.'

I remembered Carole saying that Brad had graduated from NYU film school, so I wondered if they'd met in New York, and asked him.

'Nah. LA. Where else? LA is where it's happening. I had an internship at Fox during my junior year.'

'I hope it was better than some internships where they have you answering phones and schlepping coffee,' I said.

Brad shouldered his camera. 'It was super, actually. They had me building and editing marketing presentations. I even had a brief stint working on a promo for *The Simpsons*.'

'Was Martin working for Fox, too?'

'Met him at a party in Brentwood. He was in the area, chasing down a Bigfoot sighting near Sherman Lake. He invited me to come along. I've been hooked ever since.'

'Excuse me?'

The voice belonged to a pleasant-looking young man dressed in a white turtleneck jersey tucked into a slim pair of jeans. Embroidered boats sailed around his belted waist. 'I'm guessing from the Ask Me ribbon that you're the one in charge of the setup?'

Larry Mack, the linguist.

'For my sins,' I said with a smile. 'How can I help?'

He reached into the briefcase he was carrying and pulled out a sheet of paper. 'I've got this handout but my plane was late so I didn't have time to get it photocopied. Can you take care of that for me?'

As much as I wanted to keep grilling Brad, I found myself saying, 'Sure, no problem,' and dashing off to the business center with his handout. I studied its contents as the copies shot out into the paper tray: The Sasquatch Phoenic Alphabet, by R. Scott Nelson, US Navy Crypto-Linguist. In addition to the standard letters and phonemes, Nelson had developed symbols for grunts, whistles, screams, snarls and tooth pops. Fascinating. I couldn't wait for the print job to finish so I could get back to the session.

Larry Mack had already started when I arrived so I slipped into the back row, taking a seat next to Leah Solat. I tucked the printouts under my chair.

What drifted out of the speakers over the next several minutes was a spooky combination of barks, howls and clicks that sent icy fingers scurrying along my spine. Coyotes baying at the moon, perhaps? Wolves having bad sex? Or was it Wookie-speak, the eerie blend of moans, grunts, ughs, arghs and even purring I associated with Chewbacca vocalizations in the *Star Wars* films? I'd read that Chewbacca's voice had been engineered by a student at USC from raw recordings of four bears, a badger, a lion, a seal and a walrus. Is that what was going on here, too? It was downright weird.

'I'd squatch my pants if I heard *that* in the woods,' Leah whispered to me in an aside.

I had to agree. I felt as if I'd stepped into the Twilight Zone.

At various points the vocalizations would cease and there would be the sound of hollow knocking.

Next to me, Leah cocked her head, listening carefully. 'Sounds like a major league slugger taking practice swings at a tree.'

Thinking about the branch that had likely killed Martin, I shivered.

Further along on the tape, whatever lurked in the woods began banging rocks together.

'Sasquatch speaks twice as rapidly as humans,' Mack explained, 'so we had to slow the tape down by fifty percent in order to transcribe their vocalizations. For translation purposes, we use something called the Unclassified Hominid Phonetic Alphabet invented by R. Scott Nelson. We'll have handouts for you after the program.'

'You, too, can speak Squatch,' Leah muttered.

On the dais, Larry was saying, 'There is no grammar and no syntax that we know of, but we hope that by applying some transcription standards it will help you report Sasquatch vocalizations with some consistency.

'You've heard excerpts from the tapes,' he continued, 'so now let's see what some of the vocalizations look like.'

He aimed the remote and the screen became densely filled with seemingly meaningless arrangements of letters, reminding me a bit of the DNA profiles we'd seen a day earlier during Cecelia's presentation.

NÄR LÄ
Ü KÜ DZJÄ
SÏ DZJAÖ GLÖ PÜ MËKH
RAM HO BÄ RÜ KHÄ HÜ
FÄ LIP ÄBÄSI ZIS

'What do those dots over the letters mean?' someone in the audience wanted to know.

'If you follow along,' Mack said, highlighting letters on the screen with the red dot from his laser pointer, 'they're the classic vowel sounds. Ah, eh, ee, oh, oo,' he drawled.

To me, it sounded like the chromatic vocal warm-up exercises our choir director put us through before services every Sunday morning. All that was missing here was the earnest but tonally-challenged guy in the tenor section.

With the transcription still up on the screen, Mack drove home his point by playing the matching audio clip over and over three times.

I inclined my head toward Leah and whispered, 'If he plays the tape backward will Paul McCartney still be alive?'

Her elbow bumped mine. 'And you accuse *me* of having no respect,' she hissed.

'But, what on earth are they saying?' someone in the front row wanted to know.

Mack shrugged. 'Nobody knows. Not yet.'

'Well, then. What's the point?'

'We know that whales and dolphins communicate with one another,' Larry Mack said easily, 'but we don't know what they're saying either.'

As the question and answer session segued into a discussion of humpback whale songs, I noticed that Leah Solat's thumbs were flying, actively live tweeting back to a colleague at the *Bee*.

'I thought you'd already filed your story,' I said quietly.

'Story's written. Just filling in some last-minute details.'

'Are you going home, then?'

Leah's fingers froze. 'Gosh, no. They've asked me to stay and cover the Radcliffe murder investigation. He'd done some filming around our region. Locals knew him.' She paused and skewered me with her eyes. 'What do you know about what's going on?'

I tried my wide-eyed, innocent look but it wasn't fooling her.

'You can be honest with me, Hannah. I know you were with Jake when he found Radcliffe's body. Everybody saw you two down there,' she paused. 'Until Jake covered up the camera. Nice jacket, by the way.'

When I didn't rise to the bait, she said, 'My bet? It was a bear. There are cubs around this time of year. Females are fiercely protective of their young.'

Remembering my conversation with Jake the day before, I said, 'Do bears pick up branches and use them as weapons?'

'No shit,' she said.

'You didn't hear it from me.'

After the session I tracked Brad down as he was packing up his gear. 'Ü KÜ DZJÄ,' I said.

'I think you just asked me to marry you,' he said with a grin.

Brad was heading for the next session – Monique's talk about Zana. I was going there, too, so I got into step beside him.

'I'm curious about something, Brad.'

He brushed his forelock aside and glanced at me sideways through long, dark lashes. 'Yeah?'

'How come you weren't with Martin yesterday morning? You'd been following him so closely all weekend.'

Brad shrugged. 'He told me to get lost. Said he had an errand to run in Sisters. Something to do with a house he and his wife were buying in the Hollywood Hills. Promised he'd catch up with me later.'

'So what did you do instead?'

'Ate another donut, then went up to my room to edit some of the footage I'd recorded. I'm working on a proposal for NatGeo and I want to show them what I can do.'

'Is your special for *Don't You Believe It!* still on track?' I asked, thinking about the conversation that Jake and I had overheard on the patio. 'After Martin . . . well, you know, I sorta wondered.'

'I have lots of irons in the fire, Mrs Ives. It sounds crass to say it but Martin's death opens up lots of opportunities for someone. Why not me?'

'You've come a long way in the last few years,' I said. I stopped then turned to look at him directly as a thought suddenly occurred to me. 'Say, when you were interning at Fox did you ever work on *Planet of the Apes*?'

'Ha! I wish. I got to see some post-production on *The Bachelorette*, though.' He winked. 'For my sins.'

I laughed. 'Funny, I missed that one.'

We'd reached the door of the conference room where Monique Deschamps was scheduled to give her talk about Zana in ten minutes. 'I know you have work to do, Brad, but you knew Martin better than anyone. What do *you* think he was doing down in the woods yesterday morning?'

Brad grinned. 'Easy. Staking out Jim Davis's camera. He didn't trust the guy.'

'You think Jim and Athena Davis would perpetrate a hoax?'

'Don't you?'

It had always been hard for me to picture mild-mannered, slightly henpecked Jim as a murderer and Athena as his Lady Macbeth, both with blood on their hands, but I was curious as to what Brad thought about them. 'Hardly,' I told him. 'Think about it. If the cops seize your tape and you put a copy up on YouTube for free . . .'

Brad's pitying look cut me off in mid-sentence. I was clearly the dumbest broad in all of Deschutes County. 'Wrong, Mrs Ives. It's the ticket, the absolute ticket. The vid goes viral. National news, slots on Ellen and Kathie Lee. Speakers fees at conferences like this.' He jabbed an index finger in the air just short of my chest.

'Book deals. That's where the money is. If you manage to capture a Bigfoot, agents will beat down your door in order to wave contracts in your face.'

'If Squatch is real,' I said.

His eyes narrowed. 'Or appears to be.'

'Too bad he's lying low,' I said, watching Brad's face closely.

'Who?'

'Squatch, of course.' I made a production of checking my watch. 'By tomorrow at this time we'll all be gone. Sasquatch can have the woods back to himself.' Then it was my turn to wag a finger. 'But you're a disciple of the great Martin Radcliffe so you know and I know that it's all a big steaming pile of horse pucky.'

TWENTY-ONE

Tkhina, Ochamchiri District of Abkhazia, Russia, 1890. 'Russia's domesticated ape woman, Zana, was laid to rest today near this village . . . Hunters captured her in the wild, whereupon she was sold, changed hands several times and eventually became the property of a nobleman . . . Her skin was black, or dark grey, and her whole body covered with reddish-black hair. The hair on her head was tousled and thick, hanging mane-like down her back. Her face was terrifying; broad, with high cheekbones, flat nose, turned-out nostrils, muzzle-like jaws, wide mouth with large teeth, low forehead, and eyes of a reddish tinge' . . . Zana was trained to perform simple domestic chores and became pregnant several times by various men. Remarkably, she gave birth to normal human babies, four of whom survived to adulthood.'

Obituary cited by Dmitri Bayanov. *In the Footsteps of the Russian Snowman*, Crypto-Logos Publisher, Moscow, 1996, pp. 46–52

I desperately wanted to talk to Cecelia Cloughly about the Netflix video. I also intended to quiz her, wearing her scientist's hat, about the Jim Davis tape. The more I thought about

it, the more I realized that Brad Johnson had, perhaps uninten-
tionally, put his finger on the crux of the matter. As far as Jim
and Athena Davis were concerned, it didn't matter whether the
Bigfoot they had filmed was real or not. But for Martin (and
now Brad) the big bucks lay only in proving it was a hoax.

Someone had murdered Martin, I thought, but it wasn't
Bigfoot. Bigfoot, if he existed, had simply been in the wrong
place at the wrong time.

I followed Brad into Monique's session, 'Zana: The Last
Neanderthal?' and took my usual seat at the back of the room
where I could see Cecelia if she came in. She didn't disappoint.
About two minutes before the session was to begin, the professor
wandered by the end of my row, scanning the crowded room for
a vacant chair. I hissed for attention, waved and motioned her into
the one next to me.

'Can we chat for a bit afterwards?' I asked as she settled into
her seat.

Cecelia studied me seriously over the tops of her eyeglasses.
'Sure. What about?'

'I need your professional opinion.'

'Take an aspirin and call me in the morning.'

A giggle bubbled up from somewhere. 'Not that kind of
opinion!'

'Shhhh,' she cautioned. 'Save it for later. She's about to start.'

For the folks in the audience not familiar with Zana's sad life,
Monique had prepared an illustrated slideshow. Her talk began
with a photograph of the Caucasus Mountain range, enrobed in
snow. Just looking at it made me shiver and wish I were wearing
a sweater.

'No photographs of Zana exist,' Monique continued, forwarding
to the next slide. 'Just a pen and ink drawing done years after
her death. Contemporaneous descriptions described her as an
"ape woman," but was she? One theory held that Zana was the
last survivor of a tribe of Neanderthals living for millennia in a
remote region of the Caucasus between Georgia and Russia.'

The drawing filling the screen was a close-up of a woman's
face in an eerie, Mona Lisa-like pose. Her slight smile revealed
a row of small, even teeth. With her unusual blend of Negroid
and Mongoloid features, how unlike the local population this

wild woman must have appeared, I thought. The Caucasus. Isn't that where the word 'Caucasian' – white people – came from?

'Until recent times,' Monique told her audience, 'scientists could only speculate on Zana's origins based on her physical appearance as described by people who had seen her. Reportedly, she stood six and a half feet tall with dark gray skin. Her body was covered with red hair and a mane ran along her spine. Zana had a broad face, close-set eyes, high cheekbones and ape-like, forward-facing nostrils. To her captors, she certainly seemed to be half woman and half ape. Some even claimed she was a yeti.'

Monique paused for effect. 'Then along came DNA.'

All around us, heads nodded knowingly. After Professor Cloughly's presentation the previous day, most of the audience probably felt themselves fully informed – experts even – on the role that DNA analysis played in the search for Bigfoot.

'In 2013,' Monique continued, 'Professor Bryan Sykes of the University of Oxford, pictured here with a supposed yeti scalp, reported that analysis of Zana's DNA proved she was one-hundred-percent Sub-Saharan African in origin. Sykes speculated that she could have been a slave brought to Abkhazia by the Ottoman Empire.

'Further analysis by Sykes in 2015, however, conducted on the saliva of six of Zana's living relatives and a tooth from her deceased son, Khwit, caused him to rethink that theory. Sykes now believes that while Zana was one-hundred-percent African, her DNA did not match any known African group, speculating that her people may have migrated to the remote Caucasus approximately 100,000 years ago.'

'Wow, just wow,' I said under my breath.

Then Monique burst everyone's balloon. 'Some of the professor's colleagues doubt his findings, questioning both the sources of his samples and his methodology. Others believe the press release was a publicity stunt timed to coincide with the publication of his book on the same topic.'

Next to me, Cecelia sniffed. 'First time *that's* ever happened, I bet.'

I had to smile, but not for long.

Listening for twenty minutes as Monique detailed the enslaved, often shackled, tortured life of Zana, a disabled, mentally-challenged outcast – local squires got her drunk and had contests to see who could mount her, for heaven's sake! – I felt like I needed a bath. When she bore children – alone and unassisted, bathing the newborns in a cold mountain stream – they were taken away from her and raised by local villagers. Fortunate for the children, I thought. And also, more than a century later, for the geneticists.

'Witnesses and residents of Abkhazia, including her descendants, establish Zana's existence beyond any doubt,' Monique continued, 'yet experts still wrestle with her background and biological identity. Was she simply a victimized woman suffering from a disability, a runaway African slave or even a surviving Neanderthal?'

The faded photographs of Khwit and his daughter, Natalia, that had dominated the screen for several minutes dissolved. A photograph of a Red Army soldier – looking so much like the Russian president that I figured Monique must have a sense of humor after all – took their place. 'Are there others of Zana's kind living in the Caucasus, relics of an ancient African race of humans?' she asked rhetorically.

'A curious story. In 1941, shortly after the German invasion of the USSR, a wild man was captured somewhere in the Caucasus by a detachment of the Red Army. He appeared human but was covered, like Zana, with fine, dark hair. Under interrogation he was unable (or unwilling) to speak, so the unfortunate creature was shot as a German spy. We know no more about him.'

Monique aimed her pointer and the Red Army officer dissolved, returning to the haunting drawing of Zana. 'Zana died over 125 years ago, but her unusual genetic legacy remains an enigma yet to be solved. Sykes is to be commended for applying scientific methods in an attempt to answer this question, but to the scientific world at large it is still far from resolved.'

In the flurry of questions that followed Monique's provocative talk: have they looked for Zana's bones? *Yes. In the 1960s.* Did they find them? *No.* Who were the fathers of her children? *Nobody knows for sure, although Edgi Genaba's wife raised the two youngest children and Zana was buried in the Genaba family cemetery.*

I whispered to Cecelia, 'I'm ready to go. Are you?'

Several minutes later the two of us were settled into chairs in a comfortable corner of the lobby, not far from the fireplace.

'Cecelia, before we go any further, I need to clear something up.'

'Go for it,' she said, looking a bit puzzled.

'I just spent a harrowing lunch hour up in my room watching a Martin Radcliffe video. You can probably guess which one.'

To my astonishment, Cecelia grinned. 'I certainly can.'

Thinking she was simply putting a brave face on what had to have been a traumatic experience, I touched her arm and said, 'I'm so sorry! I didn't realize the man was such an obnoxious bully. You looked like you were about to cry.'

'I was good, wasn't I?' she said, still smiling.

I sat up straight. 'What do you mean?'

Cecelia patted my hand where it rested on her arm. 'I put Martin up to it, Hannah. As a scientist, I was getting rusty. I *needed* to get out of the classroom and into the field. I'd applied for a sabbatical but the university was digging in its heels. Budgetary constraints, teacher work load, yada yada yada. A bit of institutional embarrassment on national TV was a small price to pay to get them to finally sign off on my expedition.'

'You devious wench!'

'Thank you,' she said.

'It must have been one heck of an expedition to make it worth being humiliated in front of millions of viewers,' I said.

'Oh, it was. Totally.'

I jabbed her with my elbow. 'So, don't keep me in suspense. Where did you go?'

'To the ruins of a Great House near Monument Valley, just on the Arizona side.' Cecelia paused. 'You've heard of cliff dwellings?'

'My parents subscribed to *National Geographic*,' I said, as if that answered her question.

Cecelia laughed. 'Well, one thing I'll bet NatGeo didn't tell you about was "man corn."'

'Uh, no. What's man corn?'

'Think about it,' she said.

I didn't like where my mind was taking me.

Before I could say anything, though, Cecelia continued, 'Archeologists from the University of Arizona discovered charnel deposits in this particular dwelling – food dumps dating back to the twelfth century. On analysis, the bones were determined to be human – men, women and children.'

I shivered. 'Are you saying what I think you're saying?'

'I'm afraid so. There was unmistakable evidence on the skulls and on the bones of butchering and burning, but in order to make a clear case for cannibalism, rather than a simple massacre, they asked me to come in.'

'I thought your expertise was scat.'

'Exactly. At one of the sites they uncovered fossilized coprolite, or desiccated human turds. Based on analysis techniques developed in the nineties for similar remains at Chaco Canyon, I tested the turds for traces of human myoglobin.'

'I'm assuming the results were positive.'

'They were.'

'Yuck,' I said.

Cecelia, still grinning, said, 'I love my job.'

'Speaking of jobs,' I said as I dug my iPhone out of my bag, feeling confident that I could cross Cecelia off my list, 'I'd like your opinion on something.'

'Which hat am I wearing? Scientist, musician or girlfriend?'

'Scientist.'

I tapped the Safari icon, brought Jim Davis's website up on my iPhone and clicked the link to the YouTube video he'd posted. The tape began to roll.

Together we watched the creature as it strolled to the Metolius riverbank with the now-familiar two-legged, stooped, loping gait. How it turned, looked at the camera then skedaddled.

'You're a doctor, Cecelia,' I said. 'See how he walks? Does that look like an ape to you or a man trying to walk like an ape?'

Cecelia squinted at the screen. 'Hard to tell. The quality's not the best.' At her request, I reran the video. After studying it for the forty-three seconds it took to run its course, she said, 'We need Martin Radcliffe, you know. He was the pro when it came to video tape analysis.'

'Right. But he's not here, so who would people go to next?'

'Brad Johnson, maybe? He's been working with Martin for a while, I understand.'

'I can track Johnson down later, I suppose, but right now I'm wondering what *you* think.'

Cecelia tapped the screen. 'I notice that the arms are longer than normal for a human but they could be extensions.'

'How about the feet?' I asked.

'Abnormally large, for sure. But if they're fake I'd expect him to have more difficulty walking.'

'Maybe he's had a lot of practice,' I suggested.

Cecelia seemed to be considering what I'd just said. 'Practice doing what? Walking around in fake feet? Not something one does every day, Hannah.' She paused. 'Except maybe circus clowns.'

'Can you train somebody to walk like an ape – convincingly, I mean?'

'Absolutely. I saw a documentary once, I forget how long ago. They interviewed a guy named Terry Notary – an odd name, so that's why I remember it. Notary is an actor and former Cirque du Soleil performer who starred in some of the *Planet of the Apes* movies. He ran a kind of ape school for the actors, billing himself as a movement coach.' She drew quote marks in the air. 'It was all very zen, as I recall,' she said. 'Humans are not that far from apes – I don't have to tell you that. But, in order to play one convincingly, Notary had his students start with a blank slate, lying quietly in a hammock somewhere, presumably thinking ape-like thoughts.'

She paused then furrowed her brow. 'I remember the arm extensions in particular because they so closely resembled the leg braces used by polio victims.' She reached out a hand. 'Here, let me have your phone for a minute.'

A minute later, we were looking at a video showing Terry Notary – young, handsomely appealing in a Patrick Swayze sort of way, a lock of dark hair falling oh-so-charmingly over one eye – demonstrating the use of his arm extensions to walk exactly, to my unprofessional eye, like an ape.

'Don't try that in high heels,' I said.

'You'd have to ply me with alcohol first,' Cecelia said with a laugh. 'Planet of the Drunken Apes.'

'So, what's your professional opinion of the Jim Davis video?'

She grinned. 'You're not going to let me out of this chair until I give it to you, are you?'

'Not a chance.'

'A guy in an ape suit. Well-trained but definitely a guy.'

TWENTY-TWO

'Tennessee has another wild man, much more satisfactory than the last. He is seven feet high, covered with shaggy hair, very muscular, runs away from men with astonishing swiftness, but approaches unprotected women with wild and horrid screams of delight.'

The *Elyria Independent Democrat* (Elyria, Ohio),
May 10, 1871

After she left to get ready for dinner, I sat quietly for a few minutes, thinking about what Cecelia had said. *Planet of the Apes*. Every time I turned around there was a reference to it.

How many *Planet of the Apes* movies had there been over the years? I wondered. Six? Seven? I decided to look it up when I got a moment to myself, perhaps in another year or two.

Fortunately I didn't have to wait that long.

After dinner, I intended to make a brief appearance at the Bigfoot Encounters story session on the patio. Billed as a 'no-shame zone,' the session was run like a twelve-step support group. Some folks were reluctant to join in at first, but once they knew they were among like-minded friends they opened right up. No embarrassment. No judging. Just like an AA meeting. These people really understood.

I had been lured out to the fire pit not so much out of a desire to hear stories about Bigfoot but by the aroma of hot chocolate. Tina, the server, had clearly overcome her earlier shyness. She'd deserted the hot chocolate and mulled wine serving station and was, instead, the center of attention. Keeping her voice just low enough for those clustered around the fire pit to hear, she soon held the audience of fifteen in complete thrall. I grabbed a cup of hot chocolate and stood on the periphery of the crowd, sipping carefully and listening.

'Me and my sister were visiting my grandparents on their farm near Chagrin Falls, Ohio,' she began, 'and we were playing on the swings near the edge of the woods. For some reason we both stopped playing and looked up, and there, in plain view about ten feet away, was a big, ape-like animal.'

'She should read audio books,' Susan said, joining me suddenly. 'Lovely voice.'

'Shhhh,' I said, though I totally agreed.

Tina's eyes flashed in the firelight. 'It had a wrinkly face like a chimpanzee, with a widow's peak at the hairline, you know, and really black eyes. I think it was about eight feet tall and covered all over with long, brown hair, like in those ape movies.' She paused then looked from one audience member to the next before continuing. 'We all just froze, you know, and stared at each other. Then it took off into the woods and we ran home. We told our grandparents that we'd just seen a monster but nobody believed us. Grandaddy said it must have been a bear. Gramma said we were staying up too late watching scary movies on TV so she sent us to bed early.'

As Tina continued with her tale, I was swamped by a wave of nostalgia for the summers I'd spent at that camp in rural Vermont, sitting around the campfire telling ghost stories. I leaned closer to Susan and rasped, 'Who stole my golden arm?'

'Stop it!' Susan said. 'You'll make me spill my drink!'

'I was only twelve then,' Tina said, 'and I'd never even heard of a Bigfoot. Then you know what happened?'

'What?' someone said.

'Tell us! Tell us!' chirped a tiny voice I recognized as seven-year-old Kylie.

Tina waited everyone out, building suspense like a natural-born storyteller. 'I saw that Patterson and Gimlin film the other night, that's what happened. I saw Patty.' Tina's voice, even after all the years that had passed since the sighting, quavered with excitement. 'Patty was i-den-ti-cal to that creature I'd seen all those years ago in O-hi-o.'

She sat back in her chair and folded her hands primly at her waist. Her story was done.

Susan had quietly excused herself and gone off on some errand. I took several steps backward, merging into the shadows. As the next storyteller began his tale, I sneaked away and went to my room.

I kicked off my cruel shoes, flopped down on the bed and began massaging the cramps out of my toes. When I thought I would be able to walk again, I grabbed my iPhone off the bedside table and swiped it on.

Finally, there was a text message from Paul. The *Resolute* had reached Cape May and the crew were enjoying crab cakes, beer and long, hot showers ashore.

I texted back, 'Wild and crazy times. More later.' I didn't mention poor Martin.

Before allowing myself to be distracted by a game of Words With Friends – my sister, Georgina, was cleaning my clock so thoroughly with seven-letter words like 'quizzify' and 'jukebox' that I suspected her of cheating – I got down to business.

How many times had the *Planet of the Apes* been mentioned, just today? I had already been thinking about its significance, and then Tina, of all people, mentioned it again.

I powered up Google and had a look.

Starting in 1968 with the classic starring Charlton Heston and including the 2001 remake by Tim Burton, I counted nine films: *Beneath the*, *Escape from*, *Conquest of*, *Battle for*, *Rise of*, *Dawn of* and *War for the*.

But the fact that made me gasp, fall back against the headboard and squeak 'Ohmahgawd' was this. The *Planet of the Apes* franchise was owned by Twentieth Century Fox.

Rise of the Planet of the Apes had been filmed by Fox in 2011, about the time I figured Brad Johnson would have been interning there.

I grabbed my phone with the intention of texting Jake, until I remembered Jake didn't 'do' texting on his prehistoric clam-shell. I used the bedside phone to call his room but he didn't pick up. I left a message for him to call me back.

When he did, five minutes later, I picked up on the first ring.

'Brad Johnson worked at Twentieth Century Fox about the time they were filming *Rise of the Planet of the Apes*,' I told him. 'Do you think he would have had access to the ape costumes?'

'That's quite a stretch, Hannah. You don't have to work for Fox to have access to ape costumes. Any popup Halloween costume shop would do nicely.'

I made a rude noise. 'I don't think so. Those are obvious fakes.

Even seen at a distance on a blurry, jittery video, you'd be able to tell.'

As we talked, I clicked through to *Rise of the Planet of the Apes* on a popular motion picture and television database. 'Oh, damn. It says here that *Rise of* wasn't even filmed in LA. They filmed it up in British Columbia.' I paged forward a few screens, still unwilling to give up on my theory that Brad had used his Fox connections to steal an ape suit and masquerade as one in Flat Rock. But the Wikipedia entry for the film squashed my theory almost completely. 'Wait a minute. Listen to this. *Rise of* . . . was the first of the franchise to be filmed using something called performance capture.'

'Uh, what's that called when it's at home?'

'Just a minute, I'm looking.' I scrolled down the entry, searching for an explanation, then quickly wished I hadn't. 'It says here that the actors wear gray velcro body suits with LED lights attached at strategic places. More than fifty LEDs. They're wired for sound, yada yada yada. The film is then turned over to a New Zealand company called Weta. The guy who made the Lord of the Rings movies owns it.'

'What does Weta do with it?'

'They animate it. Those chimps were one-hundred-percent digital.' I felt like weeping. Poof went my theory, shot down in flames. No Weta magic in Flat Rock Freaking Oregon.

'Back to square one,' I grumped.

'Let it go, Hannah.'

I had no intention of letting it go. 'Do you think we had a real Sasquatch down there, Jake?'

'Based on my experience? No.'

'But, the footprints? Your castings . . .?' I let the sentence die.

'Think Prince Charming,' Jake said with a chuckle. 'I can search all over the kingdom until I find a warm-blooded foot to match that cast. Until then it's just an interesting chunk of plaster.'

'I've seen grizzlies and it wasn't a grizzly,' I said.

'No.'

'That leaves a guy in a monkey suit.'

'Yes.'

'Who, then? And why?' A thought suddenly occurred to me.

'Could it have been Martin Radcliffe himself, setting up a hoax just so he could debunk it?'

'If it was Radcliffe there would have been no need for him to be wearing camouflage.'

I let that sink in.

'I think it's more likely Radcliffe got wind that something was up and decided to set a trap for Jim and Athena,' Jake said.

'That's what Brad suspected, too. But what was Martin planning to do?' I asked. 'Come streaking out of his hiding place and tackle the imposter? And what if it actually was a Bigfoot,' I said, rushing on. 'Martin didn't have any tranquilizer darts on him, as far as I know.' I paused. 'Maybe he carried bear repellant. I bought a little can this morning, just in case.'

I closed my eyes and rested my head against the headboard, trying to picture the scene, filling in the blanks left by Jim Davis's film. Davis's film was, quite literally, only half the story.

Radcliffe dressed up like Desert Storm, waiting quietly in the woods, some twenty feet behind the camera.

A shadowy, faceless someone picks up a branch so quietly that Radcliffe doesn't even turn around.

A single, powerful swing and *whomp!*. Down he goes.

'You still there, Hannah?'

'What time did Jim's video alarm go off, Jake, do you remember?'

'Nine-thirteen a.m. exactly.'

I did the math. 'Martin Radcliffe was fifty minutes dead by then.'

'So it appears.'

'Do you think he saw something? The guy wearing the monkey suit, I mean.'

'Hard to say. He stared directly at the camera, for sure, but he could have been looking at something beyond the camera too.' He paused. 'But with Martin already dead, what was there to see in the woods other than Martin's body?'

I had to agree. 'Right. The murderer would have been long gone.'

'There's only one way to know for certain what he saw. Find the guy wearing the monkey suit and ask him.'

'Yeah, sure,' I said. A moment later, I added, 'I wish we could engineer a repeat performance.'

'How?'

'Shhhh. I'm thinking.'

As I turned ideas over in my mind, all I could hear was quiet chatter leeching through the wall from a television in the adjoining room. 'What if they thought nobody took it seriously – the Sasquatch, I mean? Would whoever it was try again?'

'It's hard to say. Has Davis put his camera set up away?'

'Athena told me he's moved the camera to another location. He found what he thinks is a Bigfoot nest a bit further downstream. When he was out casing the joint yesterday afternoon something threw pinecones at him, so that sealed the deal.'

Whatever was in the woods surrounding the lodge, I thought, it wasn't throwing pinecones. It was wielding, like Theodore Roosevelt, a mighty big stick. 'Jim Davis is nothing if not ever hopeful,' I said.

While Jake nattered on about my hare-brained ideas and leaving well enough alone, something else popped into my head. 'There's something I don't get. Brad Johnson was shadowing Martin Radcliffe, sticking to the man all weekend like chewing gum on his shoe. I'm surprised the History Channel doesn't have footage of Martin taking a leak.'

Jake snorted. 'You're not going to leave Johnson alone, are you?'

'Answer me this, then, Detective Cummings. How come Brad didn't accompany Martin into the woods on Friday morning? Brad says it's because Martin sent him away and told him he had an errand to run in town. But we only have Brad's word for that.'

'Are you going to talk to him then, or should I?'

'Your turn, I think. See you in the morning?'

After we wished each other a good night I brushed my teeth, pulled a nightgown over my head and went rummaging on the desk for my Kindle. I found it hiding under the bag that contained the FLIR infrared camera attachment I'd bought as a gift for my husband. Still so keyed up I knew I wouldn't be able to sleep, I installed the device on my iPhone – just snap it in, as easy as advertised – and amused myself for several minutes checking out the hot spots in my room. My computer screen (fuchsia), the light bulbs (white) and the cold seeping out around the door of my refrigerator (deep purple). I practiced taking a few shots then switched over to the App Store. Long before Zombie Vision finished downloading, I fell fast asleep.

TWENTY-THREE

'At last he came to the edge of the little glade where the camp lay and shouted as he approached it, but got no answer. The campfire had gone out, though the thin blue smoke was still curling upwards . . . Stepping forward he again shouted, and as he did so his eye fell on the body of his friend, stretched beside the trunk of a great fallen spruce. Rushing toward it the horrified trapper found that the body was still warm, but that the neck was broken, while there were four great fang marks in the throat. The footprints of the unknown beast-creature, printed deep in the soft soil, told the whole story.'

Theodore Roosevelt, *The Wilderness Hunter.* New York, GP Putnam's Sons, 1893, p. 446

The next morning, Sunday, I awoke to the sun shining full on my face. When I went to the window to adjust the drapes I was relieved to see no sherriff's vehicle in the parking lot. Perhaps Detective Lieutenant Cook had overslept. Or maybe she'd packed it in.

The sun, which had been so dazzling a moment before, was packing it in, too. Dark clouds moving in rapidly from the west swallowed it up whole, turning a promising day dreary.

The clock on the bedside table read 8:16. Damn! I had less than fifteen minutes until I was supposed to be downstairs making myself available, so I dashed back and forth the short distance between the bathroom and the closet, washing up and dressing like a woman possessed. Hating the boring person who stared out at me from the full-length mirror, clad almost completely in black, I added a colorful scarf to my outfit, knotting it carelessly around my neck, then headed out the door.

It had almost closed behind me when I realized I'd left my name tag behind. I did a quick U-turn, found the name tag hanging on the back of the bathroom door then scooped up my cell phone, still encased in the FLIR. 'Oh, what the hell,' I muttered and tossed it into my bag, too.

Avoiding the piles of luggage stacked up in the lobby, ready for the bus that was going to take it to the airport later that morning, I went looking for Debbie. I found her packing up the last of her donuts. I paused at her table, looking sorrowful. 'I saved one for you,' she said, taking pity, handing one over neatly wrapped in a napkin.

I lifted a corner of the napkin and peeked underneath. 'Chocolate! You are a star.'

She beamed.

'You really should franchise this, you know,' I said, taking a big, satisfying bite.

'It's kind of you to say so, Hannah, but I'm happy as I am. Small scale, know all my customers. Like you. Besides,' she continued, 'I have no desire to see my face plastered on billboards all over the USA like the Kentucky Fried Colonel or something.'

'You're much more attractive than the Colonel,' I teased.

Debbie pointed at what remained of my donut. 'You'll spoil your brunch.'

'Who cares?' I polished it off. 'Where's the brunch, anyway?'

She waved toward a pair of double glass doors. 'They're setting it up on the patio, near the pool.'

'Isn't that a bit risky? Looks like rain to me.'

She shook her head. 'Nothing on the radar, according to your boss. Sun's supposed to come out again around noon.'

'Fingers crossed!' I bid Debbie goodbye, saying I hoped our paths would cross soon again.

I was half an hour too early to connect with some scrambled eggs and bacon so, fortified by the donut, I went looking for Jake instead.

The first person I ran into was Cecelia Cloughly, stepping out of an elevator, dragging a suitcase in one hand and carrying her

French horn in the other. A conference tote bag was slung over her shoulder.

'Morning, Cecelia,' I said, reaching out for the suitcase. 'Let me help you with that.'

'Thanks,' she said, handing it over with obvious relief. 'I imagine it goes in the pile over there?'

'Right,' I said. 'Follow me?'

After we deposited her bag with the others headed for the airport, Cecelia said, 'I'm leaving in a couple of hours, but if I don't get to see you before then . . .' She extended her hand. 'It's been lovely meeting you.'

'Likewise,' I said, taking her hand and shaking it. 'Stay in touch?'

'Of course.'

As we walked together toward the conference rooms, I said, 'I'm curious about something, Cecelia. Is Radcliffe's show *all* an act? Does everybody agree to go along with some sort of script?' I paused. 'There I was feeling sorry for you and Monique, for Prairie Flower and even for blowhards like Randall Frazier. Was it all for show?'

'I can't speak for everyone, of course,' she said, 'but I'm almost positive that Monique and Prairie Flower were completely blindsided. Monique Deschamps can't stand the man! You should see what he said about her book.'

I stopped dead in my tracks. 'But Monique told me Martin Radcliffe ignored her publisher's request for a blurb.'

'Oh, that's true. Radcliffe didn't blurb it but he savaged it on Amazon.' Cecelia set her horn down on the carpet, reached into the zippered compartment of her conference tote and pulled out her smart phone. She tapped the screen, waited for it to refresh then handed the phone to me. 'Read it and weep,' she said. 'Monique did.'

Martin Radcliffe had given *Bigfoot: Fact, Fiction and Fable* a one-star review.

As Cecelia watched, serious and unsmiling, I read:

> *Miss Deschamps' book claims to be 'comprehensive' but actually contains nothing new or groundbreaking. This heavily biased work is so poorly organized that I was finding*

myself continually lost, desperately in need of an index which is, of course, lacking. And speaking of lacking, where are the illustrations? The few dark, grainy images the author provides add nothing to our understanding of this complex subject. The publisher apparently has no problem charging big-boy prices for a book that, at a scant 190 pages, could best be described as a 'brochure.' And while I'm on a rant, I have news for you. 'There' and 'their' are two different words. If a publisher doesn't take the time to properly edit and spell-check a book, I don't have enough time to waste reading it.

'Ouch!' I said when I'd finished wading through Radcliffe's scathing prose. 'If I were a writer that would be enough to make me hang up my pen.'

'Or bump the man off?' Cecelia mused.

'I wonder where Monique was when Martin went down?'

Cecelia shrugged. 'You might want to ask her.'

'I plan to,' I said, handing the phone back.

'Unfortunately she left this morning,' Cecelia said.

'Well, on to Plan B,' I said, trying to hide my disappointment while making a mental note to mention the savage review to Jake. 'Are you staying for brunch?'

'I haven't decided yet,' Cecelia said, picking up her horn and heading down the hallway. 'See you later!'

'Where are you going?' I called after her. 'Brunch is the other way.'

Cecelia turned and waggled her brows mischievously. 'If you promise not to tell, I'll let you in on a little secret. At the end of this hallway, turn to the right and there's a beautiful vending machine that carries chocolate bars. Can't get them anywhere else in this godforsaken mountain outpost.

'Why are you laughing?' she asked.

'I'll explain later,' I said, watching with relief as Cecelia trudged down the hallway, lugging her horn and threading her way among conference attendees – not up to any mischief at all, but simply in search of a chocolate bar.

I was so lost in thought that I nearly collided with Brad Johnson as he emerged from the Meriwether Lewis conference room, camera hoisted to his right shoulder. He moved slowly, apparently

filming the attendees as they milled around the corridor, chatting,
drinking coffee and noshing on Debbie's donuts. When he saw
me he aimed the camera in my direction. My hastily groomed
face was not ready for prime time so I waved him off, wondering
if Jake had had a chance to corner him yet and grill him about
Martin.

Brad pivoted with a good-natured wave of his free hand and
chose another victim, a Good Ole Boy wearing a ten-gallon hat,
a rodeo roustabout gone to seed.

I found Jake easily enough, sitting on a bench further down
the hallway, sharing a cake-style donut with Harley. I sat down
beside them.

'The longer I think about it the longer my list of suspects
grows,' I said to Jake after telling him about Monique's devas-
tating one-star review. Brad's camera made another sweep in our
direction. 'Did you talk to Brad?'

Before Jake could answer, Harley, who had been lying quietly
nearby, thumping his tail on the carpet, suddenly rose to his feet
and barked. A single woof, short and sharp.

Jake's head spun around. '*Vas is los*, Harley?'

As if Jake's response wasn't fast enough for the dog, Harley
barked once again and tugged on his leash.

Jake stood up and gave Harley the lead. As I watched, the pair
hustled down the hallway following Brad who, with his back
turned to us and his camera rolling, seemed totally unaware of
the drama going on behind him.

I trailed along behind like a third wheel.

When he reached the main lobby, Brad paused and Harley
did, too. Nose pointed, ears erect, the dog sat down next to Brad,
skewering the cameraman with his dark amber eyes.

'Harley's alerting,' Jake murmured.

'Does that mean he thinks Brad did it?' I whispered back.

Brad lowered his camera and stared at Harley, looking
perplexed. 'What's up with your dog, Cummings?'

'Is there someplace we can talk in private?'

'Sure, but call off your dog. He's spooking me, man.'

We were standing just outside the double glass doors of the
lodge's business center. Except for two computers and a high-
speed printer the room was empty, so we went inside.

'What's up with your dog?' Brad asked again once the doors whooshed closed behind us.

'You tell me,' Jake said. 'On Friday I ordered Harley to track whoever attacked Martin Radcliffe. The trail dead-ended at the parking lot. But today, well, here you are.'

'Dog needs his nose checked. I didn't have anything to do with Martin's murder. He was my ticket, man! Why would I want him dead?'

Remembering the conversation we'd overheard on the patio the previous afternoon I could think of several reasons, but I kept my mouth shut. This was Jake and Harley's show, not mine.

'Perhaps you wanted to step into Martin's famous lime-green tennis shoes,' Jake said, giving voice to exactly what I was thinking.

Brad slumped, looking deflated. 'You've got it wrong.' He stared at Harley for a long minute. 'I don't know what . . .' he began. Then his eyes widened and his face brightened. He began patting his pockets. 'Harley's a sniffer dog, right?'

Jake nodded.

From the back pocket of his jeans, Brad pulled out a slim silver case about the size and shape of a disposable cigarette lighter. As Harley's back end twitched, Brad slipped off the cap, revealing two neatly rolled joints lying side by side. 'Can't arrest me, man. Marijuana's legal in Oregon.'

'Sorry,' Jake said. 'I guess Harley got his wires crossed.'

Brad shrugged and slipped the case back into his pocket. 'No problem. Glad we got it cleared up.'

After Brad left, looking smug, I said to Jake, 'Did Harley? Get his wires crossed, I mean?'

'It's possible, Hannah. Harley's an elderly dog and a bit out of practice.'

'But you don't believe it, do you?' I said, reading the look on his face.

'At this point, I don't know what to believe.' After a moment, he added: 'You hungry?'

'Famished,' I said.

'Then let's go see what the buffet has to offer.'

While Jake went off to fill a water bowl for Harley, I wandered out to the patio and located the buffet tables, loaded with an obscene amount of food: eggs, bacon, sausage, creamed beef and hash browns – compact little squares, not grated. There was fresh fruit, yogurt and hot oatmeal with all the trimmings. What's not to like? A few minutes before, my teeth had been set for scrambled eggs, but once I spotted the Belgian waffles I was a goner. I joined the line.

Instrumental renditions of Beatles tunes played softly in the background as we grazed. I hummed along with *Hey Jude* while decorating my waffle with fresh strawberries and whipped cream. Holding my plate, I looked around.

Before I could find a table two children streaked past, screaming like banshees. Another, around ten years old, lunged in front of me, grabbed a blueberry muffin and raced off after them. I wondered where the camp counselors had gotten to when I noticed another kid bouncing, fully clothed, on the end of the diving board.

This trick did not escape the attention of his eagle-eyed mother. 'Jason! You get off that board right this minute! You hear me?' I recognized Carla, the young woman I'd met at lunch the day before. Kylie's mom. Once Jason had removed himself from the danger zone, I asked, 'Did Kylie ever find a plastic fork?'

'Oh, yes. She managed to tick off all the boxes.' She indicated my plate, which was tipping dangerously to starboard. 'Please, join us.'

I smiled, sat down and dug in.

I'd eaten half my waffle when Carla excused herself to retrieve her son from some other escapade. She frog-marched him back to the table and sat him down, firmly, next to me, where he fussed and fidgeted, tearing the edges of the paper tablecloth into tiny strips then laying them out individually on his grubby palm and blowing them away.

I wiped whipped cream off my lips with my napkin, crumpled it next to my plate and went into full grandmother mode.

I reached into my bag and rooted around for my iPhone, thinking Jason might settle down if I distracted him with a game of Minecraft or The Sims.

I'd forgotten until I dredged it up, heavy in my hand, that the instrument was still encased in the FLIR. Even better! Before long Jason had mastered the Zombie Vision app and was turning us all into red-eyed monsters.

From the look his mother gave me, I was her new best friend. 'Is this seat taken or can anyone join?'

'Hi, Jake.' I introduced him to Carla, whose last name I learned was Malone.

'Have you eaten?' Carla asked him.

'I will in a minute,' he said. 'Thanks.' Then he turned to me. 'I was looking for Susan Lockley. Have you seen her?'

'She's off coordinating some last-minute changes to the airport shuttle. If you need to make a change now she's going to kill you.'

'Just want to make sure they save room for Harley,' he said, reaching down to pat the dog who, in spite of all the cheerful chaos going on around him, sat passively at Jake's heels, his ears twitching with interest.

Cecelia Cloughly drifted past heading in the direction of the meditation garden, carrying her horn. I called out to her and she came over. 'Surely you have that piece down pat by now,' I teased, indicating the case containing the horn.

She leaned in and spoke quietly. 'Frankly, crowds like this make me a little bit crazy.' She hefted the case. 'Meet my excuse to get away.'

I cheerfully waved her off.

When she was several feet away, she turned. 'Don't worry,' she called over her shoulder. 'I brought my mute.'

Five minutes later, Brunhilde was tooting farewell to Siegfried once again but softly, barely audible under the orchestral version of 'Lucy in the Sky with Diamonds' wafting out of the outdoor speakers.

'She shouldn't do that,' Jake commented as he joined us with a plate piled high with food.

'Do what?' Carla wanted to know.

'Play music. Sasquatch are attracted to music.'

I jabbed him with my elbow. 'Stop it!'

'It's true. In Muir Woods, back in 2003, some flower child was leaning against a redwood playing "Kumbayah" on a recorder when she was attacked by a Bigfoot.'

Thinking about poor Martin, I said, 'Yikes. Was she killed?'

'Nope.' Jake chuckled. 'Bigfoot grabbed her recorder and snapped it in two. Or so she claimed. Since she was stoned at the time nobody paid much attention to her story.' He paused and sipped at his coffee. 'So much for the theory that music has charms to soothe the savage beast.'

'Breast,' I corrected.

'Whatever,' Jake said. 'From what I've seen on television and Martin Radcliffe's show in particular, professional hog callers would have better luck attracting a Sasquatch than a horn player.'

'How about those guys speaking Squatch?'

'Them, too,' he said.

Although folks were still visiting the buffet – some for seconds or thirds, I noticed – the crowd had noticeably thinned.

'Mom!' Jason crowed. 'You are a zombie! Look!'

Carla was giving Jason and her zombie portrait her undivided attention when somebody started to scream, a staccato, *'Eek! Eek! Eek!'* that silenced everyone.

I became aware of several things at once.

Jake shot to his feet. *'Was is los?'* he said, putting Harley on alert.

Kylie was running toward us, arms outstretched and waving wildly. 'Mommy, mommy, Bigfoot!'

Kylie had it right. About fifty yards away, at the edge of the forest, caught like a deer in the headlights, stood a Sasquatch.

'Jake! Hurry!' I snatched my iPhone out of the hands of an astonished Jason and dashed off after the creature, determined to unmask the imposter the old-fashioned way by tearing the disguise off his face.

'Hannah! No!' Jake was seconds behind me. 'Leave him to me.'

Squatch had darted through a gap in the trees and I shot through, too. Ahead, over the sound of my own heavy breathing, I could hear thrashing and twigs crackling.

The forest closed in around me, growing darker. I chanced a look behind me, fully expecting to see Jake but, surprisingly, I was alone. I paused to listen for him but the woods surrounding me were unnaturally quiet.

I stood still, clutching my iPhone in a death grip, hearing my husband's voice in my head: 'Hannah, what are we going to do with you? Are you out of your mind?'

Probably. But I thought Jake was right behind me! My heart thudded and seemed to turn over. Where the hell was he?

I brought the phone up to my face, surprised that it was so

heavy, forgetting for a moment that it was still encased in the FLIR.

'C'mon baby,' I whispered as I swiped the phone to life. I used the app to scan the forest around me. Nothing but cool colors – navy, purple and blue. Was the damn thing even working?

I aimed at my hand – a warm, golden yellow. It was working fine.

Holding the phone in front of me, I moved cautiously forward, scanning as I went. Through gaps in the trees – dark blue foliage, the trunks outlined in neon green – I plunged deeper into the woods, praying I was heading in the right direction. Then I stopped, hardly daring to breathe. Something warm was just ahead, a reddish-purple shape, crouching near the roots of a tree.

'I see you,' I said.

Nobody answered. The shape didn't move.

I suppressed the crazy impulse to shout at the creature in Bigfootese. RAM HO BÄ RÜ kept running wildly through my mind like a mantra.

I tried an old cowboy trick. 'We have you surrounded.'

All remained quiet.

'The police are on their way.'

Silence.

'I see you,' I tried again, my voice quavering. I reached into my pocket, wrapping my fingers around the aerosol can of Bear Shot that I'd bought from Marty in the dealers' room, feeling reassured by his guarantee that the specially formulated pepper spray would 'stop a charging grizzly in its tracks.' After what seemed like an eternity but was probably only a few minutes, I said, 'Screw it!' and turned on the phone's flashlight, moving in for a closer look.

At the base of the tree lay a pile of rags.

I moved closer, stooped and picked one up. It consisted of shaggy strips of burlap and pieces of string, like an old-fashioned mop, attached to coarse webbing.

I hadn't spent almost all my life hanging around military bases, first as a navy brat and then as the wife of a Naval Academy professor, not to know what I held in my hand, still warm from the body of whomever had been wearing it. A ghillie suit.

Great. I was stuck out in the middle of the Deschutes National

Forest and whoever had been disguised with this foliage camouflage outfit was long gone.

At least my battery was fully charged and I had the Google
GPS app to guide me out of there, wherever 'there' was.

I raised the phone to switch it over to the GPS app when
something on the screen grabbed my attention, shaking me to
the core. A man's face, clearly a man's – all purple head and
ears with bright yellow eyes – peered out from behind a tree.
When I lowered the phone he was completely invisible, blending
in to the surrounding shrubbery.

If I couldn't see him without the device, maybe he couldn't
see me?

I took a cautious step forward. Something snapped under my
foot. I swore, not caring if he heard.

Whoever it was took off, crashing through the underbrush,
grunting as he ran, with me hot on his tail.

'Hey!' I shouted. Branches slapped at my face and tore at my
hair. Somewhere along the way I had lost my scarf but I wasn't
about to stop and go looking for it, even though it had been a
birthday gift from Paul.

Suddenly I was aware of slats of daylight between the trunks
of the trees up ahead. I thought I had been running in the direction of the river but as I burst out of the woods I was astonished
to find myself not on the banks of the Metolius but in the lodge's
meditation garden, just behind what I'd come to think of as
Cecelia Cloughly's bench.

Her bench was deserted. I grabbed the back of it, steadying
myself as I gasped for breath.

'Hannah?'

I looked up. Professor Cloughly stood on the lawn nearby, her
foot resting on a shape I couldn't immediately identify. 'He came
charging at me from out of nowhere,' she explained. 'So I hit
him with my horn.'

I eased closer. A man lay face down on the grass under Cecelia's
foot, both arms wrapped protectively over his head. He still wore
the bottoms of the ghillie suit, like a pair of furry pajamas.

'Damn. Dented it, too,' she said, stroking the bell of her
instrument. 'Luckily I left my concert horn at home. Got this
one on eBay for three hundred and fifty dollars.'

I prodded the fellow with the tip of my shoe. 'Who are you?'
He moaned. 'Tell her not to hit me.'

I turned to the professor. 'Don't hit him again, he says.'

Cloughly seemed unmoved. 'You ought to be ashamed. Scaring everyone like that. There are *children* here!'

I kicked him again, a tiny bit harder. 'Turn over.'

'I didn't do anything wrong,' he whimpered.

'Then get up on your feet and talk to us about it,' I said.

The guy had just begun to stir when Harley bounded through the gap in the trees where I'd been minutes before, followed by Jake Cummings, who looked relieved. What appeared to be the other half of the ghillie suit was rolled up under his arm. Harley stationed himself at our captive's feet, still on full alert. 'Where the hell have you been?' I asked, speaking to the dog and ignoring his master. My knight in shining armor had arrived a day late and a dollar short. I scowled at Jake. 'I thought you were right behind me.'

'I tripped over Jason. Stupid kid ran right in front of me. We both went flying.' He rubbed his knee then winced. 'Damn. We lost you in there, Hannah.' He held up my scarf. 'If you hadn't dropped this we might never have found you.'

'I have GPS,' I reminded him, holding up my iPhone. 'It's a good thing you have Harley.'

'Call off your dog!' the guy on the ground pleaded. 'Please! I'm not going anywhere.'

'*Pass auf*,' Jake commanded, putting Harley on guard.

Seemingly reassured he wasn't about to be eaten alive by a slavering canine, the guy lowered his arms. Several seconds later he turned over.

'Good Lord!' I said.

'You see?' Cecelia said. 'Scared me spitless.'

'Shit,' Jake hissed, turning it into a two-syllable word.

Only Harley seemed unperturbed by the stranger.

Except for the T-shirt that declared our captive belonged to the 'Sasquatch Research Team,' we were looking into the face of an ape.

The ape reached up and rubbed his temple, massaging the spot where Cloughly had conked him. His hand came away covered with dark gray paint.

I squinted, struggling to identify the person hiding under the skillful paint job. No wonder we'd been fooled. Even close up, the guy looked like a gorilla: the lowered hairline, the unibrow, the flattened nose, the full, cracked lips.

'Shannon's quite the artist,' I said as the penny dropped.

'Who?' Jake asked.

'Shannon. One of the camp counselors. This is a prime example of her skill as a face painter. And, unless I'm mistaken, once this guy takes a washcloth to his face we'll be looking at Shannon's partner in crime, Colin. The other kiddy counselor.'

Colin pulled up the hem of his T-shirt and began wiping his face with it, grotesquely smearing Shannon's beautifully executed design. 'We didn't do anything wrong, honest. It was all Brad's idea. Fire everyone up, create a little excitement.'

'Too bad somebody ended up dead,' Jake said.

'That had nothing to do with me. I was just doing a job. Dress up in the ghillie suit, walk out of the woods, make some footprints, let the camera get a look at me but not too close, then split.'

Jake helped Colin to his feet none too gently, marched him over to the bench and sat him down. 'When you made your debut the other day, were you aware that Martin Radcliffe was lying dead just a few yards away?'

Colin's red-rimmed eyes grew wide. 'God, no. Do you think I would have gone through with the prank if I had known that?'

'So what's your excuse for this encore performance?'

'Brad said it was for his film – the documentary he's making for TV. He missed filming me the first time, down by the river. He needed to capture it on film.'

Something wasn't right. If Brad had arranged for the prank, as Colin claimed, why hadn't he been down at the river bank, camera shouldered, filming away on Friday? Why did he need a retake? And, more importantly, why hadn't *he* discovered Martin's body?'

I looked at Jake. 'Where is Brad, anyway? Last time I saw him he was interviewing people at brunch.'

Jake's face registered alarm. 'I don't know.'

'He was supposed to meet me in the parking lot,' Colin said with a wide-eyed look that said he was just trying to be helpful. 'He owes me another two hundred dollars.'

'Are you some sort of idiot?' Jake bellowed. 'You dress up in a ghille suit, a guy gets murdered then Brad talks you into doing it again?' He turned to me and Cecelia. 'Sign this guy up for the Darwin Award.'

Beneath the smeared grease paint, Colin's face sagged. 'I had nothing to do with Martin Radcliffe's murder! I already told you. I didn't see anything down by the river. Just walked to the water and back, like he paid me to.'

Knowing what Jake had told me about the timing of Radcliffe's death, I believed him. Still, I thought Colin had a lot of explaining to do.

Apparently Jake thought so, too.

'Here,' he said, thrusting the rolled-up ghillie suit into my hands. He seized the young man's upper arm in what looked like a death grip, gave Harley a sign and the three of them marched down the path that led back to the lodge.

'Well, that was fun,' Cecelia said as she packed her horn back into its case.

I juggled the suit so that it fit more comfortably under my arm. 'This thing is heavy.'

'You dropped something,' Cecelia said, pointing.

A flesh-colored object lay on the manicured lawn near the spot that had been torn up by the tussle with Colin. I bent down and picked it up. 'For heaven's sake!'

'What the hell is that?' Cecelia said, moving a step closer and adjusting her eyeglasses.

I held up a molded piece of latex the size and shape of a large boot. It had five sausage-shaped toes and was tufted all over with curly, brown hair. When I managed to stop laughing, I said, 'It's a hobbit foot. Flexible midtarsals and all.'

Jake Cumming's 'Cinderella' was Bilbo Baggins.

TWENTY-FOUR

*Red Bank, Northesk, New Brunswick, Canada, 1881. 'Quite a
sensation was caused last week . . . by the appearance of a strange
and terrifying animal, which those who have seen it describe as a
gorilla . . . It is . . . about seven feet long with arms and legs, but
running on all fours. The head is a dark color and the face has
features resembling those of a human being. The body is of lighter
color and covered with hair . . . It was observed that the creature
had no tail, a fact which gives color to the supposition that it is an
animal of the gorilla family. Prof. Grote, describing the gorilla,
says it has no more tail than a professor, while the knowledge that
monkeys have tails, and the idea that these external appendages
are a badge of general monkeyhood are deeply rooted in the
popular mind. But the apes are as tailless as man and no more so.'*

The Daily Patriot (Charlottetown, Prince Edward Island,
Canada), June 28, 1881

Jake's 911 call, we learned, had reached Detective Lieutenant
Barbara Cook at Shepherd of the Hills Lutheran Church just
before the closing hymn. She skipped the benediction and
arrived at Flat Rock Lodge around eleven-thirty, taking Colin
immediately in hand for questioning. When she finished grilling
him, Shannon got the full treatment, too. I ran into the pair of
counselors in the coffee shop afterwards, drinking cappuccinos
and looking sober.

To my surprise, Brad Johnson had not made himself scarce.
Jake and I cornered him near the swimming pool and waited at
the snack bar nearby, eavesdropping on his interview with Randall
Frazier about the lava tubes of Mount St Helens. 'Ape Cave,'
Frazier was telling Brad's camera when we arrived, 'was discov-
ered in 1947 when a logging tractor fell into a sink hole.'

The interview continued – an unapologetic advertisement for
Frazier's upcoming expedition. The caves were cold, we learned,

and windy. We'd need warm clothing. Three sources of light per person.

His patience eventually exhausted by Frazier's lengthy inventory of camping supplies, Jake yelled, 'Johnson!'

Brad lowered his camera and sneered, 'Catch anything, Cummings?'

I wanted to slap the insolent smirk off his face. 'As a matter of fact, yes,' I snapped.

'We need to talk to you.' Jake sounded unruffled but I'd seen his back stiffen.

'About what?' Brad wasn't going to make it easy.

'Colin and Shannon.'

'Ah.' Brad rested his camera on a nearby tabletop. 'Everyone here is so freaking serious! It was just a harmless prank, you know. Liven things up a bit. Make the documentary I'm working on far more interesting.'

'Harmless?' I puffed.

Brad looked genuinely puzzled.

'The late Martin Radcliffe?' I reminded him none too gently.

Brad heaved a sigh. 'Martin's death had absolutely nothing to do with Colin's little masquerade. Martin didn't even know about it.'

'No connection? How so?' I asked.

Randall Frazier, who had been silently listening to our conversation, chimed in. 'Just because somebody is dressed up pretending to be Bigfoot doesn't mean that there isn't a *real* Bigfoot hanging out in the area, protecting his territory or her young.'

After hanging around with whackos all weekend I had to admit there was a certain logic to that.

'Lieutenant Cook sent me to find you,' Jake said. 'She wants to speak with you, Johnson. If I were you I wouldn't keep her waiting.'

'You may think it was a good joke, Brad,' I said, 'but Lieutenant Cook hasn't got much of a sense of humor.'

Brad sighed, picked up his camera and followed Jake back to the lodge.

I trailed behind, walking side by side with Randall Frazier, chatting amiably. In the lobby, now knowing more than I ever wanted to know about lava tubes, I made my escape and headed for the dealers' room. Susan had texted that she wanted me to thank everyone for coming and offer to help with packing up, if necessary.

The minute I entered the room, Prairie Flower motioned me over. I joined her in front of her display tables, now semi-dismantled. Cardboard boxes yawned open at her feet. Rolls of bubble wrap stood nearby, their ends trailing.

Fingering the crystal pendant that hung around her neck on a gold chain, Prairie Flower said, 'I need to tell you something.'

I set aside the box of assorted crystals I'd been admiring. 'Yes?'

'Brad Johnson killed Martin Radcliffe, you know.'

I managed a smile. Encouraging her to go on, I said, 'I suspect as much.'

'I doused his name three times,' she said. 'Every time the answer was the same. Yes. Yes. Yes.' The way she stared at me, breathing quietly, I figured Prairie Flower expected me to use my position of authority to do something about it.

But was she telling the truth, I suddenly wondered, or simply blowing smoke to cover up her own involvement in Martin's death? I touched her shoulder and squeezed it reassuringly. 'The sheriff is talking with Brad right now. We really need to leave it in their hands.'

'I didn't know Martin well,' she said, swiping away a tear, 'but even though we didn't always agree, he had finally come around to treating me with respect.'

'I'm glad you brought that up,' I said. 'Can you help me out with something?'

The eyes she turned to me glistened. 'I'll certainly try.'

'I watched Radcliffe's show – the one with you on it. I'm surprised you didn't strangle the man on the spot.'

Prairie Flower pulled a tissue out of her breast pocket and blew her nose. Was she stalling? 'It hurt at the time,' she sniffed, 'but it all turned out right in the end.'

'How's that?' I asked.

She chucked the tissue into a packing box filled with trash. 'Who was it that said there is no such thing as bad publicity?'

'PT Barnum?' I guessed.

'That's the fellow. Well, if it hadn't been for being on that show, Randall Frazier wouldn't have known about me. That's how I got the invitation to help plan his expedition. In spite of Radcliffe's razzle-dazzle, Frazier was impressed with my gift.'

'How about Radcliffe's other claim, though? About you not being Native American. That had to sting.'

'It's true, Hannah, as far as it goes, but it's not the whole story.' She sighed, sounding deflated. 'I was born in Calgary but my parents were killed in an avalanche while cross-country skiing in Kananaskis Country. I was only three so they sent me to live with my aunt in Taos. Kya'ah Tanzey was my father's widowed sister-in-law. I never knew any other mother.

'Believe it or not,' Prairie Flower continued, speaking softly, 'Martin later apologized. In writing! Pinned the blame on his staff's shoddy research. I appreciated that.'

'Being good to people is a wonderful legacy to leave behind,' I said, thinking Prairie Flower was more forgiving than I ever would have been. 'Can I help you pack up?'

When she agreed, I picked up the stacks of her books (she had sold pitifully few, I noted) and packed them neatly in the box they had come in. Except for one. 'Will you sign this for me, Prairie Flower?' I held it out. 'Twenty bucks, right?'

She smiled – the first I'd seen since I met her on Friday. 'Of course!'

That done, I began looking around for another task and noticed that Jake's plaster footprint had disappeared from the glass case. I figured he had already retrieved it.

Five minutes later, I found the casting in the trash can.

Later that afternoon, Susan and I shared a taxi into Sisters. We had no more responsibilities, so I'd talked her into leaving the lodge a bit earlier than our late-afternoon flights required. At the Cottonwood Café we tucked into some positively sinful Dutch apple crêpes, then I dragged her to Dixie's, the western apparel store on East Cascade I'd discovered earlier, so that I could fulfill the promise I'd made to myself the previous Thursday. If all went well I would soon be the proud owner of a genuine pair of cowgirl boots.

The leathers in my size included alligator, bison, calf, crocodile, goat, rattlesnake and lizard. I drew the line at elephant. And fringe. And lace. And definitely no Stars and Stripes Forever styles. 'Can you show me this one?' I asked the salesman, indicating a pair in brown calfskin with a simple but elegant stitch pattern that fit perfectly when he slipped them on my feet.

Susan watched, trying not to laugh, as I tried on another half-dozen pairs. 'What do you think?' I asked Susan as I stood and took a few tentative steps.

'Nice,' she said.

I twirled, gaining confidence. 'I feel half a foot taller.'

When I found the pair that made my heart sing – square-toed in 'rebel russet' with four rows of curly-Q stitching and a scalloped top – Susan enabled me, as all good girlfriends should, to buy them.

I tucked the legs of my jeans into the new boots, stood in front of a mirror and strutted my stuff, feeling like Crystal Gayle at the Grand Ole Opry but without the hair or the guitar.

I dropped the Doc Martens I had been wearing into Susan's hands. 'I'm wearing the boots home.'

Parked at the counter while the salesclerk rang up the sale, Susan startled me with a sharp poke in the back. 'Look who's here.'

Several aisles away Brad Johnson was perched on a stool, trying on boots. He stood, stretched and strode right past us, seemingly oblivious to our presence, heading for the full-length mirror at the rear of the store.

'What's he doing here?' I whispered. 'After what Colin told us this morning I was sure the police would have taken Brad into custody by now.'

'No such luck. I saw Jake Cummings off on the van. Apparently they haven't found a shred of physical evidence that connects Brad with the branch that killed Martin. Nothing that even places him at the scene. No witnesses. Nothing on tape. If he did it, Hannah, it may be the perfect crime.'

'No evidence *yet*,' I said.

'True. According to Detective Cook the case is still wide open.'

As Brad paced like a peacock in front of the mirror considering his purchase, I toddled over and checked the box his boots had come in. One-hundred-percent Caiman crocodile, handmade by

Lucchese in Austin, Texas. Since 1883. And only $750. What a bargain.

I was still holding the box when Brad snuck up behind me and spoke, making me jump. 'A good look on you, Hannah,' he drawled, bobbing his head at my recently acquired boots.

'Thanks,' I said, just to be polite.

'Well, ladies. What do you think? Should I get these?'

I shrugged and set down the box where I'd found it. 'Up to you, I guess. A little too expensive for my blood.'

Brad stooped, picked up the New Balance tennis shoes he'd worn into the store and lobbed them into the boot box. 'I've never owned a pair of boots before. Might as well do it right the first time.'

'Don't you . . .?' I began then clamped my mouth shut. I looked at Susan and Susan looked at me.

Brad was busy handing his Visa card over to the hovering salesman so he didn't notice.

'Don't I what?' he asked, turning around to face me.

'Uh, don't you need some kind of special cleaner?' I said, pointing to a neatly stacked pyramid of Kiwi Saddle Soap cans.

'Oh, yeah,' he said, snagging one off the top. He tossed it to the salesman.

'Good catch,' I told the guy.

The salesman grinned and headed off to the cash register.

With Brad busy signing sales slips at the cash register, I leaned close to Susan and whispered, 'He's lying about the boots. We both saw him wearing them, right?'

Susan nodded vigorously, her hair so close it brushed my neck. 'Maybe he got rid of them?'

'Why? Because they were splattered with Martin's blood?'

'That's my bet,' she said.

'He's leaving on a plane in a couple of hours. What should we do?'

'Call the cops?' Susan suggested sensibly. 'I have Cook's number. You keep Brad busy.'

'Me?' I hissed. 'What am I supposed to say?'

'Talk about anything,' she said. 'Just don't let him get away.' Susan headed outside but just before she got to the door she turned, gave me a thumbs down and mouthed, *Don't mention the boots.*

I gave her a look.

After Susan left I stationed myself at a rack of ladies' western shirts, keeping my eye on Brad and my back to the door while I slid hangers back and forth on the rack.

Brad was also in the market for hats. I watched as he tried on a Stetson – a black felt number with a rolled brim – tipping it back, further off his forehead then considering the results in a mirror. The action freed the comma of hair that usually hung raffishly over one eye. He reached up and tweaked it. Good grief. So there was nothing casual about that dangling lock – he plans it that way.

In the mirror, Brad's eyes caught mine. A slow grin spread across his face. He winked.

'Son of a bitch,' I whispered to myself. 'He thinks he's gotten away with it.'

In six long, confident cowgirl strides, I closed the distance between Brad and me. I shot him a toothy, disarming grin. 'So, the police let you go, then?'

Brad took off the hat and caressed the brim. 'Can't lock a guy up for a little practical joke, can they? If they could the prisons would be full of twelve-year-old trick-or-treaters.'

Arrogant jerk. I decided to rattle his cage a little. 'You killed him, didn't you? You killed Martin.'

Brad laughed. 'You think I'm going to confess?' He glanced around the store. 'Where's the hidden camera?'

'No cameras. Just you and me.'

Brad plopped the hat back on his head. 'Don't expect any "If I Did It" speculation out of me, Hannah. I'm not as dumb as OJ.'

I skewered him with my eyes. 'Sounds like a confession to me, Brad. Are you telling me you did it but are just too smart to get caught?'

I was fishing, expecting a clever retort, when Susan sidled up. 'Well, fancy meeting you here, Brad.' She turned to me. 'I hope I'm not interrupting anything.'

When I assured her she wasn't, Susan said, 'I don't suppose you've heard anything about who's taking over Martin's TV show, have you?'

Brad smiled. 'It's practically a done deal.'

'You think?' I said.

'Marty died with his boots on, so to speak. Who else has exclusive footage of his last days on this earth? Of *course* they want it. They'll even pre-empt one of those mind-numbing "famous for being famous" celebrity reality shows if they have to. Somebody will snap it up, guaranteed.'

Not only a jerk, I thought, but a ghoul, too.

'What do you do between now and then?' Susan wanted to know.

'Edit the footage, of course. Got a ton of gigs, weddings, anniversaries and the occasional bar mitzvah. Just waiting to hear, then I'm out of the special events biz for good.'

He adjusted the Stetson to his satisfaction then drawled, 'Well, if you'll excuse me, ladies, I have to be moseying along.' Touching a finger to the brim of his hat in mock salute he sailed past us, heading for the cashier to pay for his hat.

'Asshole,' said Susan.

'And his John Wayne imitation sucks, too.'

TWENTY-FIVE

Apex, North Carolina, March 5, 1883. 'The appearance of an unknown animal near here has caused great excitement. The footprints are a foot long and eight inches wide. The animal has been seen twice from a train. Pursuit was begun yesterday by over a hundred men. It has killed three valuable horses at Charlotte, N.C.'

The Newark Daily Advocate (Newark, OH),
March 6, 1883

Susan joined me on the sidewalk outside Dixie's and we watched while Brad made his leisurely escape in a rented Nissan.

'Where are the police when you need them?' I asked rhetorically.

'She's on her way,' Susan said.

When Barbara Cook arrived I described my conversation with Brad. 'He as good as confessed,' I concluded.

'"As good as" won't cut it, Mrs Ives. We need solid evidence.' She turned to Susan. 'What were you telling me on the phone about a pair of boots?'

I answered for both of us. 'The first night of the conference, Susan and I noticed that Brad was wearing a distinctive pair of western boots.'

'Pretty expensive ones, too, would be my guess,' Susan said.

'Anyway,' I continued, 'after Martin's murder, Brad started wearing sneakers. I didn't think anything of it at the time – even cowboys don't wear boots every day – but just now, in there, he bought another pair after telling us he'd never owned a pair of boots before.'

'We figure he's ditched the boots somewhere,' Susan said.

'We figure he was wearing them when he killed Martin,' I added.

'If he threw them away at the hotel they might still be in his room or maybe out back in the dumpster,' Susan said. 'Garbage at the lodge gets collected only once a week. While we were waiting for you I checked with the manager. They pick up on Wednesdays.'

Although she thought it was a long shot, Cook promised she'd send an officer back to the lodge to look for the boots. We described them as well as we could remember while she took notes, then accompanied her into Dixie's where, after some discussion, we pointed out a similar pair.

'Well, she didn't laugh at us, at least,' I remarked to Susan as we watched Lieutenant Cook drive away with her notes and a photograph of the boots on her cell phone.

'At least we tried,' my friend said.

'OK. So what would you do with a pair of boots you desperately needed to get rid of?' I asked.

'Burn them,' Susan said.

'Too dangerous,' I said. 'This is wildfire season.'

'Back home, I'd give them to Goodwill. Who's going to notice when they're jumbled up with a zillion other things in a donation bin?'

I raised a finger. 'Ah ha! Come with me.'

Back inside the store, I waited until the clerk had finished ringing up a red plaid rodeo shirt for a customer, then asked, 'I have a fleece jacket that I don't want to take back on the plane to Maryland with me. Is there a Goodwill donation center in Sisters?'

'Not that I know of, but if you go a block over on Main, Habitat for Humanity has a thrift store.' He checked his watch. 'They're open until four on Sunday. They don't usually take donations on a Sunday but if you explain your situation I'm sure they'll be glad to help you out.'

Five minutes later we arrived at the Thrift Store, a two-story, western-style structure with red siding and white trim. A porch stretched across the front of the building. White railings separated it from neatly planted flowerbeds where hollyhocks were already in full bloom.

Inside the store we were welcomed by a stuffed fox, standing on a log, his glass eyes twinkling in the afternoon sun. A bit creepy but this was the Wild West, after all. Racks upon racks of used clothing, arranged by size, stretched out before us. Shelves held fabric remnants, neatly folded and tied with string. Other shelves, made of glass, were covered with dishes, small appliances, cookware and knickknacks. Hats ranged along one wall, and just ahead, on our right, stood a white metal rack displaying several dozen pairs of boots.

I examined them closely. None of the boots were Brad's.

A tiger cat with a white bib slept curled up in a woven basket near the cashier. I reached out to pet it. 'Hello, beauty, and who are you?' I asked the cat.

A woman with short blonde hair and wearing a royal blue apron paused in her task – reshelving paperbacks – to answer me. 'That's Miss Jewel,' she said. 'And I'm Paula, one of the volunteers.'

I took out my iPhone and showed Paula the picture I'd taken at Dixie's of the boots that were similar to Brad's. 'This is going to sound crazy but I'm looking for my husband's boots,' I told her. 'It's *so* embarrassing but I wrapped up a bunch of things to give away and another to take to the cleaners and the stupid man took the wrong pile! Have boots like these showed up here recently?'

Paula studied the picture over the tops of her eyeglasses then called out to another volunteer who was fiddling with a jewelry display, 'Kim, do you remember that bundle we found on the porch yesterday morning?'

A dark-haired woman I took to be Kim wandered over, an Indian necklace much like the ones for sale in Prairie Flower's shop dangling from her fingers. 'The one with the man's outfit in it?'

'That's the one.'

'I put the clothes in the pile for washing but the boots are still in the back. I need to put a price on them. The Sisters rodeo is the week after next,' Kim explained with a grin, 'so we always feature our western gear in May.' She waved an arm. 'Boots, hats, shirts . . . get your complete western outfit here. They've been selling like hotcakes.'

'Could I see the boots, please?'

'Sure. I'll be right back.'

While we waited, Paula filled us in on the Sisters Rodeo, now in its seventy-sixth year. Roping, racing, wrestling, bull riding. It was the real *yee-haw* deal.

'Here you are, then,' Kim said.

Even before she closed the gap between us I could tell by the quill-pocks and the elaborate stitching that the boots she carried were, indeed, Brad Johnson's.

'Those *are* Brad's!' I cried, reaching out for them. 'Thank you! You've saved my life. I'm happy to buy them back. How much do I owe you?'

She plopped the boots onto the counter. 'They're yours, aren't they? Mistakes happen.'

I fumbled in my handbag and pulled a twenty out of my wallet. 'You must let me pay you *something*,' I said, handing the money over. 'You've gone to such trouble.'

'You want the shirt and pants back, too?' Kim asked. 'And the belt?'

'Oh, yes,' I said, feeling my face flush. I had no idea what Brad had been wearing on the morning he killed Martin Radcliffe but I suspected I was about to find out.

When Kim went to get the clothing, Paula said, 'It's a good thing the rodeo wasn't a month ago.'

'Why's that?' I asked.

'If it had been, those fine boots would have been long gone.'

TWENTY-SIX

Centerville, Illinois, September 4, 1883. 'A wild man, naked as Adam, has been roaming around the country . . . causing intense excitement and consternation among the farmers' families. His long tangled beard and matted hair, his tall athletic form and the fierce look out of his eyes make him an exceedingly unpleasant person to meet in a lonely spot . . . He was first seen by [a woman] who . . . was returning home shortly after nightfall . . . The wild man crept stealthily out of the orchard, and when near [her] buggy, made a rush to stop the horse . . . A telephone message was sent to Belleville, yesterday, asking the sheriff to come and capture the creature, young men of the settlement are searching the woods in every direction today, but some of them are not over-anxious to encounter the monster . . . Others are puzzled to decide whether it is the Missing Link or an escaped lunatic.'

The Saturday Herald (Decatur, IL), September 8, 1883

Although we nearly missed our flights because of it, Susan and I drove as fast as the speed limit would allow back to the lodge, where we delivered Brad Johnson's discarded clothing to Lieutenant Cook, preserved as carefully as we were able in a new, reusable shopping bag. She'd searched Brad's hotel room, with no results, and was extremely grateful that we had saved her from an equally fruitless up-to-the-hips delve into the brimming, malodorous dumpster.

As we drove down the long drive heading away from the lodge I felt like I was leaving Brigadoon, a magical village where myth, fantasy and reality were so closely intertwined that it was often difficult to tell one from the other.

Back home from the airport late Sunday night, I was surprised by how seamlessly I slipped back into the comfortable sanity of day-to-day life in Annapolis. The following day I battled the traffic on Route 2 to get to the hot food bar at Whole Foods. I cooked

– unimaginatively – for myself, favoring cream of mushroom soup and peanut butter sandwiches. I carpooled the grandkids to dancing lessons and baseball practice. I walked their dog.

After a week of batting around the house doing mindless chores, waiting for *Resolute* to sail back into the harbor and Paul to sail back into my life, I found I keenly missed my new friends.

I'd been tempted several times to telephone Lieutenant Cook to ask how the investigation was going but the last thing she needed was a nosy phone call from me. According to the *Nugget News*, which came out every Tuesday in an online edition, Martin Radcliffe's widow, her attorney and the History Channel's network executives were keeping the local authorities on their toes, but as yet no one had been arrested for the crime.

I'd been home for a week when the phone rang. I checked the caller ID, wondering who would be calling me from a 612 area code. Minneapolis! Jake!

Jake responded to my breathless hello with, 'I've got good news for you, Hannah.' Brad Johnson had been arrested in LA and was being extradited to Oregon to face murder charges for the death of Martin Radcliffe. 'He's fighting extradition so it may take a couple of months, but eventually he'll be cooling his heels in the Deschutes County Jail while awaiting trial.'

'Fist-pump time!' I said.

'It's a good thing the Thrift Store hadn't gotten around to washing Brad's clothing,' Jake told me.

'Was Martin's blood on them, then?' I asked.

'Not as much as one might have expected from the nature of the attack, but yes.'

'So, that proves Brad did it, right?'

'Not so fast, Hannah. If they'd gotten a warrant to search Brad's room for evidence and found the shirt there, it would have been one thing, but getting a judge to issue a warrant based solely on your intuition . . .' His voice trailed off.

'Story of my life,' I said.

'However, once Brad discarded his clothing it became fair game.'

'Score one for our team,' I said.

'On the other hand, the chain of custody was broken, so without a warrant for Johnson's DNA there was no way to prove that the clothing was actually his.'

'Damn.'

'So, now we come to the boots,' Jake said.

'Since Brad has been nabbed I'm feeling confident that the boots had something to do with it.'

'Bingo. They got lucky. They were custom-measured and custom-made by a company in El Paso, Texas, specifically for a customer by the name of Brad Johnson. They keep meticulous records down in El Paso. Want to know Brad's calf circumference? His heel, ball, high and low instep measurements?'

'Hallelujah, but, wait a minute! That just proves they were Brad's boots, not that he killed Martin.'

'Ah, but there's where you're wrong.'

'So there was blood on the boots, too?'

'Not a drop, although Brad must have worried there could be since he gave the boots away. Damn things cost over a thousand bucks.' He took a deep breath. 'No. No blood. It was something else.'

'What? What? You can be an infuriating man – you know that, don't you?'

'*Sphaerocarpos hians*,' he said.

'You're toying with me, Jake, aren't you?'

He laughed. 'Turns out those ostrich quill follicles are dandy for picking up evidence. Cook sent the boots to the state lab for analysis and that's what the lab came up with. Spores of the trumpet bottlewort. Extremely rare.'

'How rare is rare?' I asked.

'So rare the Native Plant Society of Oregon is doing cartwheels over it. Trumpet bottlewort has been reported only once before, decades ago near Corvallis, and Brad, by his own admission, has never been anywhere near Corvallis.'

I remembered noticing moss on the rocks in the crime-scene pictures Jake had taken. 'Does trumpet bottlewort look like ruffled, whitish-green rosettes about the size of a quarter?'

'How did you know?'

'I took another look at the photos you took.'

'You said . . .' he began.

'I know. I lied.'

Jake laughed.

'So that's it, then,' I said.

'All over but the shouting.'

What did folks do before email?

Jake emailed a month later. After a bidding war he'd sold his crime-scene photos to *Dateline NBC*, a true-crime television news magazine. Lester Holt would moderate the show, tentatively entitled, *The Boots that Roared*. Jake and Thad were using the money to buy a condo in Fort Lauderdale, Florida. Pet friendly, of course.

Variety announced that Rolf Maxman, the 'Silver Fox' of daytime TV's *Don't Try This at Home*, would be taking over as host of *Don't You Believe It!* 'We are delighted,' producer Leo Kopp was quoted as saying. 'Rolf has the expertise, talent and gravitas to step into the shoes so tragically vacated by the untimely death of Martin Radcliffe.'

Gravitas. One of the Roman virtues. Brad, sadly lacking in the gravitas department, would be taping weddings and bar mitzvahs for the foreseeable future, I supposed, keeping himself out of trouble while awaiting trial. According to *The Nugget*, bail had been set at one million dollars. Brad's parents had signed a signature bond to spring their darling boy from the hoosegow. If he blew town, though, they'd lose the Brooklyn brownstone and the lakeside cabin in Canandaigua.

Leah Solat's tongue-in-cheek four-part series in the *Bee* caught the eye of *Vanity Fair*. Her feature article about the Sasquatch Sesquicentennial would appear in their November issue. I emailed her back. 'Delighted! See to it that Sigourney Weaver plays me in the movie.'

After a series of auditions with two call-backs, the New Jersey Symphony Orchestra hired Cecelia Cloughly as principal horn. The instrument she brought to Flat Rock went to a needy student at Newark High School in New Jersey who, when informed of its history, promised not to hit anybody with it.

Susan telephoned via Skype from Punta del Este, Uruguay, where she was shopping for a vacation cottage. Heather's mother had passed away, leaving her only daughter a modest inheritance. The former assistant had used the money to buy Susan out. Susan was enjoying the expat community, grateful that no Bigfoots had been spotted so far in Uruguay, although she suspected it was only a matter of time. She'd been on a couple of dates with a retired neurosurgeon named Jorge De Los Santos but claimed they were 'just friends.'

I would check out the cottage *and* Dr De Los Santos on a future visit.

Paul arrived home on a high morning tide. He breezed through the front door carrying a duffle bag full of dirty clothes. After we'd had time to get reacquainted, I told him all about the conference. Needless to say, it took a while.

'The whole thing sounds bizarre,' he said, turning to me in bed and propping himself up on one elbow.

'Oh, I don't know,' I said. 'What do you think is more bizarre? Spending a weekend with a bunch of folks who truly, madly, deeply believe in something that's just a teeny bit hard to prove, or . . .' I paused then stroked his arm thoughtfully. 'I could have been wandering around in public wearing a terrycloth robe chanting *Namaste*. Or sitting half-naked with strangers in hot tubs that smell like rotten eggs.'

'Sounds good to me,' he said, 'especially the half-naked part.' And shut me up with a kiss.

TWENTY-SEVEN

Yale, British Columbia, July 8, 1884. 'Last Tuesday it was reported that the wild man, said to have been captured at Yale, had been sent to this city and might be seen at the gaol. A rush of citizens instantly took place, and it is reported that no fewer than 200 impatiently begged admission into the skookum house. The only wild man visible was Mr Moresby, governor of the goal, who completely exhausted his patience answering enquiries from the . . . visitors.'

The Columbian (New Westminster, British Columbia, Canada), July 12, 1894

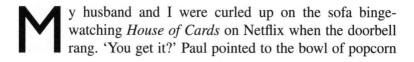

My husband and I were curled up on the sofa binge-watching *House of Cards* on Netflix when the doorbell rang. 'You get it?' Paul pointed to the bowl of popcorn balanced precariously on the bridge created by his long, lean legs between the sofa cushion and the ottoman.

I squirmed to an upright position. By the time I got to the door the UPS delivery truck was already turning right onto Maryland Avenue but he'd left a large shipping carton behind on the stoop.

'Put the show on pause,' I yelled, 'and come give me a hand with this!'

'What on earth?' I muttered as we wrestled the box into the entrance hall. The printing on the cardboard box gave no clue to its contents. 'Maybe it's a major award?' I smiled up at my husband.

A mischievous I-know-something-and-you-don't grin spread across his face.

'Are you going to tell me what it is?' I said.

'And spoil the surprise?'

'Brat! The least you can do is fetch me a knife so I don't break off my fingernails trying to get the damn thing open.'

While Paul was in the kitchen fetching a serrated knife, I examined the box like a kid on Christmas morning. It had been shipped from a company in Elk Grove Village, Illinois, but otherwise the contents remained a mystery.

Paul leaned against the door jamb, arms folded, supervising, as I slit the packing tape, opened the flaps and began flinging packing material to the floor. Something gray, plastic, as tall as my youngest grandson . . .' I tipped the box toward me and peered deep inside.

'You are kidding me.'

Paul shrugged. 'Seemed appropriate somehow.'

I figured my husband hadn't consulted with Prairie Flower about the availability of the Sasquatch garden figure I'd seen offered for sale back in Flat Rock, Oregon, so I asked, 'Where on earth did you get it?'

'Bought it from one of those mail-order catalogs that are always cluttering up our entrance-hall table.'

'I'm speechless.'

Paul grinned. 'I could have bought the life-sized one, of course. But it was six feet tall and cost over two thousand dollars.' He paused. 'Plus shipping.'

Paul helped me extricate the statue from the box. When it

stood in our entrance hall in all its polyester resin, hand-painted glory, I said, 'I know just where to put him.'

'Or her?'

'Don't be silly.' I pointed. 'This guy's got abs.'

Although the Squatch weighed only about twelve pounds (according to the packing slip) I let Paul carry it out into our backyard. Following my instructions, he installed the statue in the back corner of our garden, near the wall. The following April, when my azaleas bloomed yellow and fuchsia and white, the Squatch would be stepping casually out of them.

'You realize, don't you, Paul, that this means an end to back-yard garden parties? Except for family picnics, of course. The family already knows I'm nuts. My friends simply suspect.'

'You'll have to name him,' Paul said after a moment.

I studied the ridiculous object, thinking how unlike a Sasquatch he probably looked, if Sasquatch existed. 'His name is Martin.'

Paul's arm snaked around my shoulders, drawing me close.

'NÄR LÄ KÜ,' I said, leaning into him.

'What does that mean?'

'According to a former US Navy linguist, it's Bigfoot speak. I like to think it means, "I love you" but I could just as easily be saying "please pass the salt."'

Paul's laugh rumbled around the garden like rolling thunder. 'NÄR LÄ KÜ back at'cha, Hannah Ives.'